BACK
TO THE
GARDEN

MEGAN WYKES

WINNIPEG

Back to the Garden

This book is a work of fiction. Names, characters, businesses, organizations, places, events, and incidents either are the product of the author's imagination or are used fictitiously.

Design and layout by Matthew Stevens and M. C. Joudrey.
Cover illustration by Robin Moline.
'Inch Worm' song credit: Frank Loesser.

Published by At Bay Press May 2023.

Library and Archives Canada cataloguing in publication is available upon request.

ISBN 978-1-988168-97-5

Printed and bound in Canada.

This book is printed on acid free paper that is 100% recycled ancient forest friendly (100% post-consumer recycled).

First Edition

10 9 8 7 6 5 4 3 2 1

atbaypress.com

Dedicated to Saskia
for showing me the depths of love and courage.

1

On what first appeared to be an unremarkable evening, sometime between dinner and the kids' bedtime, Cynthia dropped a bomb. She said to her husband, in a matter-of-fact sort of way, as she poured leftover milk down the drain and stared out the back window: "You should move out. This isn't working."

Paul was seated at the kitchen table, peering up at the ceiling, watching the smoke from his cigarette converge around the broken light fixture. He failed to respond. A bead of sweat slowly rolled down his spine. It had been an unseasonably sweltering month, May 1971, and the kitchen was, by his estimation, hovering around ninety degrees Fahrenheit. He would have killed for a fan.

Was he surprised, outraged, or saddened by what his wife of six years was saying? Not really. Instead, he was increasingly captivated by an idea that swirled around in his mind as if pressing for resolution while, at the same time, dancing around it: If love were a liquid and could be contained, as in a large vessel, then each time his wife tore into him with one of her snipes or jabs, the emotion would reduce by one drop.

He contemplated the idea that love, once vast and unshakeable, could measurably diminish over time, as he noticed her, out of the corner of his eye, rallying for another onslaught. At this point in their marriage, he could imagine the bottom of the water-bearing vessel, as clear as day, glistening like mother of pearl.

"What, exactly, isn't working?" he finally asked, even though he knew the answer. She was the only one of the two brave enough to call it out. Was bravery even the right word? he wondered. More like efficiency. She was the more efficient of the duo. Typical, he thought. Typical of her to cut things off right before you hit rock bottom. My God, he suddenly realized, that's exactly what she's doing: cutting her losses. He felt surprised, and disappointed perhaps, that he hadn't anticipated this strategic move on her part. The woman, her life, the way she approached everything, was tactical. There was no fucking around, no time wasting, no cloud watching, or navel-gazing. He winced at the idea that his wife had, for God knows how long, been keeping score on his shortcomings, and felt a wave of shame.

"You and me. C'mon, Paul, you know we haven't seen eye to eye for ages. This can't be news," she said, sounding frustrated. For a second, it looked like she was about to cry.

"Is this about my opting out of social work?" he pressed, wanting to hear her say it. In some perverse way, he needed to get into the muck of it, to tease everything apart and look at it, all the nasty bits and pieces, one disappointment after the next. And was this how she truly felt about their life together – a string of disappointments? The idea hit him like a ton of bricks. He had always imagined their life as a kind of adventure where he and his wife could feel comfortable enough with each other to explore different avenues, embrace unexpected opportunities where fate presented a variety of circumstances. But now, by what she was saying, she clearly thought that he – or one of them – should be driving the ship.

"You mean your flunking social work? Well, yeah. But it's more than that, and you know it." Her tone was becoming edgy.

He could tell she was, on one hand, holding back, but on the other, desperate to lash out at him. With her, there was always a storm brewing inside.

"It's all of it. Your books and ideas …" Her voice trailed off. "Everything's a cutting-edge theory or some feverish debate. I'm sick of it." She looked out the window again and gripped the edge of the sink as if to ground herself.

God, she really must be pissed this time, he realized, noticing her knuckles turning white.

"You don't have to be flippant," he said, extinguishing his cigarette and rising from the table, inching his way into her airspace around the sink.

"You're so fucking predictable, Paul," she said, retreating to the threshold of the room and clinging to the doorframe as if intending to block his exit. "Don't you see? If it's not this thing – some great new plan for humanity – then it'll be the next thing … You're floundering. You've always been floundering. I was an idiot not to see that."

He flinched. Floundering? That was over the top. Did she really see him as some kind of hopeless cause? How are people supposed to know about the world, have a philosophy or approach, without these kinds of investigations? He wasn't trying to conjure a plan for humanity necessarily; he was just trying to understand things and, from there, build a path forward. She was making him sound crazy.

Paul took a moment to shake off the insult. Defensive and hurt, he also felt compelled to win her back, in some small way, by offering some breadcrumbs, some concrete plans that had been percolating.

"Look, Cyn, the group therapy idea's solid," he said. "I'm using Aunt Lillian's money she left me in the will. That'll last for months. I'm not touching our savings. Plus, I've already booked the rental space. All I need now are the participants. I'm ready. You'll see." He made a mental note to check if the Victoria-Royce Presbyterian church, in the Junction area of west Toronto, had actually confirmed his rental of the basement.

"It's like you're convincing yourself. Why do you always have to be saving the world? This group therapy idea sounds like quackery. I've never even heard of it."

"I've told you before. It's brand new. I read up on it." He knew he could make a difference with this approach in a way that he couldn't if he had stayed in social work. Not with all its rules and regulations, its hierarchies. "With this new kind of therapy, I feel I can really, and more honestly, help people work through their issues," he said, trying to determine if that even counted in her mind.

"Yes, honesty, of course," she said sarcastically.

"Everything has to be so goddamned authentic with you, doesn't it?"

He thought about the water-bearing vessel, the analogy, once again. He considered his diminishing capacity for love. What was he even fighting for anyway? He wondered if, or under what circumstances, his vocation could be considered a success in his wife's mind. Yes, he was trying to win her back from the edge by sharing his aspirations to run the new therapy sessions, but it seemed to be having the opposite effect.

He had to acknowledge that Cynthia was partially right about his immersion in books and theories, but he couldn't help himself. He knew perfectly well that he was wired that way. He collected ideas and waited for their application in the real world. For him, the ideas didn't necessarily need to be anchored, applied, or with immediate purpose. They could find their anchor years, even decades, later. He was patient that way.

"There's nothing wrong with theories," he said, attempting to defuse the argument, curling his shoulder-length hair around his ears to stay cool. The room seemed increasingly oven-like. "They're supposed to help us find our way in life."

"Jesus, Paul," she said, sighing, "you're the most lost person I know."

Wow, he thought, first floundering, now lost. Cynthia had a streak of cruelty, he had always known that, but this was beyond the pale.

She turned on her heel and left the room.

Paul remained at the table, his chest feeling very tight, his eyes welling up, the pain of her words sinking in. Was she serious about ending their marriage? He felt blindsided by the idea, crushed at the thought of ending things and feeling, all of a sudden, abandoned.

Just then, he spotted five-year-old Evan half-hidden behind the kitchen door.

His son was frozen, standing tall like a soldier in the corner of the small kitchen, wearing his Scooby-Doo pyjamas that desperately needed a wash. His right hand, in mid-air, had a stranglehold on a miniature grey dinosaur; his chubby fingers held the stegosaurus up as if suspending time. His chin was quivering. His eyes were wide and questioning.

"Oh, Jeez, Evan," Paul stammered. He knelt down and hugged the boy, kissing his soft brown hair. "I'm sorry you heard that. Mommy and I were just talking."

"Fighting," Evan mumbled into his father's shoulder. "You guys were fighting."

"No, not really. Adults sometimes need to talk. They sometimes disagree. And that's okay."

"Mommy's mad."

"We may raise our voices, but we care about each other. And, most importantly, we love you and Jason very much." He thanked God that Jason, at eighteen months, was too young to have understood the argument.

He could feel Evan's shoulders relax a bit. He looked into his son's watery eyes.

"It's okay. Everything's fine," he said, even when he knew nothing could be further from the truth. Despite feeling blindsided, he had to admit that this spring had been a train wreck. He and Cynthia were fighting all the time, although this argument had been a doozy. She had never before asked him to leave.

As he held his son, Paul wondered if he had enough psychic energy or sheer willingness to love, or continue loving, his wife after all these years – only a half dozen, but it seemed like an eternity. He forced himself to consider if he were still in love with her, or if he merely wished that love were still, somehow, attainable.

He extracted a grape Popsicle from the freezer, split it in half with a butter knife, handed one half to Evan, and led him out the back door, where they sat on the stoop, so the inevitable drippings wouldn't sully the kitchen floor.

"Mommy said we can't eat sugar before bed. I brushed my teeff," Evan admitted.

"This time, it's okay."

Father and son sat and ate in silence – Evan, intently focused on consuming the frozen treat as rapidly as possible; Paul, lost in thought as his Popsicle transformed into a watery mess.

Cynthia's words still echoed in his mind. He was very hurt but starting to rally. She really didn't understand his new approach at all, he thought. He wanted to do everything differently from his training; he wanted to start something completely new. But this, he now realized, might entail revisiting his training, his MA supervisor, and his ill-fated sojourn in social work.

* * *

Paul, who tended to look favourably on everyone, had never liked his MA supervisor, Vladimir. Not really. He lamented his negative feelings toward the man who was, by Paul's estimation, a half-generation older. He had tried very hard to like him, but their approaches to social work, and life, were profoundly different.

Regrettably, it was Vladimir's job to assess Paul; this man would determine whether or not Paul graduated. To do this, he shadowed Paul in one-on-one meetings with clients who were interfacing with the system for the first time. He also observed Paul when he was running sessions, such as a family intervention where a child was slated to be removed from the home, due to a parent's abuse or neglect, and placed in foster care.

Vladimir had been a physician in the USSR. After he defected, he attempted to pick up his career in Canada, but was told that he would need to start all over. So instead, he retrained in social work. This wasn't a great fit, in Paul's eyes. He could sense the man's resentment. He knew that Vladimir felt the job was beneath him, because his supervisor let it show from time to time.

Vladimir's philosophy on dealing with people was brutish. The man lacked finesse and had limited interpersonal skills. He was blunt, which he would have rationalized as being direct, in a good way. He often said to Paul that a social worker's job was to inform people of the facts of the system. What people did with this information was their problem. Even the word *problem*, Paul thought, revealed a great deal about Vladimir's mindset.

One particular file had driven a wedge between the two men – a case where a stepfather had been inappropriately touching an eleven-year-old girl. The mother didn't believe her daughter when she confided in her and, as a result, had refused to alert the authorities. Instead, the girl's teacher had reported the situation. Paul feared that things might escalate if they, as social workers representing the interests of the child, failed to act. They did act, but it was in the subtleties where they had failed, Paul firmly believed.

Vladimir's philosophy didn't leave room for emotionally charged considerations that cropped up in this case, such as: How does a person inform an awkward preteen that her stepfather's going to jail to stop him from molesting her? – How, when the girl's mother had sided with her spouse, and had begun to perceive her own child as some sort of temptress? It was clear the mother would have sooner seen her daughter, who wasn't old enough to shave her legs, removed from the family home than see her breadwinning partner forced to leave the house.

The tears and upset seemed to perplex Vladimir, who responded by retelling all parties how the system worked: The dad would be removed, and the trial date would be set. What else was there to say? "Why are these people crying?" he had asked Paul on several occasions during this harrowing case.

Paul, by contrast, was utterly drained. On the final meeting in the molestation case, he had to excuse himself and splash water on his face before he could return to the room. The intensity of this case was crushing to him. He couldn't imagine how people lived, day to day, with that kind of trauma.

Paul was aware that, unlike Vladimir, he operated on instinct and gut feelings. He sensed what these people really needed was reassurance, a hand to hold, a moment's silence to acknowledge their pain, a safe place to land. He could see the fear in the young girl's eyes. He believed that she needed to be assured, convinced, that this was the right move, that things would turn out much better once the stepdad was out of the picture, once the mom had cooled down. But this family had never known anything close to peace. It would be very hard to change their dynamics.

When the session was over that afternoon, and the family slowly headed toward the elevators as if retreating from a long and bitter siege, the girl ran back to the office and hugged Paul.

He reciprocated and patted her head, very nearly overcome with emotion himself.

Vladimir scowled. Social workers weren't supposed to touch clients, he often said. Paul had broken a cardinal rule. Vladimir gave Paul a failing grade on that particular case, citing that the girl, accustomed to sexualized relationships with male authority figures, was projecting onto Paul, and for that reason alone, he should have refused her embrace.

Paul was, naturally, repulsed by his superior's suggestion. He argued that somewhere along the line, this child needed to know that there are good people, good men, in the world.

This "F" grade was a permanent tarnish on Paul's transcripts. He didn't graduate with his cohort, but he didn't care. He still viewed Vladimir's judgment, and perhaps to some extent the whole of social work, as fundamentally flawed. People needed to connect. That was the point of everything, wasn't it?

After that case, Paul decided that he could not carry on in traditional social work, and that he wasn't cut out for anything involving the custody or welfare of children, which would rip his heart out over time. Having his own children only exacerbated this feeling; every child he saw reminded him of Evan or Jason.

Instead, he decided that he wanted to focus on helping adults – potentially more complicated than kids, but at least this way, he could level the playing field, approach his clients as partners in the process of getting well. This was not a popular modus operandi, he realized, but he had to go with his gut.

What Cynthia failed to realize was that he wanted to reinvent social work, to make it better, less hierarchical. No, he hadn't quite given up on it. He just wanted to try something novel; return to basic principles, and then start fresh. He had read a great deal about new psychological therapies where all parties were equal; where there was no clinical leader, per se; where people just helped each other. He liked the sound of this.

Paul knew he wasn't the good-for-nothing that Cynthia clearly saw when she looked at him. No, he was a man with a plan, and his ideas for the group therapy sessions had evolved into a concrete undertaking.

*   *   *

After he and Evan finished their Popsicles, Paul tucked his son into bed. Brushing teeth and a final pee didn't seem to matter in the grander scheme of things. He watched his son

crawl under the covers. Evan had a kind of joy and content-
ment that he admired. Children really could live in the
moment. It was possible. Evan seemed to have forgotten the
fight he had witnessed, and he was now eagerly awaiting the
nightly ritual of his father singing the "Inch Worm" song.

Paul tucked the thin cover up to his son's chin, just the
way he liked it, even on the hottest nights, then wiggled his
peter pointer finger right above Evan's little nose to animate
the magical inch worm.

Evan squealed with delight and grabbed his father's
hand.

Paul began singing very softly,

Inch worm, inch worm
Measuring the marigolds
You and your arithmetic
You'll probably go far.

Inch worm, inch worm
Measuring the marigolds
Could it be you'd stop and see
How beautiful they are.

After Evan drifted off – as always, around the second
rendition of the song – Paul kissed his son's sweaty little
head; exited the bedroom, leaving the door open a crack
(so if any monsters crept out of the closet, they could leave
peaceably); and turned back to the task at hand. In the living
room, he picked up a pen and paper, and began drafting an
advertisement for the group therapy sessions. He planned to

post the ads on telephone poles and in grocery stores around the neighbourhood right after he confirmed the space rental.

These ideas filled Paul with hope for the future. He could make a difference, after all; he could be a positive force for change, even when his personal life was in shambles. This took the sting out of Cynthia's words. He would show her that his ideas had merit; he could win her back. Chaos could be good, refreshing even, he told himself. It could catapult him into a more positive space – one where his wife would be proud of him again, where he could recapture all the good things that brought them together in the first place. This didn't seem unfathomable. In fact, he was banking on it. He willfully blocked out the part of his mind that wandered, kicking and screaming, into the darker possibilities. He disregarded the tiny voice inside his head that dared to ask: What if the experiment fails?

2

The start date for the group therapy sessions, May 24, crept up on Paul. He was excited as he raced to the Victoria-Royce Presbyterian church, anxious to meet the individuals who had signed up for the three-month experiment. He arrived at the church a few minutes early, having walked all the way from Roncesvalles. He could have taken the streetcar and bus, of course, which would have been much cooler, but he figured that walking would help him to organize his plans and prepare for the first in the series of sessions.

Just seconds before entering the building, he was distracted by a commotion. A woman, farther up Medland Street, seemed to be having a delusional episode. She was talking loudly, in the throes of an emotional discussion with an imaginary person. Passersby were sidestepping her, even crossing to the opposite side of the street to avoid her.

Paul stopped, wondering if he could help the woman, but decided against it when she appeared, at a distance, to have stopped acting erratically. She ceased the conversation, suddenly, and started walking south as if nothing out of the ordinary had transpired.

He went in the side entrance of the church and headed down the stairs.

The minute he entered the basement, he snapped the fluorescent lights off to keep it cool.

The heat of the day was losing its bite. With the approaching dusk, the sun had softened from a raging noon-time inferno to a honey-coloured orb. This light filtered through large windows near the ceiling, which, he figured, would be at ground level if he were standing outside.

The absence of the irritating hum from the lighting was replaced by something enchanting: evidence of human activity above ground. He must have missed this when he raced into the building. He could now hear the freckled laughter of local kids who had hijacked the ice cream truck. He picked up the whirr of the Annette Street bus. He traced the sound of a guitarist whose acoustics likely trickled out of some nearby bedroom window as the singer struggled with a Stones song – "You Can't Always Get What You Want."

Wiping the sweat from his forehead with the back of his hand, he ventured into the centre of the Victoria Royce-Presbyterian's expansive underground room, taking in its details.

A chalkboard had been washed clean from the day's activities. Rainbow-shaped lines, repeating rhythmically across the surface, evidenced a swift cleaning. Below this, a row of shelves overflowed with picture books.

One wall displayed remnants of Santa, Rudolf, and the Easter Bunny. These faded paper images had curled in the extreme humidity. Like the last leaves of autumn, they were tenuously clinging to the wall. Paul's entry had created a slight breeze that, in fact, caused Santa to descend, ominously, to the floor. The adjacent wall was covered with Bristol board cutouts of animals: koala, giraffe, lion, butter-fly, turtle, snake, rabbit.

He sat down on one of the chairs scattered around the room, slightly fearful that he might break its miniature frame, obviously made for children, and waited for the others.

This was good. Arriving early would allow him to formulate his thoughts more readily. He still didn't feel completely prepared.

Within minutes, a thirtyish woman with a mass of ginger hair, which curiously ensnared a pencil around her ear, entered the room. His first participant!

"Good idea," she said.

"Sorry?" he asked, scrambling to get up from his tiny chair.

"Keeping the lights off."

"It's an oven out there today."

"I'm Claire," she said, extending her hand.

"Paul. Welcome to the first group therapy session. Please fill in the contact information sheet, here, so I can be in touch if I need to cancel a session. This is one hundred percent confidential." He handed her a piece of paper, extracted from his Army Surplus bag, to jot down her information.

"Cool." She began digging in her shoulder bag, evidently looking for a pencil, then realized that the writing utensil was stuck in her hair. She filled in the document, then sat down rather unceremoniously on the floor.

"You don't look like a therapist," she said, smiling slightly.

Paul glanced down at his favourite ultra-thin butterfly shirt and cut-offs that were frayed along the edges. He was suddenly aware that his hair hadn't seen a comb in a while. His sandals were on the verge of disintegration, and his toenails were, admittedly, a tad long – not dirty, but long.

"I think that's a good thing," she clarified.

A moment or two later, a slender, dark-haired man entered the basement and introduced himself as Simon. From his attire, Paul surmised that he was some kind of a bureaucrat who had come to the session directly from work.

"You look familiar," Claire said to Simon. "I can't put my finger on it."

"Sorry," Simon said, evidently unable to confirm any previous meeting they may or may not have had. He seemed uninterested in finding the connection, as he glanced out the window.

To Paul's surprise, the next participant was the woman who had been talking to herself on the street just moments earlier. Entering the church basement, she introduced herself as Beata. She appeared to be in her late fifties. She looked Nordic; she was tall and strikingly attractive. She emitted an aura of softness that seemed motherly or nurturing. Her straight silver hair was cut neatly around her face and well off the shoulders. She wore sky-blue culottes, a plain yellow t-shirt, and a necklace with a large, unprocessed chunk of amber.

Clearly, she had composed herself. Or perhaps he had been mistaken about the outburst. In any case, Paul tried to put the unsettling scene out of his mind and focus on the task at hand.

Realizing the tiny colourful chairs were sturdier than they seemed and, in fact, entirely stable for adults of an average build, Paul encouraged everyone to pick a chair and settle in. The group formed a natural circle in the centre of the room. Claire chose to remain on the floor.

"This space is a nursery school from nine to five," Paul explained.

"Santa's had a bad day," Simon said, pointing to the fallen poster.

Paul smiled, to acknowledge the joke, but no one laughed outright. There was a feeling of apprehension hanging in the air.

"This may be the extent of our group," Paul said, glancing at his watch. It was 7:10 pm. "Very good. Let's start. Why don't we begin with why you came today, and what you're expecting to get out of these sessions."

No one volunteered any information. They looked at him with a fair degree of doubt or even suspicion. This caught him off guard. But, he rethought, had he honestly believed that they'd simply come in and share their innermost feelings right away? He realized that this was preposterous and began thinking of ways to earn their trust.

"I should say that I'm not an authority, per se. I'm just facilitating. I'm not a social worker or a shrink. I want this to be completely nonhierarchical. We're all equal members of a team that helps its members through sharing our feelings."

Again, crickets. Everyone was glancing around the room to avoid Paul's gaze.

"Okay, why don't we just go around the circle and introduce ourselves? Simple enough. Say a few words about who you are, what you're all about, where you're at, what floats your boat."

The group remained unresponsive. Perhaps the request was too vague?

"Okay, I have a way to open up a little … and this'll be fun," he suggested, trying not to let the edge of panic take hold. "When you introduce yourself, tell us, in just a few words, the best and worst thing in your life right now." He had read somewhere about this icebreaker. People don't necessarily need to get to the heart of things right off the bat; they just need to get used to talking in the group. The rest will flow more naturally.

The idea flopped. The group seemed instantly stressed. Simon, in particular, had a look of horror on his face, as if bloodletting were on the agenda.

"Well, I can start. To make things easier. My name's Paul. Best thing: my two boys, Jason and Evan. No doubt. Worst thing? Hmm. I'd have to say the failure of true Communism. I happen to believe that one day, it might work out the way Marx intended." He thought of citing his marriage as the worst thing, but decided against it. Maybe another time.

"Biographical tidbits? I'm interested in nonhierarchical egalitarian work with adult clients, talk therapy. What else? This past spring, I've been learning about Maslow's hierarchy of needs."

"I read about his work," said Claire. "In a psych book."

"Yes, he was an American psychologist who wrote a paper in the 1940s that said, in short, humans have a set of needs, in a particular order, where one need has to be fulfilled before others. For example, food and shelter are necessary for humans to next develop a sense of belonging, identity, esteem, and eventually be self-actualized."

He stopped himself from rambling. He could imagine Cynthia rolling her eyes. He actually heard her whispering: *No one gives a shit, Paul.*

"What's self-actualization?" asked Simon.

"I'd say it's feeling fully alive. Reaching your potential."

"Makes sense," said Beata. "You can't feel good about your life until there's food on the table. First things first."

"Exactly," Paul said. "I'm interested in finding this through group therapy," he added. "I might also say that this is the first time I've launched such an effort."

"Wait, you've never done this before?" asked Simon, looking nonplussed. "We're the guinea pigs?"

"I wouldn't put it like that," Paul said, feeling uncomfortable with Simon's take on things. "I see this as a social experiment. It's terribly exciting, really. Now, who's going to go next? Just a brief introduction. Painless, I promise."

Claire jumped in. "I can start. I'm an editor, a word nerd. Grammar slammer bammer," she said, quoting a popular television show. "I'm sorry – I shouldn't joke. I know I need to stop doing that. If I make light of why I'm here, pretend as if everything's fine, I'm wasting everyone's time," she said, chastising herself. "I have a bad boss situation. There, I said it. What else about me? I live in the area, always have." She was visibly nervous now. "I – I don't know what else to say ... I read a lot." She began rubbing her palms. "I need to read. For work, I mean," she ended awkwardly.

"That's great, Claire," said Paul, trying to make her feel at ease.

She struck him as someone who might not have many friends or, more specifically, as someone who lived for her work, which isn't the same thing, but it ends up having the same outcome.

She reached into her shoulder bag, extracted a package of cigarettes, and lit one. Paul noticed that her hands were shaking, and one of them appeared to be injured.

Simon seemed hugely pleased that she had broken out the smokes, as if it gave him permission as well.

"What the heck," said Paul, joining the others. "We should feel at home here. Go ahead and smoke." He got up and found what looked like an ashtray resting on the edge of the chalkboard.

This changed the mood, and everyone seemed to relax. Only Beata failed to light up. The rest puffed away in near silence for a few moments. It was a curious kind of collective letting-go, which brought with it a tentative sense of togetherness, a fragile bond, Paul realized.

It was Beata's turn next, if they were going around in a clockwise circle, but Paul was unsure of how to approach her and what to expect. Was she really the same woman he had seen in the street, acting erratically?

"Beata, what would you like to tell us about yourself?" he asked.

She took a deep breath. "Hello, all. I work at the

Ontario Crafters' Guild," she began. "I have two children: Aisha, twenty-two, and Etienne, twenty. You can probably tell from my accent that I'm originally from Holland. I moved to Chicago when I was a child."

"Kids live in Toronto?" asked Simon, now on his second cigarette and warming up to things.

"No, they're back in the States. I'm afraid we don't share the same politics," she said. "My late husband and I moved the family here from Chicago six years ago to avoid Vietnam. My husband Jafari – Jaf – was originally from Kenya, then London, so we had no reason to stay in the States.

"I'm here as a result of my children's prodding, their concerns. They're lovely kids, very mature young people, but they worry about me, I suppose, my coming to terms with … things. My husband's untimely death, you could say."

She looked at Simon, indicating she was done and it was his turn to share information.

Before turning his attention to Simon, Paul considered Beata's situation. If she were, indeed, the distraught woman he had witnessed prior to the meeting, then she clearly had some major issues going on. Had everything been triggered by her husband's death? He wished he could speak to Beata's children to understand their concerns but, of course, that would be impossible. He would have to figure out her situation, whatever that may be, in relative isolation.

"My name's Simon, as you know. I work in the Marriage Licensing Office at the New City Hall, which is … entertaining. I issue the licenses."

"Anything you'd like to share about your life?" Paul asked.

"I'm renovating my home, an 1880s cottage in

Cabbagetown," Simon added in a way that sounded more like a question, then concluded: "That's me, summed up."

So, why was Simon here? Paul wondered. He wasn't terribly forthcoming about his life, and Paul saw no evidence of trauma or distress. He made a note to dig deeper. Maybe they could start with Simon next time, he figured.

Paul then elaborated on the ideas behind group therapy and the approaches that he was hoping to apply. He encouraged all of them to think more about why they had shown up today and what major issues they would like to bring forward to the group over the course of the summer.

Their time was suddenly up. Paul was surprised how quickly the hour evaporated. No one, except him, had actually answered the question about the best and worst things in their lives. He would need to work on this.

When the session ended, Claire, Simon, and Beata left the church almost immediately. Paul remained in the basement, dumping the ashtray, and straightening the chairs. Still ruminating about Beata's perplexing situation and Simon's reluctance to disclose any real details about his life, he was in no hurry to get home.

In truth, he felt a little overwhelmed and he was trying not to let insecurity take root. This group therapy endeavour was harder than he thought it would be. In some ways, his training as a social worker had done little to prepare him. And since he was trying to buck against the system, to create something new, he found himself swimming between theory and practice.

The idea that he could inadvertently damage these people, beyond what they'd already endured, terrified him.

But what, exactly, had they endured? He had no idea. The hesitation and lack of trust that he could feel from all three of these people concerned him greatly. Hell, he wasn't even sure they would show up for the next session. His summer-long experiment just might end at inception.

3

This was the day Claire had been dreading for months: the annual review. And it began on a very rocky footing.

"Rewriting the Milgram experiment was stupidity itself," Maron said before Claire even had the chance to sit down in her boss's office. "Surely, you must know that."

Maron's dark hair was bound restrictively at the top of her head in a bun, which made her ice-blue eyes bulge unexpectedly. She was wearing an orange corduroy pant-suit that looked just a little too tight. To Claire, her attire seemed an odd selection for such a hot day, especially since the publishing company wasn't air-conditioned.

Claire oozed into the chair. "I thought the rewrite was necessary," she said, knowing this was a weak explanation. "From an editorial perspective," she added, realizing this was an unnecessary clarification since all her work was editorial.

She could feel the blood rushing from her head, that sinking feeling as if she were about to faint. Her hands began to tingle. She folded them on her lap in such a way that they looked interlocked, when, in fact, the thumbnail of her right hand was digging into the meaty flesh of her left palm.

She knew the pain would dissuade her from crying. It would focus her attention away from the words that the two were exchanging, draw her thoughts far from this suffocating office. It was, she realized full well, a perverse way to take an emotional step back from a situation. She had developed this now-automatic mechanism many years ago as a way of handling acute anxiety, from which she had suffered since childhood.

The "incident," the Milgram rewrite, was set in motion months earlier when Claire received a manuscript for an introductory psychology book. The author was a well-known psychologist at an east coast university. A fully tenured academic.

The manuscript, however, required a major edit. One section in particular, which described the Milgram experiment, was profoundly muddled. Claire realized that the best thing to do would be to start from scratch and rewrite the whole chapter, which she did.

The book was published a few months later. Then things went wrong, and got exponentially worse. The professor was doing a national media junket related to a spree of corner store robberies in British Columbia. The interviewer, keen on the deviance angle, went off script and asked the scholar about his recently published psych book. The professor, bless him, gave credit on national television to his "crackerjack editor, Claire."

This was the point when the war between Maron and Claire truly began; this was ground zero.

Claire often considered what she could have done differently to avoid the strife this caused. In doing so, she frequently returned to Dr. Stanley Milgram and the dark nature of his work.

In preparation for the rewrite, she had learned a fair amount about Milgram. He was a young professor of social psychology at Yale in the early 1960s. He was interested in authority. His experiment, which Claire studied meticulously to describe it to the best of her abilities as a non-academic, was relatively simple: The subject or study participant was to take the role of the "teacher" and be told that the test was about memory and learning. In a lab setting, this person had to pose a series of questions over an intercom to a "learner," someone who was hidden in an adjoining room. This learner was, in reality, an actor hired by the research team to perform a very convincing mock situation.

So ran the experiment: Each time the learner failed to answer a question correctly, the teacher was instructed (by the experiment's overseers) to push a button that would dispense electric shocks, in increasing voltages, to the learner, as punishment.

Claire was fascinated by the fact that the teacher could, with each incorrect answer and the prescribed punishment, hear the learner's (the actor's) mounting screams through the wall. Over time, as the voltage increased, the learners – all convincing thespians – began to beg for the experiment to stop, but the teachers continued following the orders of the overseers. A few of the teachers were upset by what they were doing. Some quit the experiment and refused to administer the electric shocks.

Milgram submitted his experiment to a scholarly journal in 1963, under the title "Behavioral Study of Obedience." It, naturally, ruffled a lot of feathers. He was denied tenure at his alma mater, Harvard, due to ethical breaches.

The experiment, however, gained profile in the public's mind. People were developing an appetite for this sort of thing, it seemed to Claire.

"But what in God's name possessed you to rewrite the experiment?" Maron asked, forcing Claire back into the conversation, the annual review.

Maron's arms were crossed, and her elbows rested gingerly on the surface of the large desk. She hunched over the paperwork and peered at her subordinate unflinchingly.

If nothing else, this woman, only a few years older than Claire, was threatening. Claire hated the way she was always putting her off her game. Maron's energy seemed to radiate from her body and occupy all surrounding space. Like heat rising or water falling, this phenomenon was some kind of law of nature. This travelling energy was a nervous sort, frenetic and toxic. After meetings with her boss, Claire often felt highly agitated, like she needed a good cry or wanted to call her mother just to hear her voice.

Unsure how to answer the question, Claire wiggled her thumbnail deeper into her palm and looked down at the floor, focusing on a random fleck of dust.

She wished she weren't like this; she wished she had more protective emotional gear to rise to the challenge of someone like Maron. But Claire's efforts to avoid confrontation were based on one central idea, to which she clung: She believed that if she were able to look at a situation from all angles, unpack the incidents on the battlefield, ruminate on the outrageous unfairness, then she might be able to tease apart the components, and do something constructive with this new knowledge.

This, of course, took time – another nail in the coffin when it came to workplace strife. Agility was key here. During an argument, Claire was aware that she likely appeared frozen, when she was, in fact, thinking things through and weighing the options, deliberating. She feared that being static, or stone-faced, made her look simple-minded. She was afraid that Maron had pegged her as *not that bright*.

Claire hoped that one day, possibly through these kinds of Herculean machinations, she could fix things. But, in her weaker moments, she sensed that this was an illusion. Deep down, she feared that this cycle of analysis was never-ending; that it would fail to progress in any meaningful way because it always circled back on itself; and that she might not be able to fix herself.

Claire's most dramatic attempt to heal herself was always on her mind, like a haunting. A few years back, she had checked herself into a psychiatric hospital. It had helped, but the healing wasn't permanent. It wore off, plain and simple. Claire's basic nature returned.

The memory of the hospital swirled around in her mind as she tried to stay positive and focused during the annual review, but it was becoming difficult.

"You know people have been talking about you," Maron continued after a considerable silence. "Yes, I've met with others … and the consensus is disappointing. I'm afraid I've been forced to start taking action, papering your file."

"You're serious? I – I've been here for two years."

"Well, you haven't been working for me for all those years. I run a tight ship."

"I see," Claire said, hating herself for acquiescing. What else was there to say? How else could she respond?

She felt desperate for a break and considered asking permission to step outside for some fresh air, but she suspected that it wouldn't be allowed. The review had just started, after all. They had only been in the room for ten minutes.

Just sit here and look like you're absorbing information, Claire told herself. She was beginning to feel angry, close to tears. This emotion welled up in her and made her want to look away, to shield herself from Maron's piercing gaze. She glanced outside, welcoming the temporary reprieve. Beyond the floor-to-ceiling window of her boss's office, a set of cotton candy clouds drifted in slow motion across an unfettered sky.

Suddenly, Maron's telephone rang. As it turned out, she was supposed to be chairing a meeting in two minutes, so she concluded the review.

"This isn't over," she said threateningly.

Claire whispered a vague response and fled the room, forgetting the paperwork on Maron's desk. As she rose and turned to leave, to her horror, she realized that her boss's door had remained open for all Editorial to hear. Her heart sunk. Surely everyone in the office had caught the tone of the conversation, if not the sordid details.

She kept her eyes on the floor as she walked to the women's washroom, her hands tightly clenched. She didn't want to make eye contact with her peers, many of whom seemed to think Maron was a good boss. (How was that even possible?) She pushed the washroom door open with one shoulder and stood over the bank of sinks.

Her hands, still cupped together, were illuminated under the near-surgical light. Slowly, into the nearest sink, she released the small pool of crimson that had settled into her left palm. The blood first clung to the sides of the porcelain sink, but then Claire twisted on the cold-water tap, and it was swiftly washed away. She turned her attention to digging the blood out from under her thumbnail.

"Never cried," she said to herself in the mirror as she ran more water into the wound. The throbbing was replaced by a cool, numbing sensation. "Never. Fucking. Cried."

Claire left work early, still shaken by the review, still nursing her sore hand. As soon as she reached her apartment in the Junction, she extracted a beer from the fridge and then headed to the balcony. Exhausted, she flung open the screen door, sat down on the green and yellow folding lawn chair with a heavy sigh, and lit a cigarette.

The temperature was almost one hundred degrees, despite the approaching dusk. The air didn't seem to be moving. A cicada started up as Claire stared at her wounded palm. The cut looked very red around the edges.

Her hands were shaking. She knew that she was still experiencing the tail end of an elongated anxiety attack spurred by the review. She held the beer bottle up to her forehead and cheeks, grateful for the coolness against her face; then took a sip; sunk back into the flimsy chair; and put her feet up on a milk crate.

This third-floor balcony was Claire's sanctuary. The trees were so close that she could easily touch a variety of ash and maple foliage. The oaks were much higher and out of reach, but they created a dappled light that she craved – in part because of the coolness that the shade provided, in part because of the aesthetic.

She looked at her watch: 7:45 pm. She opened a second beer as the smell of hamburgers from neighbourhood hibachis wafted up. This charcoal scent mingled with that of chlorinated water from nearby hoses. She could hear the sprinklers starting up, one after the next, and the water rhythmically splattering against fences and backyard garages.

She loved this area of the city, the Junction. Most of the homes here were built in the first decade of the twentieth century, when the population mushroomed around the West Toronto Railway Station.

The High Park subway station had opened two years ago. This expansion connected the area more to the metropolis, but the west end was still considered to be on the periphery, which was fine with Claire. Keeping the world at bay, in a sleepy section of the city, was part of her survival mechanism.

Five beers and a half dozen cigarettes later, she decided to skip dinner and go for a walk. The drink had quelled her anxiety, but she was now substantially drunk. She stumbled out of the apartment and headed to Ravina Gardens.

At street level, the air was even more static than it had been in the apartment. But at least it was a notch cooler.

Claire wandered the winding streets of High Park, often glancing west to appreciate the tangerine glow of the sun as dusk approached.

She plunked herself down on a wooden bench at Ravina and watched toddlers in the wading pool taking one more dip before their tired-looking mothers would rush them home and off to bed. Older siblings were clustered around the swing set drinking 7UP, the boys too overheated to wrestle. A trio of giggly teenaged girls walked in front of Claire, trailing a jet-stream scent of Johnson's baby oil, no doubt having spent the late afternoon tanning. One of them had a transistor radio. A couple of shirtless dads, their torsos made leathery from lawn maintenance over the unusually hot spring, were poolside, talking baseball and watching their wives tend to the kids.

Claire observed the families, feeling like an interloper. Under the full influence of the alcohol now, she leaned over the back of the bench, half falling off the wooden structure; pointed to the gaggle of men; and said to the nearest exhausted mother, "I honestly can't imagine being saddled with one of those leathery-backed Cro-Magnons."

The woman, shocked at first, slowly nodded her head and said, "Honey, it surprises me too."

After a while, still feeling drunk, Claire got up to further stroll the neighbourhood. Maybe she could walk it off.

She passed one of Paul's advertisements for group therapy stapled to a telephone pole. This was how she had originally found out about the group. She assumed the others had done the same. The ads were up all over town, it seemed.

She re-examined the copy. She loved catching typos, and the urge to find such a mistake often overtook her. This ad, however, failed to deliver. It read:

> Tired? Sad? Psyched out? Do yourself a solid. Try Group Therapy. It's new! It's experimental! Victoria-Royce Presbyterian church, Annette and Medland Streets. Mondays, May 24 to August 23, 7:00 – 8:00 pm. No bread? No problem. It's free. All hang-ups welcome.

The text was written to attract hippies – that was clear. She wondered if that was Paul's intention. Was he a hippie? He certainly looked like one with his long hair, crazy butterfly shirt, and disturbing toenails. At the first group therapy session, he looked as if he'd stumbled in from a Grateful Dead concert.

Walking home, Claire began to sober up. Once again, she inspected the painful cut on her palm. Clearly, her current coping methods weren't saving the day. She wondered about group therapy. Paul seemed nice enough, but did he really know what he was doing? Would it be worth going back for the next session? She wasn't sure.

4

It was two hours into her workday, and Beata was seated at the lightbox, studying a sheet of twenty-four slides (stained glass windows) under the magnifying glass. She was supposed to be writing descriptions of the pieces but found it difficult to concentrate.

Instead, she was considering this newfangled therapy idea. Should she return to Paul's group? She knew that she was in mourning, but, paradoxically, opening up about the loss of her husband, Jafari, was her biggest hesitation. She felt that she needed to keep something of Jafari for herself, something entirely private. She feared that talking about him would cheapen or diminish their relationship, as if the act of disclosure would reduce their history to something mundane and in no way exceptional.

If she were to continue with the group, she supposed that she should, as hard as it may seem, share her story, and start at the beginning. In truth – or rather, under the right circumstances – she loved to talk about the early days.

Jafari had been an accomplished scholar on faculty at the University of Illinois. She was intensely proud of this fact. Educated at the London School of Economics, he was interested in developing African nations that were lacking consistent infrastructure. This was the subject of his PhD: a comparison of five such nations.

Early on in his career, his work had been published in a number of high-profile international journals – a detail that Beata never failed to mention to anyone who would listen. It helped that he spoke fluent Swahili. Coming from Kenya, a country where sixty-eight different languages flourished, he had both versatility and accessibility that Western scholars simply did not possess.

Beata had always viewed Jafari as a rising star. She could feel it in her bones. After all, at twenty-five years of age, he had been offered full tenure over the telephone – long-distance by one of the deans at U of I. This was when Jafari was still living in London, before he had even had the chance to defend his PhD, and a few months prior to meeting Beata.

It was an exciting time on campus at U of I. Optimism was high. The College of Liberal Arts and Sciences, which hired Jafari, was comparatively young, having opened its doors in 1946. By the early 1950s, when he arrived, there was pressure to expand, to offer more diverse courses in the humanities and social sciences.

As a sociologist whose perspective was chiefly economic, Jafari had been hired to teach in the growing anthropology studies program. It wasn't exactly his field, but the sociocultural component in this area of study was expanding, as was the discipline of sociology in general, and he found a way to teach what he was most interested in by providing compel-ling course syllabi that met the approval of his superiors.

Jafari's whirlwind courtship with Beata, who was employed as the secretary in the anthropology department, wasn't a secret. The two drove to work together almost every day that first fall. They were married before the New Year rolled around.

The student body wholeheartedly accepted the marriage and the resulting children, Aisha and Etienne, who were born within the first three years of the marriage. Faculty members, however, were not as welcoming. Acceptance of an interracial marriage cut across specific lines, it seemed. Anthropologists, having built their careers on study-ing different races and cultures, were accepting on the whole. Sociologists, being in a newish area of study that had stemmed from anthropology but wasn't completely embraced by the mother field, displayed mixed sentiments. Many in this group, curiously, tended to view the marriage under the umbrella of deviance.

Off-campus racism was alive and well. Beata recalled two incidents with great bitterness. Once, she and Jafari were asked to leave a wedding reception at an upscale restau-rant, unbeknownst to the bride and groom, who were dear friends. They got up from their table, chicken dinners half-eaten, and left silently, not wanting to cause upset to the bridal couple.

On another occasion, they had just seen the movie *East of Eden* and were walking from the theatre to the car, arm in arm. A middle-aged Caucasian woman walked right up to Beata – with no hesitation whatsoever – and spat on her shoe. "Marry your own kind," she whispered through her teeth, then scurried off.

America had disappointed the couple in more than a few ways. Jafari, in particular, became disenchanted. The final straw was in 1965. The notion that Vietnam, which he believed to be a wholly manufactured war, could steal their young son away from them was a complete abomination. Although the States had already been involved in Vietnam – the bombing of North Vietnam had begun – the first US combat troops were sent over in March 1965. This date, to many, marked the real beginning of the war.

So, after many late-night conversations and much handwringing, Beata and Jafari decided to leave the country and build a better life for themselves and their children in Canada. Four years later, after they left the States, Jafari's instincts about conscription were proven right: The lotteries began in December 1969 for those men born between 1944 and 1950. Etienne was born in 1951; he would have been next.

Relocation was not without risk. They moved to Toronto without securing jobs. Jafari had some connections at the University of Toronto in the anthropology department, but nothing solid at the time of the move.

Thankfully, this department was going through a renaissance. A few high-profile academics had recently been hired. One of these scholars was South African-born social anthropologist Isaac Schapera, who had been a research assistant to the well-known anthropologist Bronisław Malinowski while completing his doctoral studies at the London School of Economics – Jafari's alma mater.

Jafari was familiar with this man's research on Botswana, and one of its languages, Tswana. Schapera drew his research, in part, from the unpublished work of David Livingstone, which fascinated Jafari, as well as missionary journals.

Having met with Schapera, and clearly hit it off with the scholar, Jafari was invited to guest lecture at U of T on more than one occasion. Students loved him, Beata always pointed out. He was a tremendous orator who interacted with audiences exceptionally well. He explained complex theories, qualitative and quantitative research, and detailed field notes, in such a way that made the material come alive.

On the heels of this success, Jafari became a part-time sessional lecturer. There were hints that the next time the department had an influx of cash for new hires, he would be top of the list.

Beata, meanwhile, had secured a position in the Resource Department of the Ontario Crafters' Guild, a non-profit organization representing weavers, potters, wood workers, glass artists, and more. The Guild was located in a slightly rundown house on Dundas Street across from the Art Gallery of Ontario.

She had landed the position at the Guild after half-heartedly submitting her cover letter and résumé when the kids were in school and busy with friends, and Jafari was becoming more entrenched in his studies. To her, it seemed like a good time to launch back into work.

Functioning as a librarian of sorts, Beata helped visitors find information about crafts in the province through the slide library maintained in the Resource Centre. She also oversaw a government-funded initiative, the Liturgical

Project, which documented religious objects across the province, from chalices to robes, stained glass windows to pulpits. As long as the pieces were functional – the definition of craft, as opposed to art – then they were fair game. She catalogued and photographed them, as well as provided brief but engaging write-ups.

Beata wasn't trained for this kind of work and, in truth, she was a little surprised when the Guild offered her the job. But there was a sense that no one was particularly trained to work at the Guild – the president was a glass blower from the UK; the vice-president was a furniture maker who built dining tables from driftwood that he found along the shores of Georgian Bay; the membership manager was a weaver ("fibre artist," as she preferred); and the human resources manager, who doubled as the financial officer, was a metal worker and knife maker. To Beata, it was a circus-like environment, but she was made to feel welcome right from the start.

Within a year of moving to Toronto, the family had settled in nicely. Aisha and Etienne were set up in local schools, having made friends easily. Everyone was happy. This was another golden point in time, second only to their courtship – one on which Beata frequently dwelled.

Everything changed, of course, when Jafari suffered his fatal heart attack, the cause of which was an undiagnosed abnormality. When it happened, he was at his desk in the corner of their bedroom by the window, writing an op-ed on Africville.

Immediately after he died, when she returned to the apartment from the hospital without him, she tore the paper into many small pieces, as if it had somehow caused his death. But a few hours later, she Scotch-taped it back together and, the next day, framed it. These were his last thoughts in this world, his last penmanship. His handwriting in particular took on a special meaning for Beata. Every time she discovered another handwritten scrawl – from lecture notes to a shopping list – she squirrelled it away for safekeeping.

She suddenly realized that she hadn't moved from the lightbox in two hours. Her back was aching, as she had been slumped over all this time. This rehashing of everything, the whole of her life with Jafari, wasn't helping when she did it in isolation, she concluded. She knew that she had to get better and, with this, she realized that she needed to return to Paul's group. There was too much at stake.

5

With reluctance, Paul accepted the fact that he and his wife were entering into uncharted territory: a trial separation. It seemed as though their marriage had run out of gas. In some ways, neither partner appeared willing to undertake a final push or grand gesture to stay together. Calling it a trial period, however, made it sound less permanent or final, not so scary, as if they could ease back into their married life, unscathed, at any point in time.

Two days after the big fight with Cynthia, when she asked him to move out, Paul was flipping through the classifieds, looking for apartment rentals, as the kids watched cartoons in the den. Something caught his attention: an ad for a flatmate in a communal living situation down Roncesvalles, not far from his current house. It appeared to be an actual, functioning commune! Now, this was something he could sink his teeth into.

Paul recalled, with fondness, the day he discovered Karl Marx, in the school library, at the tender age of twelve. One of the opening lines of the *Communist Manifesto* had stuck in his head – "The history of all hitherto existing societies is a history of class struggles" – although, at the time, he had had to look up the word hitherto in the dictionary. Undaunted, he ploughed through *Das Kapital* over the Christmas holidays that year, which his uncle looked upon with great suspicion.

Despite the fact that the finer points of dialectical materialism would have completely evaded young Paul, to this day he believed that these documents altered his worldview. They gave him a lens to interpret the world. The haves and have-nots, the division of the globe by the bourgeoisie, the enslavement of the proletariat – all of these things painted a vivid and very dramatic picture.

Perhaps now, at age thirty-five, he could "harvest" the ideals of Marxism. He decided it was about time to see what old Karl had actually meant; it was time to live a Communist truth and try communal living in earnest.

He called the landlord immediately and was accepted into the household as the new tenant over the telephone, which seemed a bit odd to him, but he brushed away any doubts. Maybe this was the way real Communists conducted business.

The initial transition, the physical move, was simple, rudimentary. He merely pulled up from the basement the largest brown suitcase he owned – a wedding gift from Cynthia's parents – and threw in about twelve books that he was hoping to read over the summer; a few bits of clothing, underwear, pyjamas, the purple and orange tie-dyed shirt that Evan had made him for Father's Day; and his so-called

Jesus sandals, as Cynthia had dubbed them in happier times. Bedding, fresh towels, soap, shampoo, toothbrush and paste, and his list was complete. He was ready.

On one of the cooler evenings that week, when Cynthia had taken the kids to see a movie, Paul walked with his brown suitcase, from his modest family home on Garden Avenue to the new house, only a few streets away in Roncesvalles.

* * *

On his walk, he went over his last conversation with the kids. Before Cynthia took them to the movies, she had given him a few minutes alone with them. It was a surprisingly gracious gesture. As she left the room, she brushed past Paul and he caught a closer glimpse of her. He could tell that she had been crying. Her demeanor had changed since the big argument. She was much softer, fragile, not so sure of herself. As she left the room, he could see by her slumped shoulders and matted hair that this had taken a heavy toll on her.

He turned his attention to his sons. Jason was already asleep in the umbrella stroller, the heat having exhausted the wee lad. Paul suddenly realized that his youngest would likely not even remember a time in his life when he lived with his father, and that idea just about brought him to his knees. He looked out the window to steady his emotions before turning back to his eldest.

Evan was alert, excited for the movie.

"You know that I'm moving out – just down the street, very very close – for a little while, right?" Paul said, trying to sound casual. Cynthia had already explained some version of this to the kids.

"Yup," Evan chirped. "Mommy's taking us to see *Willy Wonka and the Chocolate Factory*."

Paul scanned his son's face for any hidden grief. He found none and was forced to conclude that Evan didn't grasp what was happening. He didn't want to press the issue, so he hugged him and said, in a truly unnatural tone, taking the lead from his son's exuberance, "You know I love you and I'll visit a lot, right?"

"Yup. Can we have some chocolate, some M&M's, to go with the movie?" Evan squirmed out of the hug, eager to get to the theatre.

"You like the red ones best, right?" Paul asked, knowing the answer. He gave Evan a slightly crumpled two-dollar bill.

His son's eyes lit up with the possibilities. This was a lot of money.

As his wife and kids trundled off to the theatre, Paul vowed to stay true to his promise to see the kids as often as possible.

* * *

The Edwardian mansion on Indian Road, his new home, was set far back from the street. It was a little rough around the edges. The front lawn was burnt to a crisp through lack of care and insufficient watering, while at the same time, overwhelmed by a variety of weeds that evidently thrived in the desert-like environment.

He walked up the interlocking brick pathway to the front door, admiring the red and green stained glass above the entryway. At the door, he set his suitcase down and, suddenly realizing the rumpled state of his butterfly shirt, began pressing down the paper-thin fabric with his palm so as to flatten it against his chest. He wanted to appear a worthy candidate for communal living. Then he reached for the doorbell.

On the threshold, he told himself: Keep an open mind. Everyone has something to teach and learn; we're all students of life. This could be the start of something very new and different, the next chapter in his journey.

John, the young-looking landlord, opened the door. He looked pretty buttoned up, markedly conservative for being a Communist, Paul thought. The man shook Paul's hand and invited him to have a short chat in the living room. The other two flatmates were out at the moment, but they would be attending the commune's first meeting the next day.

The chat was, indeed, brief. Next, John showed Paul his bedroom, a medium-sized space on the main floor with a window that looked out into the backyard. He then excused himself, and left Paul alone to unpack and settle in. The bed was comfortable, and he fell asleep reading the first chapter of Arthur Janov's *The Primal Scream,* which, despite the alarmist title, put him straight to sleep.

It was, however, not a restful slumber. He tossed and turned all night, worrying about the kids, about the therapy sessions, about his new home. He rose sometime after midnight to get a glass of water in the unfamiliar kitchen, not bothering to switch on the light. He stood in the room, which was eerily illuminated by the moonlight filtered through the sheers, feeling lonely and bewildered.

The commune's inaugural gathering was held the next morning. Paul, exhausted, tried his best to rally for the meeting.

"This assembly of the commune is officially called to order," said Larry, the second flatmate, as he took charge.

Larry appeared to be around ten years younger than Paul, perhaps just out of college. He was thin with greasy, shoulder-length hair.

This young man, Paul realized at the very start, was hard to read and often flippant. He had introduced himself as an unemployed animal photographer. This, Paul knew, was a lie. He could tell by the way Larry had said it.

When Paul introduced himself as a reformed social worker, Larry burst out laughing. "Holy cow, a contributing member of society," he said.

Paul wasn't sure how to respond, so he elaborated on his employment predicament: "For the summer, I'm trying a bit of an experiment. I've rented space in a church in the Junction for a three-month-long group therapy session."

"My parents would love you, man," Larry said. "You do something real. Not like from outer space." This response equally perplexed Paul.

"Today's house meeting is about, well, important stuff to remember," said Rachel, a breezy blonde, who giggled as if she had forgotten the "stuff" already. She was a young-looking folk singer who often played at the Sir Nicholas Tavern on Roncesvalles. Paul had hazily recognized her when they were introduced, although at first, he couldn't put his finger on where he had seen her. She looked like a sixteen-year-old version of Joni Mitchell. Paul wondered if this was intentional. Was she really that young? He soon learned that she hoped to play Yorkville, but felt that she needed more practice, which was true. She had a lovely soprano voice – all of a sudden Paul recalled faintly hearing singing through the walls, when he had got up in the night for the drink of water – but her guitar playing needed serious improvement.

"Do we have a schedule for the jobs around the house and the division of labour?" Paul asked, cutting to the chase. The first meeting was not progressing as rapidly as he hoped. The group tended to wander off in a million directions. This was all he really wanted to know: the Marxist foundations, and how this commune actually operated.

He felt slightly awkward seated on the opposite side of the kitchen table. The others were nestled across a wide banquette, their backs against the row of windows through which Paul could see the backyard.

The morning sun, reflected off the neighbour's windows, shone into the kitchen. The light settled on the not-so-pleasant elements of the room: the stacks of unwashed dishes in the sink, the newspapers and sheet music piled high on the table, two overflowing ashtrays, and a substance that looked like dried vomit in the corner by the stove.

Someone had an impressive collection of *Science* magazines, but, judging from the present company, Paul imagined that these were the forgotten chattels of a previous occupant. The April 2 issue lay open. He absentmindedly read the title: "Plasma Physics, Space Research, and the Origin of the Solar System" by Hannes Alfvén.

"Good idea," said John, the buttoned-up landlord. Paul had surmised that the twenty-five-year-old couldn't afford the rent by himself, with his wages as an entry-level accountant.

"Could you coordinate this schedule of chores, Paul?" John asked, passing the buck. "You seem eager to contribute."

"Sure," Paul said, grabbing a pencil and paper from the counter. "What are we looking at? Bathroom cleaning, kitchen dishes, cutting the grass – that's seasonal – and snow shovelling later on, same category really. Groceries … What am I missing?"

"We grow our own food," said Rachel. "Out there." She pointed in the direction of the backyard.

Paul had not yet ventured into the back of the property, but he could make out a substantial lot with a large maple tree. The space beyond the tree appeared to be divided right down the centre, with one side more lush and well-tended than the other. Returning to Rachel, he noticed that she looked tired; her eyes were unnaturally red.

"Yes, I saw that in the classified ad," Paul said. "What crops are you cultivating?"

"You're a social worker, right?" said Rachel. "Well, I guess this is kinda in your line of work: social."

"She means recreational," John clarified.

Larry roared with laughter.

"I'm afraid I don't understand." Paul was perplexed.

"Cannabis." Larry seemed eager to share. "The breakfast of champions, man."

"We grow vegetables too. Tomatoes, peppers, carrots,

potatoes, and beets on the southern side," John said. "But the northern side is devoted to three strains of pot. Two from Columbia and one from Mexico."

The tutorial suddenly turned more serious.

"Mexican pot's very *now*," Rachel explained its popularity to Paul.

"We started them from seeds, in the basement, under special lights, then transplanted when the sprouts were about a foot high. Once outside, it's all about irrigation," Larry went on to explain the set-up, as if he were describing an engineering feat of epic proportions, not unlike the irrigation system of the Egyptians, siphoning water from the banks of the Nile and distributing it to a vast geographical plane.

"Three strains?" Paul asked, unfazed. "Okay, cool."

"For different purposes," Rachel said. "I like the 'Mellow Yellow.' That's the relaxing kind."

"I'm a fan of 'Fuck You Up,' which I personally named," Larry said proudly.

"What's the third kind?"

"'Job Interview.'"

"Why's that?"

"'Cause that's what it's good for," Larry said, as if stating the obvious. "When you do an interview, man. Takes the edge off."

After the meeting, Paul ventured out to look at the "crops." His initial view of the space, from the back window, had been correct: It was divided down the middle with a small row of cement pavers running the depth of the yard like a backbone.

The southern side was bone dry. The cracked earth sported the carcasses of what were formerly some kind of leafy vegetables. Carrots, tomatoes? Paul could not determine what the dead bits were, because they all looked the same: pale green, straw-like, beyond rejuvenation by several weeks. There could be no salvaging this year's crop of God-knows-what.

The northern garden, by contrast, was a veritable oasis. Ground-level fortification was secured by a tiny row of barbed wire meticulously demarcating the boundary of the lot. He guessed this was likely in place to keep out any animals – rabbits or raccoons, perhaps.

Beyond this seemingly impenetrable threshold, Paul saw rows and rows of robust marijuana plants, lovingly hydrated, the evidence of which was present: three or four hoses with sprinklers attached, set aside, poised for the next day's watering session.

The rows were mathematically precise. The sections delineating the three marijuana strains were clearly indicated by placards attached to the top of three wooden poles. They stood perpendicular to the earth, like sentinels, reading: "Mellow Yellow," "Job Interview," and "Fuck You Up."

He was surprised at the state of the plants. He had presumed that they wouldn't fare well in the harsh Canadian climate. But here they were, large as life. Perhaps the exceptional heat of this spring had bolstered their survival.

He chuckled to himself, half curious as to how this set-up – albeit well-hidden from the road – hadn't been detected by law enforcement or square neighbours, and half impressed by the rigour with which his flatmates had clearly approached their harvest. This was serious shit, he thought. It didn't bother him in the slightest that it was illegal. He was amused more than anything.

He stood in the centre of the yard as the sun beat down, took off his jersey and threw it over his shoulder, then mopped his brow with the sleeve. He remained there for several minutes, standing on one of the cement slabs, scratching his head about the particular place in which he now found himself – this strange house. He reminded himself to keep an open mind.

6

"Simon!" Claire called down the street.

The second group therapy session had just ended. It was May 31. She had decided to go back, after all. And this time, the group felt a little more natural; people were beginning to relax very slightly. The session had even gone on beyond the allotted hour.

She was pleased to discover that the temperature had changed while they were inside. Annette Street was cooler now. The night had descended and brought with it a waft of surprisingly fresh air, the calming sound of crickets, the smell of earth. The streetlights cast a honey glow over the area, with trees encroaching around the delicate light.

As she skipped up beside Simon, she looked over her shoulder to make sure that Beata was far behind and out of earshot. She couldn't see Paul at all. Maybe he had stayed back to clean up.

"The psych hospital," she said. "I recognize you. Do you remember we talked about the Van Gogh print?

How inappropriate it was?"

She couldn't recall the specifics of the conversation – it had been a few years ago – but she did remember Simon. It struck her suddenly in the middle of today's session. The memory of him came back to her as clear as day. He had left an impression on her. She knew that he was in a lot of pain at the hospital.

"Van Gogh painted the Asylum in San Remy, yes. I remember now," he said, laughing. "I'm sorry. I was out of it back then."

"Me too. The meds."

"We thought the print would motivate us to lop off our ears. It was a bad choice of art ... And a very bad joke."

They continued down the street without speaking, just taking in the night.

"I'm glad you're okay," she said after a while. By this, she meant alive.

"You, as well. But clearly, we still need help – hence, group therapy."

"I'll give it a go, for sure," she said. "I've got to get a handle on my anxiety."

"Fear of the future. That's tough."

"What do you think of Paul's approach?" He was still asking participants about the best and worst things in their lives. To date, only Beata had answered the question, although her response was somewhat riddle-like: Jafari and Jafari.

"You can tell me," Claire urged. "Practice on me before the next session."

"What are your best and worst?" Simon pushed back.

She sensed that he would be inclined to tell her, at some point, despite the apparent resistance. The chemistry of their hospital chat had been reignited. They really did click.

"Best thing: still looking for that," she said. "Worst thing: bad bosses. I think it might be me, attracting them. They're drawn to me, what can I say?" she joked again, then caught herself. "I don't know how to deal with difficult, aggressive people. My current boss is the worst ... And you?"

"Best: I think I'm resilient. But sometimes it's hard to find strength. Maybe I'm not actually resilient, but I need to be. Believing I'm not would be self-sabotage," he said.

"Resilient ... against what?"

"Society," he said. "How's that for an issue?" He stopped walking all of a sudden and began rubbing the back of his neck, glancing around nervously as if confirming that they were, indeed, alone on the street.

She was puzzled. It looked as if he were about to say something but wasn't sure.

"Simon, I –" she began after a few moments, wanting to fill the silence, to ease his obvious discomfort. Without thinking, she put her hand on his shoulder.

"I'm gay, Claire. It's not something I want to share with the group ... This isn't ancient Greece or Paris in the 1920s. Being homosexual is distinctively out of fashion.

"My job at City Hall ... is challenging," he continued. "I could lose it if anyone found out. That's a very real thing. I need an income. I have to be realistic."

"Is that under threat? Is anyone suspicious?"

"A few macho shitheads in the mail room. They're just horsing around, but there's an undercurrent."

"That's a horrible irony, when you think about it."

"How so?"

"I mean, there you are, working in City Hall, granting marriage licenses to heterosexual couples, when your own private life has to be a secret." Her mental wheels were turning. She wanted to find a way to help Simon.

"Not many people, straight or gay, would think of things that way," he said. "You know, Claire, it looks like we're both struggling with aggressors."

She nodded as they walked another half block without talking.

"If it would help," she began slowly, "I could pretend to be your girlfriend. At work, I mean. I could visit, paint a picture of your domestic life."

Simon appeared stunned by her suggestion. Claire worried that she had offended him.

She studied him, objectively, under the streetlight. He appeared tailored and professional, having come from work prior to the session, but underneath there was a different story. She realized how far he had come from the hospital experience. It was like night and day, although when he spoke about his workplace fears, she saw the look in his eyes. There was a pessimism, a despair, inside of him that threatened to blanket whole cities. It was the fear of the return of the darkest days.

"T-That's very kind of you," he stammered. "If we were to do this, we can't tell anyone. I don't want the folks in group therapy to know."

"Okay," she said. "Although they seem pretty nice. Welcoming, that is."

"No one can know about me, Claire," he pressed. "No one can find out."

They parted shortly thereafter, Claire evermore determined to figure out how to make the girlfriend scenario a reality.

That night, she dreamt about the psych hospital. This was a recurring dream: She was back inside. It wasn't clear if she had never left, or if she had left and she was returning. In these dreams, she could actually smell the place. It was a particular blend of disinfectant and vomit or sickness. She could recall every detail of it, as if the institution had taken root in her subconscious mind in a way that was permanent and inescapable; it had become a part of her.

When she awoke, she couldn't stop thinking of the hospital. She often had flashbacks about the place, usually triggered by upsetting events. The idea of going back still plagued her, and she supposed it always would. But this was different. It was as if she needed to revisit it. Perhaps group therapy, and certainly reconnecting with Simon, had brought it all back.

The hospital was located at the corner of Lakeshore Boulevard West and Kipling. It opened its doors in 1889 and it was originally known as the Mimico Branch Asylum, part of the Provincial Lunatic Asylum based on Queen Street West. In 1964, its name had been changed to the more respectable Lakeshore Psychiatric Hospital.

Its architect, Kivas Tully, had also planned Old Trinity College at U of T. His style combined Romanesque aspects, such as broad arches and heavy columns, with Gothic elements and ornamentation. The grounds of the hospital, conceived of as a "therapeutic landscape" essential to recovery, were planned down to every last detail. There was even an on-site cemetery, as morose as that seemed.

When she was an inpatient, there were rumours about an underground tunnel system where staff could quickly travel between buildings, called cottages, when the weather was poor. (Cottages 1 to 5 were originally for female patients, while Cottages A to E were for males, she was told, but over time the patients were separated or classified in a different way, by their diagnoses.) There were whispers of the existence of a subterranean railway that delivered food from the main kitchen, which turned out to be true, but it had been removed in the 1930s.

Despite its grand exterior, the interior of the old hospital had seen better days. The original walls were constructed of brick that had been painted a jaundiced yellow – no doubt, some administrator's attempt to cheer patients' spirits, though the insipid hue had the opposite effect. The walls were scuffed and beat-up looking, tarnished by the handrails of the beds often rolled from one room to another.

The fluorescent lighting in the hallways flickered off and on like a nervous tick. This had put Claire on edge. Within the first hour, she knew that she wasn't in a regular hospital, as if she needed reminding.

In the lounge, called Moorehouse, patients could watch television during certain hours, but only if they were deemed well enough; play cards; try their hand at the piano; read books from the modest library, which was really only a few bookshelves; and receive visitors, although this was very rare. The hospital was a place no one wanted to visit.

The wards were quiet on the whole. The silence was broken, occasionally, by the outburst of a patient – screaming, crying, or even singing or laughing. This was followed by near complete silence, which meant sedation, Claire soon realized.

Staff members were truly trying to help the patients, she sensed, but at the same time, they seemed overwhelmed.

Claire, a short-term patient, developed a good relationship with two young nurses in the ward, Becky and Francine, both around her own age. They were very kind to her – doing things with her that girlfriends would do, Claire imagined, never having had a great many close friends, such as chatting about various dreamy movie stars or painting each other's fingernails. Claire often wondered if, on the outside world, they would have been friends. But the outside world wasn't something a person generally thought of as a patient, at least not in the beginning. Scheduled dates for discharge came and went, and over the weeks and months, this led to the sense that time had been magically suspended.

Claire's internal journey during this time in the hospital was arduous. She was overcoming her anxiety, one step at a time, retraining her brain not to sink back into familiar loops, replaying events, mistakes, regrets, over and over.

Occupational therapy, which she enjoyed, took place in Cottage 3. This treatment was designed to help patients develop coping mechanisms and, ultimately, to help them with their transitions back to the outside world. After these intense daily sessions, she liked to visit Moorehouse as a way of decompressing.

This was where she first noticed Simon. She knew immediately that he was in a bad way. He had been admitted to the hospital the night before, yelling loudly. The commotion had cut into the darkness in the early hours of the morning, just after midnight, upsetting a few of the patients in nearby cottages.

The next day, when she saw this slender, dark-haired man in daylight, she knew that he wanted to die. His wrists were bandaged; she realized that he had attempted suicide. This was also clear from the blank expression in his eyes and the way he sat, motionless, with his shoulders caved in. He looked like he had already given up on everything, like he didn't want to be sitting in this hospital common area, in his room, or anywhere, in fact.

Over time, she noted his pattern of behaviour in the hospital: He sat by the window most days, spoke to no one, picked at the bandages on his wrists. He seemed very far away.

When Claire initially approached him, the first thing she noticed was his eyes. The dark circles under them and the pinkish hue that bled into the edges. He wasn't crying at the moment, but it looked as if he had been doing so for weeks.

She wasn't sure what to say when she walked over to his chair from across the room, so she said nothing. She just stood there looking at the artwork beside the window, digging her thumbnail into the palm of her hand.

"I believe that's a Van Gogh," he said, with a wry expression. "It's the halls of his insane asylum."

She giggled nervously.

He looked down at his bandaged wrists, turning them upwards as if to shock her. "At least I still have my ear."

She tried not to shudder, not to let the sinking feeling in her stomach reflect in her facial expression. But she could sense tears welling. She looked away. The two of them stared at the painting in silence for a long time.

Claire later learned, from Becky or Francine, that she was the only person Simon had ever spoken to at the hospital, including the doctors. She found that hard to believe, because he didn't seem to have trouble talking with her and, by comparison, her experience in the hospital was all about talking. Once the floodgates were open, she told the doctors everything. And these psychiatrists dug deep. Like all good Freudians, they went back to the beginning, back to childhood.

Claire was a terribly nervous child who had found school difficult due to the necessary compromises – not related to making friends, although these were rare, but related to her own work, her own striving for excellence.

By the age of six, on any given evening, long after the dinner plates had been cleared, Claire could be found at the dining table, practising her cursive writing. She recounted this, with great fondness, to the doctors.

At Claire's own insistence, her teacher, Miss Johnson, had provided handout copies of the cursive writing that was also tacked up above the blackboard in the classroom. The teacher later reported to Claire's mother (and Claire found out eventually) that the teacher had perceived this request as odd, but she knew that her nervous little student wanted to practise at home. In fact, the teacher had found it endearing, and Claire had become the woman's favourite pupil that year.

Then came Claire's first explosion: One evening, at the dining room table, she noticed an inconsistency in the home copies of the cursive writing compared to the school version, which had been imprinted on her brain. Likely, this deviation was the result of different printers with slightly divergent fonts, she later realized. But this inconsistency caused Claire such profound consternation that she shredded several hours of work, sobbing violently as she did so.

Her mother had witnessed this tantrum, and informed Claire that her behaviour was "not normal for a six-year-old." So, her mother took her to a psychiatrist – telling no one, of course. Claire understood, even at the time, the great weight of stigma.

Years later, in her sessions with the doctors at the Lakeshore Psychiatric Hospital, Claire surmised that in 1946 virtually no one sent their kid to a shrink, so her mother must have been desperate, must have felt that she needed drastic intervention to fix her daughter. It was also possible that, given the fact that all shrinks in Toronto were male, her mother sought a man's authority or intervention, since Claire's father had died three years earlier from complications related to polio.

Had the loss of her father triggered the first twinges of anxiety in Claire? This was the topic of many sessions with Claire and her doctors, but it was impossible to determine, because her memories of the man were reduced to mere shadows, with loose recollections attached to them. You could hardly say her father had an impact on her life, other than the void that his death had introduced. Claire could only vaguely remember sitting on his lap while her mother played piano at Christmas; feeding the ducks with him in High Park; and playing, together, with Lucky the family dog – a horribly ironic name, as the animal was hit by a car the same summer her father died.

But her dad's death took a tremendous toll on Claire's mother. Claire could see this, even back then. Later, she more fully realized that to be widowed with a young child during the war meant that her mother needed to work very hard to get food on the table, to keep her factory job, and to make sure they wouldn't fall destitute and end up in the poor house. Doctors theorized that it was possible her mother's stress and worry were passed on to her, the only child, but Claire thought it would be fruitless to speculate on it. This Freudian stuff had its limitations, and surely everyone had suffered during the war.

Whatever the root cause of her anxiety, Claire knew that her mother had genuinely believed a psychiatrist could help. The woman had idealized the great promise of a doctor.

Claire distinctly remembered the setting of this visit: The doctor's office was in a beat-up back street near College and Spadina. The psychiatrist, Dr. Barlow – most likely the only one her mother could afford – was an elderly, grey-haired man who smelled like cigarettes and Crown Royal, and who came up with a solution for Claire right away: Strike the child when the outbreaks occur. He demonstrated this on the spot, springing into action with little warning, even though at the time, Claire wasn't showing any signs of a tantrum. One minute, she was seated alongside her mother in a chair facing the doctor's desk; the next, she was being beaten by a strange old man in a white coat.

Her mother did not intervene. She did not prevent Dr. Barlow from hitting her child. This, more than anything, was fodder for Claire's sessions at the Lakeshore Psychiatric Hospital because it had caused her such distress. She couldn't figure out how a mother could seemingly turn her back on a child like this.

Both Claire and her mother left Dr. Barlow's office in tears that day. They took the streetcar home, Claire's non-stop crying drawing the attention of many onlookers. The fistful of bloody tissues in her hand and her sobs left many feeling uncomfortable, it seemed. She could sense their eyes on her, while her mother, meanwhile, stared out the window, looking as if she wanted to be anywhere but on this particular streetcar at this particular point in time.

In the end, her mother failed to adopt the prescribed treatment, and the two never returned to the cheapest shrink in town. She never expressed to Claire that she thought Dr. Barlow had been wrong. Perhaps there was still a question in her mind?

The unspoken lesson for Claire, as she unearthed in therapy, was to hide the self-loathing, to mask her expectations of perfectionism or at least not act out when she failed to achieve perfection in her cursive writing, or in any other such exercise. These emotions were to be, from that point forward, concealed. She would create private, secretive ways of fixing herself, like holding her breath or digging her thumbnail into her palm. And with these new methods, Claire was able to function for many years, well into adulthood.

She hoped that this fix would last forever, and in fact, she had counted on it. No such luck. Her hospital stay was triggered by one event in her life as a novice editor – one particularly malicious person she encountered – decades after her introduction to the psychiatric world. The battle-ground was the workplace – Claire's very first job in publishing. She was set up in a different publishing house than the house where she currently worked. She had been working there for several years, during which time she had produced around twenty-five textbooks. She felt at home and appreciated. She had become close to a small cluster of authors, many of whom were working on subsequent editions of best-selling textbooks.

A new boss, Alice Sickhart, was brought on board that year. It was clear from the start that she was someone trying to prove herself in the workplace, trying to rise in the field by cutting others down. Publishing was a male-dominated field, and women in the workplace, in general, were a minority. Perhaps Alice, a woman even younger than Claire, thought it necessary to appear tough, like a man. Perhaps she felt threatened by Claire and possibly other women in the office, Claire had often wondered.

Whatever the reason, Alice clearly took issue with her. Sensing this, Claire stayed away from the woman, giving her space to fill her new position, to make it her own.

But Alice invented ways to get into Claire's business, tried to trip her up, and found fault with everything she did. Nothing really stuck, until one day a particular political science textbook was in production, one week away from its publication date. There were many backorders, as the sales team had done a stellar job pitching the book to professors across Canada for their courses, slated to start in a few weeks. The schedule for the book had been accelerated. And for this reason, Claire felt a lot of pressure. She often asked herself, in retrospect, what she could have done to put the brakes on this manuscript before the shit hit the fan.

Then, just as the book was being printed – literally, whirring through the press – an underling, a fucking goddamned eager-beaver poli sci student who was doing a work term at his uncle's printing shop, recognized something familiar: a turn of phrase in chapter two on the structure of Canadian parliament.

Plagiarism was deadly in publishing, everyone knew. The mere whiff of it destroyed everything around it, bringing houses to their knees, discrediting editors, and ensuring they would never work again. Plagiarism, in publishing, was akin to pedophilia in the classroom: a sin beyond all others.

Claire could still recall, with great lucidity, the Grinch-like smirk that spread across Alice's face when she admitted that plagiarism had been discovered in the poli sci manuscript. Both women knew this was career-ending for an editor.

Claire went home that day and cried for hours. She couldn't sleep, couldn't eat, couldn't get out of bed. After her off-putting experience with Dr. Barlow as a child, she did not want to turn to the world of psychiatry, but she felt she had no other options. The rational part of her brain, which was struggling to calm the waters and make wise decisions about how to get better, presumed that this world had likely improved, become more humane, over the years. She still had great trepidation but was willing to put aside her fears. One week later, having been granted a medical leave falsely attributed to back pain, she booked herself into the psychiatric hospital.

The owners of the publishing house, who had always liked Claire, were merciful, although they were also saving their own skin. The book was cancelled. The academic buyers across Canada were told that the manuscript needed more development, while the sales team dusted off another poli sci textbook and unceremoniously pushed it on professors. The author-professor was promptly fired, and the book contract was made null and void. His employer, a west coast university, was unaware of what had transpired – again, the publisher couldn't divulge the story without tarnishing the house. If the university had discovered this case of gross negligence, the professor would have been fired, his tenure revoked.

This was more trouble than most houses see in a lifetime of publishing, and it had landed squarely at Claire's feet. She was, after all, the editor directly responsible for bringing this manuscript to the house, and for developing it and very nearly publishing it. She was painfully aware of the calamity she had caused.

Taking a medical leave related to a physical (back) problem was the only option. She couldn't tell anyone – friends, authors, editors, and associates – that it was a mental leave. If she did, she would never work again. No, this way, she would just slip out of society for a while, unnoticed, as people thought she was resting in a "normal" hospital or even at home, then slip back into the world with no one the wiser. Problem solved.

Claire could recall her day-to-day life in the hospital as if it were yesterday. It had been a curious time in her life. (No one ever expects to be in a psych hospital, after all.) Living in the institution was monotonous. The days blended together. But that was okay with her.

At first, even though she had checked herself in to the hospital, unlike many others who were forced into the place against their will, Claire was mildly suspicious of the scheduled "therapeutic" sessions with the psychiatrists and psychiatrists-in-training. Her childhood experience had left a pronounced halo of doubt in her mind.

But the psychiatrists in this hospital were good at their jobs, she soon concluded. It was, after all, a quarter of a century after her first interaction with the system. She forced herself to trust these new doctors, forced herself to tell her story.

When she first arrived at the hospital, she felt acutely embarrassed about the state of her palms, but she soon realized that self-harm was common in a place like this. Residents often sported deep scratches, burns, cuts, bruises, and scars from a lifetime of self-inflicted injuries to their arms and legs. It was safe to assume there were additional wounds hidden under many of the pale blue, hospital-issued gowns. In this way, Claire fit in well.

The doctors, naturally, pressed her as to why she cut her palms, and at first, she couldn't answer. In some ways, it was as if another person were doing it, she was so completely unaware. But in time, she realized that she was distracting her conscious mind by hurting herself as a way of avoiding conflict, or mentally checking out of the intensity of a stressful situation.

After six weeks, her hands had completely healed, and she had been armed with new techniques to address aggressive confrontation, to find her words with adversaries, and to stop herself from shutting down altogether when prodded by difficult individuals in the workplace. This was what she told the doctors, half believing it herself.

She knew, deep down, that it wasn't a complete fix. It was one thing to learn techniques, but another thing altogether to fully embrace this new knowledge, to actually change deep down. But Claire thought of herself as a quick study and swallowed the idea of recovery as long as it got her out the door. The rest, she figured, would happen over time.

Moreover, by the beginning of week six, she was becoming increasingly fearful that, for some reason, she wouldn't be allowed to leave. The "lifers," overmedicated zombies for whom there were no release dates, haunted her thoughts. She wondered about their diagnoses, and whether they were like her, suffering from anxiety, but only worse. If she stayed in the hospital longer, would she become like them? Not knowing their medical histories made her invent horrific scenarios where they had once been functionally "normal," like her, but over time, were reduced to catatonic states.

Shortly after that, by week seven, she stopped taking the meds, signed the requisite release papers, got the fuck out of there, and never looked back. Until now. The similarities between Alice and Maron were uncanny, despite the fact that Claire's encounters with these challenging bosses were years apart. In many ways, Maron was far worse than Alice. Alice's compulsion to climb up the corporate ladder seemed almost superficial, or at least impersonal, compared to the depths of destruction that Maron initiated against Claire, the delight she took in singlehandedly shattering her underling's confidence.

Claire found it hard to believe that she was, once again, under the thumb of a malevolent female boss. How could this be happening for a second time? Why must women undercut each other in their career trajectories? Was there no sense of sisterhood? Had the sexual revolution, putting women in the workplace and thereby theoretically levelling the playing field with men, forced us to compete against each other?

Claire was dumbfounded, although optimistic this time around. In a way, the stakes could not be higher for Paul's group therapy – a last hope for her.

7

The morning sun dappled ever-changing fragments of light into Beata's kitchen. This was her favourite time of day. On weekends, she often found herself, as if by surprise, deposited on the banquette that wrapped around the bay window – arguably the loveliest spot in the Indian Grove apartment, nestled deep inside the flat, well away from the front door.

"I'm having a bit of a wobble," she confessed to Jafari, wrapping her hands around the Raku mug that he bought for her when she first started working at the Crafters' Guild.

She peered into her apple cinnamon tea, inspecting the small fibres that had floated to the top. She sighed, not sure how to continue, or rather where to start. She glanced out the window into the neighbouring trees, as if she might be able to find her words dangling in the elegant leaves of the willow that swayed very slightly in the early morning breeze. The heat of the day hadn't descended yet, although a thick, earthy scent was detectable, hinting at what was to come.

Beata knew that something was wrong with her. She could feel it. Something chaotic and unpredictable was clutching at her ankles, threatening to sweep her away. She saw the way people sometimes looked at her on the street, the way they stared and pointed, particularly children, who seemed fearful of her, and teenagers, who laughed unabashedly. She chose to ignore them, but it hurt her feelings nonetheless.

She couldn't put her finger on the problem. So, she focused on the one thing she cared most about in the world: her kids, Aisha and Etienne. She wanted them back in Toronto but didn't know how to do this, how to talk with them about it. She needed to solve this issue, their departure to the States.

She turned her gaze back to the table, looking directly into Jafari's brown eyes – a chestnut hue that always seemed to catch the light in unexpected ways. When he removed his glasses, as he often did during their lengthy conversations, she marvelled at how extraordinarily large his eyes were, how far his eyelashes extended, each one captured, fleetingly, in the sunlight, right down to its colourless tip.

She let her eyes rest on him, take him in, for a few moments. His afro, grey and always neatly groomed, rested playfully on his shoulders. He was wearing his favourite sweater. Reds and greens. His attire was odd for this time of year, but she didn't question that, or anything. He was, simply, here.

"The kids," she said, letting her words out like a slow leak.

He adjusted his position on the banquette, tilting his head as he always did when he was intently listening. She knew this conversation would be hard for him. He was proud, for lack of a better word, of his close-knit relationship with his children. He adored them to the bones.

"I – I fear I've let you down," she said, her shoulders drooping.

"Now, you know that's not possible, m'dear," he said, resting his hand on her forearm.

She loved the timbre of his voice, the comforting tone, and the particular way he said "m'dear." There was no replacing that voice. It was etched into her brain, woven into the fibre of her personal narrative, the way she saw her life and imagined it to be: the story of their collective lives. It was familiar to her on a primal level – unmistakable in the same way that a baby's scent is to its mother. Inhaling this scent, as if it were a part of her own body reconnecting to something deep inside, this distilled everything to a base, animal-like identification: You came from me.

"I have some bad news about the kids," she began. "They've gone back to the States."

He nodded gently, as if he already knew. She could see, without the need for words, that he empathized with her. They sat very still in the kitchen as the sun rose, each lost in thought.

She was thinking about how much had changed since Jafari died. When it happened, it was as if the world became suddenly unrecognizable, irretrievable, as if everything were violently and abruptly altered, a different piece of a wholly different puzzle.

In the early days after his death, she wasn't herself when she gazed into the bathroom mirror. It was as if some stranger was staring back. What did it mean to be standing in the washroom staring at the hollowness of a former person – a carcass, really – who was, to the outside world, functioning at near full capacity? Didn't people see that a huge part of her had died as well?

In fact, she asked herself why she wasn't dead along with him, because it didn't seem possible that she could still be here when he wasn't. It was an abomination.

She had refused to take time off work directly after his death for fear of losing funds for the kids' education, and for fear of breaking the rhythm of this fresh but unwanted reality, this false new world where she skated along the surface of things. Just keep running, she told herself. Keep moving forward. Hour followed hour; day followed day. You couldn't stop the clock.

Part of her drive to continue was that she felt at home at the Guild. She could focus her thoughts here. She had a sense of comfort from the moment she laid eyes on the building, an 1890s, Queen Anne-style house. She felt at peace here. In its prime, she figured, it would have been a sumptuous single-family dwelling for Toronto's elite. However, now, over seventy years later, it was showing signs of serious decay. The paint was peeling, and bits of gingerbread had broken off. The brickwork was covered in a few layers of soot – so much so that the building, at a distance, looked nearly black. The low-ceilinged basement, which always smelled slightly moldy, was home to the curatorial staff. The small bathroom served as a makeshift space for washing wine glasses during gallery openings – probably not the most sanitary environment, but it sufficed. The main floor, with twenty-foot ceilings and ornate crown moulding, was ideal for the gallery space.

The Resource Centre where Beata worked was on the second floor. She liked the space because it was dominated by a large bay window that overlooked Dundas Street, which always had considerable foot traffic related to the Art Gallery across the road.

She enjoyed organizing the Resource Centre. This consisted of a wall of cabinets overstuffed with the alphabetized files of craftspeople across Ontario, divided by media: glass, metal, fibre, wood, pottery, etc. Most of the files contained slides of the crafters' work. Beside the files, she had made way for a new lightbox with a magnifying lens and a not-so-comfy stool.

Beata's desk was tucked into the corner of this space. She had introduced several pothos plants that had taken over the area with their droopy vines. A crafter friend had supplied macramé hanging baskets to support a few ferns that were strewn up by the bay window in a haphazard fashion.

In this space, Beata often met with people seeking to commission major works like boardroom tables or stained glass windows for churches, restaurants, banks, or private homes. She met with craftspeople who were beefing up their files and adding slides to their portfolios. She sometimes collaborated with a local photographer to document the exhibitions for the Guild's newsletter, *Crafters of Ontario*.

Of these three groups of visitors to the Resource Centre, she preferred the craftspeople and the photographer. The patrons – Toronto's "blue bloods," as Jaf always said – could be a challenge with their specific demands and frequent design changes. Patrons usually underestimated how long it would take a furniture maker, for example, to build a twenty-foot dining table, especially when the desired wood had to be imported from faraway lands. They would commission pieces of curly cherry maple with Makassar ebony inlay, bubinga, east Indian rosewood, and chevron avodire, but they had no idea how long it would take to round up these fine materials.

Beata's favourite initiative at the Crafters' Guild was the Liturgical Project. This was what kept her going to work every day after Jafari passed away. This project meant that she was a regular visitor to some of the most sumptuous religious establishments in the region, often with an exclusive pass to archival materials that members of the public would never have had the opportunity to see. In spite of her anti-religious stance – likely the result of her no-nonsense Dutch upbringing and a practical streak to her personality – she was becoming surprisingly attached to this project.

She reported on her progress each week at the Guild's staff meeting. To date, she had documented 398 stained glass windows, 478 chalices, 386 vestments, 164 pulpits, and 15 chuppahs.

The flip side of Beata's dedication to her work after Jafari's death was harder for her to acknowledge. Part of her refusal to take a break from the job was that she found it difficult to be alone in the apartment. Before they left for the States, the kids had their own lives and were often out with friends, leaving her by herself. She didn't regret for a moment the fact that they seemed to have moved on in a way that she could not.

To Beata, the living room and all of its contents – the armchairs, the old sofa, the family photographs, even the half-dead plants and discarded newspapers – came with their own historical stamp. The armchair where Jaf always opened his Christmas presents, where he sat with his morning coffee and read the paper with his left leg dangling off one side, plaid slippers akilter. The scuff in the wall where, on moving day, the box spring for their king-sized mattress had become wedged against the bathroom door in the narrow apartment. (They bent the frame of the box spring slightly, and it was eventually forced into the bedroom.) The spot on the hardwood floors where she and Jafari had knocked over a candle while dancing to the Beatles' *Rubber Soul* album, released just before Christmas that year – this had left the green wax mark after oozing into the grain of the wood. (This proved impossible to dig out without damaging the floor, so they left it.)

At first, after Jaf died, the mere act of looking at these things was excruciating to Beata. She could barely stand to be in the apartment, with or without the kids, her grief was so crushing. If she were to glance at these items and fully realize that the memories connected to them could never be re-enacted, an unfathomable panic seized her, overwhelming her senses, making her nauseous. This feeling of horror and despair resided inside her, coming in and out of focus with a will all its own.

On weekends without the distraction of work, in the early days after Jafari's death, the only reprieve for Beata was to leave the apartment. The kids often questioned her as to why she took off unexpectedly, without even telling them she was leaving. She began taking long walks in High Park. She started doing this one Saturday, only because she'd run out of options. And yet, to her surprise, shortly after the first step outside of her building, she felt an undeniable sense of respite. As she walked south on Indian Grove toward the park, the feeling sunk in: relief. She was grateful to the point of tears.

On her walks, she often peered up into the sky, trying to figure out what had changed, why she felt better. Perhaps the openness, the atmosphere, the vastness of the sky offered some kind of proxy for peace or serenity. She wasn't sure what the mechanism was, but it worked for short periods of time – while she was outside walking – and this allowed her to step back into her own life, like a stranger returning to a childhood home, in small but manageable portions of time. She couldn't explain this feeling to the kids or even to herself, or rationalize it in any way, but it was real.

Sensing that she had unlocked something almost magical, she began walking in High Park along the same route every time. It commenced down Spring Street. Here, Beata didn't focus on the gently sloping road, nor was she aware of the families, small children, and dogs that shared this space with her in the urban park. Instead, she looked up to the very tips of the trees, mesmerized by their collective sway. She liked the idea that many other people, many generations now long gone, had witnessed this same scene for decades, even centuries, if you were to consider a time before the park was formally constructed.

Something about this idea compelled her. It was as if the trees, due to their age and their timelessness, allowed her to get a glimpse of what lay beyond death; as if death itself were a construct, like time and space, which could, under the right conditions, be unlocked or dismantled.

This realization led to Beata's obsession with time, which took root a month or so after Jafari's death. She could feel that her stress and sadness about the apartment were morphing. She allowed herself the luxury of thinking differently, as if the objects in the apartment and the apartment itself would return to life, to meaning, if time were somehow altered and Jafari could, once again, occupy the same time and space as she. After all, she reasoned, it was only time that prevented them from being together.

This was a sea change, a turning point in which she was rescued from utter despair. The park, she believed, had saved her life. She returned as often as possible. Even over the unseasonably hot spring of 1971, which brought one scorching day after the next, the park had never failed her. She marvelled at the lush and exquisite foliage that offered every colour of green from lime to emerald to moss. She often stopped and closed her eyes as if to extract and distill the full effect of nature. The removal of one sense, sight, enhanced the others. She inhaled the deep earthy scent that further enveloped her into this wondrous alternate reality.

One evening, in early spring, a murmuration of starlings over Grenadier Pond had left her breathless. The way the birds flew overhead, as the sun filtered through the lower branches of the trees on the western shore, struck a chord with her. She watched the birds for several minutes, holding her breath. How did each starling know exactly when to twist and turn within the larger flock – a grouping that could have been in the hundreds, according to her fleeting calculations – to facilitate the collective, dancelike movement that swept over the water so effortlessly? How was this even possible? she wondered as she stood on the shoreline by the willows.

What secret in nature were these birds so clearly in tune with? This, when we humans, by contrast, can't connect to anything! We are so unlike these beautiful creatures, she thought. We are operating in near complete isolation, plodding through our lives as singular individuals, like distant moons no longer connecting to their home planet.

If time were to evaporate, she realized that night while watching the starlings, then she too could connect. And this was how she had more or less chosen to live her life from that point forward. She felt badly that she had not yet explained this to her daughter or son but feared they would never understand. This was too private; her grief was too personal, and she felt the need to safeguard it, even from her own children. Whenever they suspected something was off or feared for their mother's mental well-being – both Aisha and Etienne may have caught her talking to herself on a few occasions – Beata sensed that their concerns were accompanied by judgement.

"What are you thinking about?" Jafari asked. "Your head's far away, m'dear, I can tell."

The question jolted Beata back to the breakfast table, the morning conversation with her husband.

The sun was becoming oppressively hot in the kitchen nook. She realized that she would soon need to turn the fan on and close the curtains.

"The kids, I think they don't like that we talk. The way we talk," Beata said, noticing her tea had gone cold.

"Hmm."

It seemed to Beata that the idea was resonating with Jafari.

"Maybe I haven't been handling things very well with the kids," she suggested. "But I feel we're at loggerheads. With Aisha in particular, as you would expect."

"She often takes the lead, with Etienne following to avoid conflict," Jafari agreed. "We know this."

Beata wanted to tell him that after his death things got worse, but she held back. She wanted to tell him that last winter, roughly four months ago, their daughter had acted on her rebelliousness. One morning, Beata had found Aisha's bed empty. When she, in a panic, asked Etienne if he knew where his sister was, he caved and told her the whole story: Aisha had reached out to an old school friend in Chicago with the idea of moving back. Her friend was working part-time in a radio station run out of the University of Illinois, and she subsequently alerted Aisha to a job opening. The day the job was posted in the university newsletter, the friend had called Aisha and read her the advertisement over the telephone. The following day, Aisha took her passport from her parents' cabinet – without consultation, which incensed Beata – went to the Greyhound bus station at Bay and Dundas, purchased a ticket for Chicago, and left. Aisha met with the station manager and interviewed for the position. But two days later, when her daughter sheepishly returned, Beata had said nothing. It was clear that the job had not panned out.

By the time spring rolled around, however, Aisha's escape plans had evolved. She announced one day in April – on a seemingly normal morning around the breakfast table – that she was leaving, or more precisely, that she "couldn't wait to get out from under this roof."

"Sometimes I really hate you," she had said to Beata in a half whisper, that day over breakfast. "You must know you're crazy. This isn't normal." Her clenched jaw was the only indication of the sentiment simmering beneath the anger: a deep sadness. She was trying not to cry.

The thing that mystified Beata most about Aisha was the anger. She fixated on it. What have I done to elicit such a response from my daughter? she asked herself. The apparent ease with which her daughter painted everything black and white greatly disturbed her. It was as though her daughter had reconstructed her younger life as a kind of unbearable prison when, as Beata saw it, she and Jafari were very liberal and laissez-faire parents. They had given their children tremendous freedoms. This, in light of the fact that the two kids, now young adults, still lived at home, made the rebellion all the more perplexing to Beata.

The feeling that her daughter was slipping away instilled in Beata a cavernous, unsettling feeling. After so many years of closeness, she felt, their story had somehow and inexplicably been rewritten.

Etienne, Beata reminded herself, was much quieter, to the point of being reserved. Despite his youth, he had a propensity for remarkable insights precipitated by considerable silences, in which he would be working through a particular problem. Unlike Aisha, he bided his time in conversation and deliberation; he didn't charge in like the two women of the family. Perhaps this was a reflection of having grown up in the shadow of his older, more reckless sister, or perhaps it was just his natural temperament.

"The idea of moving back to the States isn't about the war," he had said to his mother, by way of explaining his sister's growing disdain and the strife it was causing the three-person family.

"We're not as political as you are, or as dad was. Aisha's more upset about … Well … the way you are these days."

"The way I am?" Beata had exclaimed, frustrated by her son's evasiveness. Sometimes gaining information from Etienne was excruciating. "Just tell me what you're saying!"

"I mean since … you know," Etienne had muttered, then walked away, making it clear that he wasn't interested in continuing this line of discussion.

She was deeply confused by this conversation, and she pondered it often. What had Etienne meant by "the way you are?" Was he referencing her long walks in High Park? Her silences around the apartment? Or worse, had he or Aisha intentionally eavesdropped on one of her private conversations with her husband? This idea raised her hackles. Wasn't it enough that she had agreed to try the group therapy sessions for the sake of her kids? Had they forgotten that commitment? What did they want from her?

Returning to Jafari in the kitchen, she measured her words: "I suppose some things have got worse, Jaf," she admitted.

The heat in the kitchen was now overbearing. The light spread into every corner of the small room. She got up and closed the kitchen sheers, glancing out the window. The distance between Toronto and Chicago seemed greater than could be measured in miles. How would she ever get her children back?

"What should I do?" she asked Jafari, knowing that the dye had been cast. The day would, again, be overtaken by a particular kind of sadness where the world would slowly become unrecognizable to her.

"Just tell me what to do," she pressed.

To her, it was inconsequential that Jafari had died one year ago or that his remains were buried in Parklawn Cemetery under a one-hundred-year-old oak tree.

She peered into his eyes once again from across the table. She counted on his sound advice. She was, in fact, waiting to hear from him.

8

"Cyn, I understand you're busy at work," Paul said with a sigh. "I'm not asking you to join us. You don't even like the Toronto Islands. But I wouldn't mind taking the kids, now that the weather ... the heat might break ... I don't see how these things are related: your work and my having the kids for a bit."

He was standing in the kitchen of the communal house on Indian Road, bound by the mercilessly short cord of the only telephone in the place. This was a regrettably public location for these sorts of negotiations with his wife, he thought, as he began picking at the insipid wallpaper that looked like it had been there for a quarter century.

Behind him, Larry, Rachel, and John were eating breakfast and deeply embroiled in some outrage that Paul didn't particularly want to know about.

At one point, he plugged one ear with his finger as he pressed the receiver against his other ear, struggling to hear Cynthia, even though she was yelling. Every once in a while, he flapped his arms in the direction of his house-mates to indicate a desired reduction in noise. This, of course, made no difference.

Why was it so hard for him to see his children? Cynthia seemed to be resisting the co-parenting plan that the two had decided on when he left the family home. What was really going on? Paul was becoming increasingly agitated and paranoid. He had promised Evan that he would visit regularly, and he had every intention of keeping that promise.

But this was Cynthia's pattern; this was their dynamic. Her fiery nature was one of the characteristics that had first attracted Paul. He knew this, and he often reflected on the irony of it, wondering if the seed of attraction for all relationships was also the nail in the coffin, given five or more years of compromise, disappointment, unexpressed expectations. And if so, did all relationships have a life span? Were we, as humans, not really suited for monogamy? In previous eras, people didn't live long enough to fall into this trap. If we lived in medieval times, Paul reasoned, we'd be dead by now, at thirty or so. He found this idea strangely refreshing.

"I would appreciate a little quiet when I'm on the phone, guys, please," he said, consciously calming himself after he hung up the telephone.

"We're keeping that wallpaper, you know," said John. He seemed mad.

Paul pivoted around to discover that he had, during his conversation, inadvertently picked off a large swath of the flowery wallpaper around the telephone. He didn't remember doing this; it was as if someone else had committed this crime. Somewhere along the line, he now realized, he had subconsciously assumed that the paper was to be removed and the kitchen painted. He suddenly remembered that these renovation plans were for the kitchen in his family home, not his present dwelling. This made him all of a sudden very sad. He was reminded of having watched a documentary with Evan about salmon returning to their birthplace, to spawn, then die. (At the time, he had to make an excuse to leave the room because he got too choked up.)

He retracted immediately. "Gosh, I'm sorry ... It was a difficult conversation ... My wife and I ..." he said, then stalled. Why the sudden concern about appearances? he wondered. This place wasn't exactly the Ritz. He glanced at the sink, overflowed with cutlery, flatware, and beer bottles, marvelling at the depth of the disconnect between order and the lack thereof when it came to issues of cleanliness in this rambling Edwardian house.

Eager to contribute to communal living, Paul had washed the dishes for five nights in a row. As an experiment, he had left them last night, to see if any of the flatmates would pick up the slack. Nope. This was the outcome, he now realized. What would Marx think? This was not the way communal living was supposed to be. Everybody was supposed to be pitching in.

Rachel, Larry, and John stared at Paul, destroyer of wall-paper, incredulously.

"It's Dorothy fucking Draper," said Larry.

Was he serious? Paul wondered. Larry always seemed sarcastic, his delivery deadpan, but he could not be sure. And who the heck was Dorothy Draper?

"It's the Hampshire House collection," John said. "Mother chose it."

"I'll replace the wallpaper," Paul offered.

The group was silent for a few awkward moments. Then Rachel's attention turned elsewhere. She extracted a lock of blonde hair from her cereal bowl and lit a cigarette. Paul found it odd that she ate a children's cereal, Kellogg's Kream Krunch, made with chunks of freeze-dried ice cream, just like the astronauts ate. The idea turned his stomach.

Rachel still reminded him of Joni Mitchell. Though, she had a sort of breeziness, a lightness that was optimistic if not a little vapid – wholly unlike the real Joni Mitchell, whom Paul considered to be a creative juggernaut.

In the pause in conversation, a half-naked stranger sauntered into the kitchen, a tragically short towel hugging his waist. With the larger matching towel, the man was drying his very long, black hair. His shoulders were still speckled with water from the shower.

No one offered an explanation as to this person's presence. Paul assumed he must be one of Rachel's musician friends.

"Peace, brother," the man croaked in Paul's general direction. He then helped himself to some coffee and motioned to sit down at the table. The smaller towel fell to the floor just as he approached the seating area. Unconcerned, he simply sat down to join the group, unfettered by his nakedness. He kissed Rachel on the top of her head, then wrapped his hair up in the larger towel, turban-style.

Paul noticed that the man's eyes, now visible with his hair pulled away from his face, looked incredibly red and runny. They oozed. The condition, whatever it was, looked painful.

Is that what pink eye looks like? Paul wondered, suddenly identifying the towels. These were the very same he had brought from home! His towels. His goddamned towels touching, scraping up against, those dreadfully infected eyes.

"G'morning," Paul mustered, trying to bury his feelings of annoyance.

He wondered if bleach could adequately cleanse the towels, or if he should just throw them out. He imagined burning them outside around a hastily constructed fire pit. His vision of communal living did not include sharing eye infections.

"We have a crisis on our hands," John said, summing up the breakfast-time discussion for Paul's benefit.

"We needed to call an emergency communal meeting, man," said Larry, highly agitated.

Rachel nodded, looking equally concerned.

"A raccoon," said Larry, gesturing out the back window. "It ate our garden. Our fucking garden ..." his voice dwindled.

Paul glanced out the window to see a very-dead-looking raccoon on the patio slab closest to the house. The animal was upside down, its paws reaching to the heavens, a curious smile on its face.

"The vegetables?" he asked.

"Worse: the pot."

"Which one?" asked Rachel's man friend, evidently aware of the three strains that Larry and others had been meticulously nurturing.

"Job Interview," said John.

"A wise decision," said Larry, lowering his head in respect. "Those furry buggers are clever."

Paul sat down to join them, lit a cigarette, and realized, suddenly, just how different his flatmates' lives were compared to his own. He felt old, for the first time, in his new dwelling. This so-called "emergency meeting" on the death of a raccoon and the loss of some marijuana simply did not measure up to his definition of a crisis.

"No shit," he said, resigned.

It was week two of Paul's new living arrangement. And in this short time, he had learned a fair amount about his flatmates, even without particularly wanting to.

For example, John, the landlord, hadn't financed the place after all. No, his mother had paid for it, Paul figured out from a bank slip carelessly left on the kitchen counter one day. Funny, he thought, because John had positioned himself as some sort of a superstar in the accounting world, if that were even possible. In reality, he was working as a teller at a bank in Little Italy. Paul had managed to discern this from John's inflated description of his job as "essential front-line service."

Larry, the self-identified animal photographer and all-around hippie, was a peaceable sort, although his sarcasm was hard to interpret. Paul wondered, however, if the man were suffering from the effects of years of near-constant marijuana use. What does that do to a person's brain? Paul mused, looking at Larry, who was, at this very moment, speaking eloquently about the raccoon's presumed final moments.

To Paul, Larry was an enigma on several levels. How did

the man subsist? Did he work at all? And why did he give a shit about the raccoon?

There were a few breadcrumbs, however, to Larry's story, which offered Paul a small but significant glimpse into the man's life: As soon as he moved in, Paul realized that his shampoo was disappearing at a rapid rate – more so than he'd ever noticed back home with Cynthia and the kids. He wondered if one of his new flatmates were stealing his supplies, but immediately dismissed the thought, feeling horrible for having imagined such a thing.

Then, over breakfast one day, he noticed that Larry's hair had taken an unexpected turn. It was no longer greasy. Instead, it was quite fluffy and a lovely light brown colour.

At first, Paul was angered by this revelation – and there was no doubt that Larry was the person who had been siphoning his shampoo, day by day, because Rachel used Gee Your Hair Smells Terrific and John had his own bathroom with his own supply, presumably. But over time, Paul had a rethink. So what if this young man is stealing my shampoo? he asked himself. Larry clearly didn't have two nickels to rub together. No, by week two, Paul had accepted the fact that Larry was stealing his shampoo, and, further, that he could live with this minor theft.

"How will we rebuild?" Larry asked, as if discussing post-apocalyptic survival options. He was looking at Paul, as the eldest of the group, evidently expecting him to have a plan at the ready.

The others turned to Paul as well.

Paul, meanwhile, was having an epiphany. The real problem, he mused, was the three of them in combination.

Each one of his flatmates was nice enough, individually, except for John. But when you put them all together in this particular environment, with the dirty dishes and pink-eye-encrusted towels, the communal living experiment became increasingly challenging.

Paul still believed in the Marxist dream, but he just needed to work out a different way of cohabiting with these particular folks.

He rallied for his flatmates. "I think for this thing to work, we need a division of labour," Paul began. "With actual work, I mean."

"Not that again. The to-do list," Rachel sighed. "You sound like my dad."

"I mean, hear me out: Let's go back to our main goals. We want to be self-sufficient, right? Grow our own food – not pot, as the focus. I mean, I'm all for it, but you need to eat first."

"I'm not sure that's my priority," Larry stated honestly.

Ignoring him, Paul continued, "Communal living is based on everyone contributing. Do we all agree with that? Can we unite around this idea?"

"That's heavy," from the stranger. "Don't guilt people out, man. Don't mess with karma."

This statement perplexed Paul. Wouldn't contributing to a common goal mean good karma, after all? He didn't have the patience to get into a debate about karma or Buddhism. If any "ism" were most relevant to a commune, surely it was Marxism.

"Has anyone ever read Marx?" Paul blurted, his frustration showing. He was particularly irked by Rachel's man friend having chimed in.

"We're not stupid," John said, putting on an air of authority. "You mean the guy who led the Russian Revolution."

That's a laugh, thought Paul: John the bean counter turns intellectual, like Nietzsche's fucking Übermensch.

"That was Lenin," he said flatly.

"Well, I sure hope he gets back with McCartney because their music was absolute magic," said Rachel, suddenly emotional. "Don't get me started on the Beatles' split!" She rose from the table, dabbing her eyes as she fled the room.

"Now look what you've done, Pops," said the stranger, his pus-filled eyes shooting daggers at Paul. He stood up and strutted off in a huff, his bare white bottom visible to all as he followed Rachel out of the kitchen.

Realizing the conversation had ended, Paul rose from the table. He knew he would never get his towels back, nor would he want them. Cancel the fire pit.

He stared out at the smiling dead raccoon. "Vladimir Illyich Lenin," he said under his breath.

9

Paul mopped his brow, glanced down at his crinkled butterfly shirt checking for sweat stains, and lit a cigarette on the steps of the Victoria-Royce Presbyterian.

It was June 21. The first official day of summer. The weather was sticky, although the heat had broken over the weekend, more often than not, with a violent thunderstorm. This day, Monday, had seen three such storms. The sky had adopted a semi-permanent bruised colouration, Paul noted. It gave him an uneasy feeling inside, a blend of melancholy and apprehension.

He entered the church and found that all three participants, Claire, Beata, and Simon, were already situated in the cool but clammy basement. All three had returned, without fail, each week for one month. Paul was very pleased about this, but today the energy of the group seemed low, he noticed right away.

He countered this with a genuine smile that lifted his own spirits more than anything. "Hello, hello," he said warmly, switching on a single bar of fluorescent light, then sitting down on one of the chairs, half laughing at the Lilliputian proportions of the furniture.

The group formed a circle in the centre of the room. They had retained the exact arrangement of the very first meeting, Paul realized. Claire was, as always, seated cross-legged on the floor.

"Welcome to the fourth group therapy session," he said as he put out his cigarette in the ashtray that had been left on one of the chalkboards by an absent-minded childcare worker.

He quickly surveyed the participants. Simon was, again, wearing his work clothes: black pants à la Beatles 1965, a crisp white shirt, and blue tie with a City Hall pin on the lapel. Perhaps he felt most at ease in these clothes, Paul imagined. Claire had her hair tied up with a rubber band and a pencil through the loose knot, well positioned for ease of access in case some sort of editorial emergency presented itself. Beata, always artily dressed, sported a maxi dress made of multicoloured linen. Some colours clashed.

"Anyone heard of primal therapy?" Paul began casually, pulling a newspaper clipping out of his Army Surplus bag.

"Scream therapy?" Claire asked. "I edited a chapter on it last year."

"American psychologist Arthur Janov, the guy who dreamt up this new approach, believes that pain is caused by repressed childhood trauma," Paul explained. "And the cure or treatment is getting in touch with your feelings. Screaming is one way people can get their feelings out. Others may cry or rock back and forth."

Paul noticed that Simon and Claire looked at each other as if they could have shared an experience or wanted to say something but refrained.

"The article's about John and Yoko embarking on this particular path under Janov's guidance," Paul continued. "I'm interested. I'm thinking of vehicles that we could use, here, as a way of connecting to our emotional selves, and realizing our similarities as human beings. Through this connection, we can help each other. Make sense?"

"Yes," said Beata, who seemed engaged. "But I'm not sure I want to scream."

"Okay, let's hold that thought, save it for later," Paul said, undaunted. He was determined to find an approach for this trio, a way to help them, and perhaps to help himself along the way.

He tried another tack: "Thomas Anthony Harris, author of *I'm Okay, You're Okay* – which I don't completely dig because his Transactional Analysis is pretty Freudian – believes that the brain records memories like a tape recorder."

"I like that title: *I'm Okay, You're Okay*. It's hard to find good book titles these days. Everything's taken," said Claire. Then she looked sheepish. "Sorry – occupational hazard."

"He's basically saying no matter how messed up we are, or how much damage we suffer and impose on others… we're going to be okay."

"Relevant in today's times, what with Vietnam," Beata said.

"He was part of a larger movement to support group therapy," said Paul. "After I read that book, I wanted to try this kind of approach."

There was a growing anti-psychiatry movement, which Paul was concurrently investigating, but he found that it didn't offer any framework he believed to be constructive for the group. He nevertheless understood the sentiment: Sociologists like Erving Goffman and Michel Foucault had studied the damage inflicted on patients, the destructive power of psychiatry. It was, after all, a pretty young discipline.

"What interests me most is this: that the pendulum's swinging away from old-school psychiatry in a way that takes power from doctors and puts it in the hands of patients," he said. "This movement is markedly political, centred around questioning authority." This was something Paul deeply believed in: liberation from hospitals, from stigma, from medications, and the pharmaceutical world. This was a step in the right direction. Power to the people.

"In any case, if we're not feeling like a good scream, let's start our work around the circle, give updates on our week," Paul suggested. "We'll keep these possible approaches on hold, for future consideration, which will be, of course, a democratic process."

From the corner of his eye, at the exact point when he said "around the circle," Paul registered a quiver from Simon, as if the man's body had received a low-voltage bolt of electricity. He recognized that, even after all this time, he'd still have to be sensitive and not force Simon to contribute.

"Good, let's begin," said Paul. "Do you want to start, Claire?"

"Okay," she said, re-crossing her legs.

Paul noticed that she didn't begin immediately but took a few moments to construct her thoughts, while absent-mindedly working her thumbnail into the palm of her hand.

"I'm still struggling with my boss," she admitted. "As I said in last week's meeting. She's papering my file with complaints, some kind of workplace grievances, against me."

"Do you think this is true?" asked Beata. "The way you said it, just now, you had some hesitation …"

"I have no way of knowing. There have never been any complaints against my work from academics. Not that I know of."

"So, this woman is threatening you with pretend complaints?" Simon asked.

It appeared to Paul as if Simon were on the cusp of participating. Jumping in like that was a good sign. If not bringing his own story, then engaging with other people's stories was healthy, he figured.

"Maybe, but once it's in my HR file, it will become real, whether it's true or not. It could be grounds for firing me," said Claire.

"Do you think that's her aim?" Paul asked. "I'm just trying to get a handle on her headspace."

"Yes, but I don't know why."

"The need to be dominant," said Simon. "That's aggression."

It seemed to Paul that Simon knew a little more about Claire's story. He began to wonder if they knew each other, either before these sessions began or perhaps they had been in touch in between sessions.

"We can't control other people, but we can control our reaction to them," Paul said, leaning into the conversation. "How do you react when your boss tells you these things?"

"I'm keeping it together, as far as she knows, but that seems to make things worse. The Milgram experiment definitely brought things to a head."

"What's that?" asked Beata.

"It's a psych experiment that I rewrote for one of my textbooks. It's about people being told, or pressured, by an authority figure, to hurt other people." She spent a few minutes summing it up for the group.

Paul was, of course, familiar with Milgram's work. "Why is this particular experiment so important to you?" he said. "I ask you, here, to strip away any overthinking, answer from your gut, and don't worry about perceptions or interpretations. Just be in the moment."

"Because it's important to get it right? I don't know."

"You mean important to describe all aspects of the experiment correctly?"

"Yes."

"So, again, why's this experiment so important? I mean, you edit a lot of psych books, I assume, and I'm sure that all of them contain these sorts of experiments."

"This one's different. It's about the abuse of power."

"Do you identify with one of the players?"

"Maybe."

"Which one? The person who's taking the orders or the one who's giving them?"

"Taking them."

"And who's the other player, the one who's issuing the orders?"

"My boss."

"Very good. And who's the "learner" in the experiment, the one receiving the shocks with every wrong answer?"

This stumped Claire, Paul could see.

"Who's actually being hurt?" he rephrased.

"I'd have to say me," she said touching her palm. "Can I be both the teacher and the learner?"

"Whatever makes sense to you." He noticed her thumbnail digging into her palm as she spoke. It was as if she was unaware of it. The injury that he had noticed before suddenly made sense to him.

"That really does ring true, Paul." She looked as if she were very nearly overwhelmed.

"Now, if you were in the experiment, how do you think you would react to the authority figure?"

"I'd like to think I'd rebel. But I might be too afraid."

"How would you rebel? What would you say to your boss?"

"I won't do what you're asking me to do."

"Now, translate that to your actual work situation. What do you really want to say to your boss?"

"You're wrong. About everything. I don't deserve to be fired."

"That's great, Claire. You can ponder that idea for next week: how to question authority."

"I need to think about this," said Claire.

Paul noticed that she suddenly seemed exhausted. He wondered if he were oversimplifying things or pressing her too hard. "Feel like a good scream? To let off steam?" he offered.

"No thanks, I'm cool."

She did not look convinced about questioning authority, but he saw a glimmer of hope. That was all he could expect at this point, he realized.

"Beata, why don't you update us about your week, the challenges with your kids," he suggested, eager for everyone in the group to participate.

Beata nodded, rubbing her amber necklace like a rosary. "My daughter's still angry with me, as is my son, to a lesser extent."

"What's the source of her anger?" asked Paul.

"I know she's grieving her father's death. And so, I forgive. But I'm also … coming to terms with things."

"Do you feel her emotions are misdirected? Is her sadness changing to anger and directed at you?" asked Claire.

Paul was encouraged that Claire seemed interested in drawing parallels, finding ideas that everyone in the group could identify with.

"Transference, very good," he said. "This is, according to Freud, how a person unconsciously redirects feelings from one person to another," he added.

"There's more to it," Beata said. "She feels that I'm not moving on … adequately. I sense she's embarrassed of me."

Paul recalled seeing her talking to herself, ranting in the streets, prior to the first therapy session.

"She's probably not fully aware of her motivations," he suggested, not wanting to criticize Beata's daughter too heavily. "Death, or any great loss, makes us behave in a wide variety of ways. We each find our own path. There's no right or wrong way, Beata."

"But why did she have to leave, return to the States, with Etienne when Vietnam's still such a threat? How could their thinking be so skewed? The war's so wrong-headed."

"You can't control their politics. They're adults," said Simon, surprising Paul with his vehemence.

"No, and nor do I want to control them. It's just the venom behind their actions …"

"Can you give us an example?"

"Etienne sent a letter," Beata said extracting a tattered-looking piece of correspondence from her purse. "Aisha doesn't like the way you're acting, it says." She spoke from memory, her eyes welling up.

Paul stepped forward and reached out to pat her on the shoulder, not wanting to press her beyond her limits. As soon as he did this, he was reminded of Vladimir telling him that a social worker shouldn't ever touch a client. But it would have seemed unnatural, or even coldhearted, not to acknowledge Beata's pain with a small physical gesture of support, he reasoned. To hell with the training – he was going to lead with his emotions and relate to these people, human-to-human.

Beata's situation worried Paul. Her grasp on reality seemed flimsy at times. He had seen it the first day, before the first meeting, but also noticed it when she spoke about her husband. She continually referred to him in present tense.

"Expectations, on both sides, often muddle things," he said softly. "Some of this will take time."

He considered his own children – as young as they were – and contemplated how they were handling the split and whether his wife could be, in her own way, poisoning them against him. Of course, he had no evidence of this, but it was something he feared, given Cynthia's volatility.

"We're all damaged, sometimes by the people closest to us," he continued. "But we return to essential communities, like families, that are connected to our sense of identity and belonging. Sometimes this takes time. Your daughter will get there, as will your son, Beata."

"I'll skip the primal screaming this week, Paul, if you don't mind," she said.

"Why don't we take a break," Paul suggested.

Everyone stood up to stretch their legs. Simon, Claire, and Paul seized the opportunity and lit cigarettes.

Paul noticed, once again, that the tension dissipated almost instantly. Even Beata, the non-smoker, looked slightly relieved, although he knew that she had divulged a mere sliver of her story. There was only so much ground that could be covered in one hour.

He watched the group members, as they paced around the church basement. He realized that an undeniable, although tenuous, bond was slowly growing among the individuals. It was palpable to him, after four weeks of sessions.

This feeling, however, was deflated when Simon spoke at the end of the break.

"I'm going to pass again this week," he said. "We're almost out of time anyway."

Simon seemed, by osmosis, to be exhausted by Beata's story. It was as if he had a limit of sadness or discord, and the threshold had been exceeded.

Paul nodded. "Whatever you're comfortable doing," he said, then added, "This is a safe place. Know that. So, maybe next week, Simon, you'll share a little."

"Anyone want to go for a beer, after?" Claire asked. "Are you allowed to do that, Paul?"

"Don't see why not," he said, making a mental note to, perhaps, consult with a few school chums at some point – the social workers who had actually graduated from the program.

But he didn't see the harm. This group was designed to be egalitarian in nature, self-helping, and nonhierarchical. It wasn't "run" by an authority figure (himself), so there should be no conflicts of interest or boundaries crossed.

"We're all equals here," he summed up.

He also wondered if Simon would be more forthcoming in a different environment. He believed that going out for drinks with this group could be a good thing from that perspective.

"On a Monday night?" Beata said. "What bars are open on a weeknight?"

Paul was surprised she didn't know any places. He wondered if any of her friends or family drank alcohol, and presumed, now, that she must be more conservative than he had first imagined.

"I know a place," he said.

*   *   *

It was close to dusk when the group headed out the door. The air at street level, on Annette, was charged with pre-storm tension.

No one had a car, so they boarded an eastbound bus that would deposit them at Dundas West Station, and from there they could travel south. All four gravitated to the back of the bus, which was almost empty. To Paul, it felt like an adventure, like they had been let loose from school, playing hooky. He noticed that Simon in particular looked almost joyful.

On the bus, they chatted about this and that, Simon speaking about his renovation and Beata inviting everyone to an upcoming gallery opening. Claire seemed keen on attending this event. Paul noticed that she was looking at him intently on the bus trip. It appeared as if she were about to ask him a question, but she must have decided against it.

Contrary to Beata's conviction that no one consumed alcohol during the workweek, the Sir Nicholas Tavern, down Roncesvalles, was packed. As they walked in, Carole King was playing full blast over the speakers.

Despite the fact that the tavern was his pick, Paul had always thought the place had a strong medieval vibe, which was sort of cheesy. This was most likely due to the knight in armour standing in the corner and the crest of arms mounted on the eastern wall opposite the door. The tavern's coffee-brown brick interior also featured several Spanish-looking archways that dominated the space. The candles at each table illuminated small areas within the darkened room and, collectively, created a network of honey-coloured constellations for each seating area.

Since it was Claire's idea to go out for drinks, she ordered a jug of beer for the table and an orange juice for Beata. Everyone except Beata dove in when their drinks arrived.

"So, what's your story, Paul?" Claire posed the question as the four huddled around a small round table in the centre of the room. "You're starting to know everything about us, warts and all, and we know little about you."

Paul thought deeply before answering.

"Fair question. Professionally, you know I dropped out of social work. It wasn't a good fit. On the home front, I have two little boys. Evan, five years old; and Jason, eighteen months." He paused and took a breath. "My life's taken an unexpected turn, you could say. My wife and I have separated. I've moved into a communal house near here. It's okay on most days. Not really what I was expecting …"

Paul's description of his life definitely smoothed over the rockiness of his current status with Cynthia, who seemed to be battening down the hatches and preparing for some kind of an all-out war that utterly confounded Paul in its amplification. These days, whenever he had called to collect the kids, it felt as if she were doing everything possible to stand in his way, that his mere existence was irksome. Wasn't moving out supposed to quell the fire? he asked himself, when instead, it had only fanned the flames, leaving him even more dumbfounded about what was truly happening. He was also increasingly worried that their marital problems were trickling over into the kids' lives, introducing a new level of toxicity. Did the kids overhear any of these nasty phone conversations? He wasn't concerned about Jason, but Evan would have understood what was being discussed, even at his young age. Either way, Paul had no way of knowing where Evan was in proximity to Cynthia at the time of the conversations. (He still lamented the fact that Evan had witnessed the very worst argument in the kitchen, back in May.)

"Things are a little messy right now," he concluded.

Claire nodded thoughtfully. "We're all on a journey, aren't we?"

He felt it was only right to divulge a portion of his personal life to this group. These people were, as Claire pointed out, sharing their lives with him, and if this were really an egalitarian, nonhierarchical effort, then Paul would need to reciprocate, let it all hang out every once in a while.

That said, the deeper he got into these sessions, the more he realized that this was a delicate balance. In hosting or facilitating the group therapy sessions, was he leading them? Was he the head of the group or was he one of them? If pressed, at this particular moment in time, he would have to say that he was the de facto leader, admittedly lacking credentials, at the meetings themselves, but he was also a member of the group now that they were out of that setting and seated in a bar.

In fact, being an equal in this way might inspire a deeper sense of trust from the others. He remembered how, after the first meeting, he had wondered if the participants would even return to the therapy session the following week. Yes, he reasoned, hanging out together like this could strengthen the connection and build greater trust.

"Did you two know each other, I mean before our group started?" Paul asked Claire and Simon. "I noticed a kind of familiarity."

"We met a few years ago," Claire said, "in a hospital."

She seemed to be a little loose-lipped, thought Paul. He wondered if she were drinking on an empty stomach, having edited through lunch or something. He caught the waiter's attention and ordered some French fries.

When he turned back to the table, he noticed that Simon was staring at Claire with a look of horror on his face.

"What?" she said in response. "We're among friends, we can surely –"

"No, no, no," Simon insisted. "You don't say something like that and just leave it dangling there for speculation."

Paul tried to smooth the waters. "We can drop it, honestly." But he began to wonder what kind of hospital they were talking about.

"I'm sorry. I fucked up. I really didn't mean to …" Claire fumbled.

"You have no idea why I was in there, do you?" Simon asked, almost angrily.

"Well, no, not really," she admitted.

"My parents had stopped talking to me. I told them I was in love with someone – stupidly thinking that piece of information might make sense to them."

The way Simon said "someone" told Paul that he might be referring to a man. Paul wondered if Beata had caught this as well.

"I didn't know," said Claire.

"Then that person left. The family drama was too much, I guess. We'd been together for eight months. That's a lot of time, you know."

"I'm sorry, Simon, truly." She was near to tears. She reached out to grab his hand.

The two said nothing for a few moments.

Paul was sure, now, that they were referring to a psych hospital. He thought about saying something, but he didn't want to appear to be brushing the subject under the rug.

"I overreacted," Simon said after a few minutes, gripping Claire's hand more tightly. "I'm sorry. I never talk about anything. Publicly, I mean. It's hard to … to open up about stuff. You'll have to be patient, Paul, in group therapy."

Paul smiled. This was a huge breakthrough for Simon. After one month of sessions, at last, the man opened up a little bit. This alone, was worth the trip to the Sir Nicholas.

Simon ordered another jug of beer for the table. "A gesture of goodwill. A toast to Claire's best intentions."

Beata seemed to be disapproving of the rapid consumption of alcohol.

Claire smiled, sank back in her chair, and crossed her legs as if she were sitting on the ground. "Everything's cool," she said.

Her hair had fallen out of its makeshift ponytail. The elastic must have broken somewhere along the line. The omnipresent pencil dangled even more precariously around her left ear.

The music ramped up a notch. At one point, Claire and Simon took a turn on the small dance floor but they were laughing too hard to continue. Everyone seemed super thirsty, so Paul ordered a third jug of beer for the table. It was his round, to be fair. He didn't want to look like a mooch.

After an hour or so, Simon took his leave and stumbled out of the tavern, realizing it would take him a fair chunk of time to travel across the city. As he left, he squeezed Claire's shoulder affectionately and nodded goodbye to the others.

Beata headed out as well, never having touched her glass of orange juice. Perhaps she suspected it was spiked. She looked as if she were decidedly unimpressed with the tipsy state of the others.

Claire remained at the table beside Paul, rocking back and forth with the music. She didn't look like she wanted to leave the Sir Nicholas anytime soon.

Now that the others were gone, and with more than a few beers in him, Paul unabashedly studied her features. Her flushed face lingered only inches away from his own. She was surprisingly pretty in an unorthodox way; her attractiveness was wholly natural. Her loose hair had a floral smell. He noticed that she was perspiring, ever so slightly, along the brow line, as he felt a drop of sweat slide slowly down his own neck.

"I think it's really cool what you're doing," she said, half yelling in his ear to make herself heard over Van Morrison's "Tupelo Honey." "The group therapy thing. I can really dig it."

Her breath was warm on his neck. Her lips tickled his ears and brushed up against his hair as she spoke. He imagined glistening drops of condensation from her breath on his skin, perhaps a few dribbles of her spit in his hair. He decided that he liked this bit of messiness very much. It was natural and undisciplined – the complete opposite of Cynthia.

In the warm haze of drunkenness, he felt catapulted forward by the music, the spit, the candlelight, and the flowery smell of her hair. It was too much for him to resist. He kissed Claire.

"I'm sorry, I love this fucking song," he mumbled by way of explanation, as he wrapped his arms around her waist and buried his face in her neck. When he closed his eyes, it felt like the room was spinning.

"What?" she half yelled, intertwining her arms around his neck and sloppily plunging her fingers into his hair.

Within seconds, they were on top of each other, their limbs recklessly intertwining. Someone's elbow knocked the candle off the table, but the tinkling sound of broken glass barely registered to him.

"Van Morrison," he mumbled. "I'm sorry, but you're quite delicious."

In his zeal, he kicked the table leg and it gave out. The contents – the beer jug and glasses – crashed to the floor. But all he could think about was Claire's breath on his neck.

"You live around here, right?" she asked.

Once more, her mouth against his ear rendered him powerless to answer direct questions. He lunged at her again, unable to pull himself together.

"Paul" – she broke off the kiss – "why don't we go back to yours?"

"Yeah, let's split," he agreed. This was total Claire, he realized: Say what you mean, mean what you say. He appreciated her frankness and couldn't believe his luck. He cursed himself for not washing his sweaty butterfly shirt, or his hair for that matter – no shampoo. *Damn you, Larry!*

They got up to leave, suddenly realizing all eyes were on the two of them. Paul saw the nonplussed waiter, who had evidently witnessed the blundering, inelegant seduction alongside a handful of patrons. The surly young man mouthed to the maître'd, "FUCKING HIPPIES," as he rested a serving tray on his hip.

Paul slapped some money down on the nearest table. "Here's some bread, man. Sorry about the mess," he said in the waiter's general direction.

He and Claire traversed a perilously serpentine course out of the restaurant, hand in hand, laughing hysterically, half tripping around the tables.

Paul then led the way to his house, stumbling through the empty streets. Where had the time gone? he wondered. It seemed close to midnight. After he urinated on the front lawn of his communal home – which seemed, at the time, the most logical thing to do, so as not to wake his flatmates – the two crept into the house. The front door was unlocked. Good thing, he thought, feeling less than confident that he could have located his house key.

They tiptoed through the foyer, past the living room, down the hall, and into his bedroom. Here, they peeled off each other's clothing with remarkable speed. In the near complete darkness of his room, he caught a few glimpses of her milky skin, the curve of her hips and outline of her breasts, on the way to the cool sheets.

10

In the following days after she slept with Paul, from time to time, Claire replayed the evening in her mind. Some fragments of the night were, admittedly, void. She did not completely remember how they got from the pub to Paul's house. She had no regrets, as he was a sweet man and a generous lover even in their drunken haste, but she knew it was a one-off, a bit of fun. They were, after all, two consenting adults.

By Thursday, once her head had sufficiently cleared, she decided to go to Simon's office to play the role of his girlfriend. She took the day off and made plans with him before he left for the office that morning. Still feeling badly over spilling the beans to Paul and Beata about their shared hospital experience, she was determined to help Simon in the only way she knew how.

She realized that creating a fake life like this was morally questionable, but there didn't seem to be any other way to play this. A person couldn't just come out and say they were homosexual, after all. Not in Simon's workplace, not in any workplace, school, or church. This kind of thing would annihilate someone's career, to say nothing of his or her social life. Look what had happened with Simon and his own family! No, this was the only way she could help, she figured, given the circumstances.

Claire had never been inside the New City Hall before, although its construction was completed more than six years ago. The futuristic shape of its exterior intrigued her. The two concave buildings that framed the space looked like giant parentheses to her, the consummate editor.

As soon as she walked through the doors of the government building, she was taken by the expanse of the place. It was all width and girth. The ceilings were low, but the space was nevertheless broad, open concept, with a few gargantuan cement pillars. Fluorescent lighting infused the space with a cold blue aura. The floor was cobbled grey brickwork.

Advancing into the interior, into a tall atrium, Claire realized that the building was constructed around a core: a cone-shaped feature that looked, to her, like a giant mushroom. This off-white structure was glowing, lit from below, and surrounded by flags. The effect was eerie, as if she were inside a spaceship. The height of the atrium made her feel, suddenly, small and insignificant.

Pivoting around in search of signage, she realized that the marriage licensing office was closer to the main entrance, and happily retreated from the mushroom.

This administrative space was dominated by a series of cubicles, rows and rows like corn crops, behind the main information desk. Worn-looking grey carpet stifled any ambient noise, making it feel as if she were in a near complete vacuum.

She caught her reflection in the glass door of the mail room, and this helped her to refocus her thoughts. She studied her attire. She had dressed today knowing that she would be meeting Simon's co-workers – a few of whom had viciously taunted him. She had to look the part. This was the goal, from which she was determined not to deviate: to present a cookie-cutter view of dating and mating in the heterosexual world.

To play the role of the girlfriend, she had exchanged her bell-bottoms in favour of a dress. She owned one shift dress, purchased for a distant uncle's funeral a few years back. It had a high collar that contained starch or some such product that greatly irritated the skin around her collarbone. It was a navy blue colour, close to black, and it covered her knees, which made it distinctively out of fashion. It was neither mini nor maxi. But that didn't matter. Style took a back seat.

She spotted Simon from a distance. He was stationed behind the front reception desk directly under the "Marriage Licenses" sign. Dressed in his neat, black suit with a simple grey tie, he was looking down, no doubt attending to some administrative form. To Claire, he appeared small and pale in the fascist environment.

She suddenly wanted to rescue him from this horrible place. She remembered their first encounter at the hospital – Simon, back then, a crumpled version of what he was now. He had come a very long way from those dark days, Claire realized, but he still seemed far away from anything like happiness.

His face lit up when he saw her. He looked as if he were

a drowning man being thrown a life jacket, which wasn't far off the mark.

"Hi, hon," she said as she approached his workstation.

She noticed a few co-workers look up from their desks, taking interest in her arrival. There appeared to be a lull in office activities. Was it always this slow on a Thursday?

"Hello, dear," said Simon, playing his part.

She scooted around the edge of the reception desk, kissed him squarely on the lips, and gave him a friendly squeeze on his shoulder – a private reassurance that this was going to work out just fine.

She smiled and stepped back to take in the sight of him, nevertheless remaining very close – intimately close – to send a clear signal to on-lookers: Yes, we are a couple.

Simon appeared shell-shocked by the kiss, and she feared she may have overplayed the impromptu gesture. They hadn't discussed this theatrical event in any detail over the phone that morning. She was, after all, improvising.

"Ready for lunch?" she prompted.

"Yes, yes, I am," Simon said. "And I've taken the afternoon off." He grabbed her arm and began leading her back down the hallway.

She wondered if he had changed the objective, suddenly and spontaneously. It seemed as if he wanted to evacuate the building as quickly as possible. Had he forgotten the introductions around the office? Maybe this was as much as he could handle today, she considered, unwilling to abort the mission at this early juncture.

"Why don't you introduce me to your friends?" she gently suggested.

"Oh, yes, of course," he said, swinging back around.

A small group of onlookers had formed out of nowhere; six people had advanced down the hall toward them in a matter of seconds. This group of two women and four men was now standing in a semicircle around the couple.

Claire recognized the problem one, the main bully, right away. He was a burly, red-haired man who stood with his thick arms folded across his chest, his legs planted far apart on the stone grey carpet in a way that rooted him to the ground as if he had laid claim to it.

"Everyone, this is my girlfriend, Claire," Simon said.

She wondered if they should be using a pseudonym or alias – another detail that the two had failed to work out in advance.

"Nice to meet you," said a middle-aged woman with bad teeth. "I'm Nancy."

As the two women shook hands, the elder's lanyard quaked, making her glasses bounce around on her breasts from one side to the other.

"I'm Janet. Good to meet you," the second, much younger, woman said as she extended her hand for a shake. "We work front desk with Simon."

Claire got a relatively good feeling from the women. Although they both appeared conservative – or perhaps it was just the environment rubbing off on them – they were nevertheless approachable. They seemed to want to meet her in earnest, to know more about Simon's personal life. Perhaps his world became more accessible to them, now that they were being told that he was "normal" – that is, heterosexual. Perhaps they had always had doubts about his sexuality, Claire considered.

"Bob, Willy, Doug, and Brian," Simon said, pointing out the remaining co-workers – Brian being the red-haired bully.

The men grunted hello, apparently assuming a handshake was unnecessarily formal. "Mailroom," someone said by way of explanation.

Claire couldn't help noticing that all of them wore very similar black suits. They were the same right down to the buttons and the lapels. She now realized that by emulating this look Simon was blending into the bureaucratic environment.

"Girlfriend? I didn't think you had it in you." Brian guffawed directly at Simon.

"We plan to marry in a year," Claire said, hugging Simon's arm and pretending that she hadn't heard Brian's comment or failed to catch the undertone.

"After we've saved enough money for a down payment," Simon added. He sounded surprisingly natural, Claire realized. Perhaps he was loosening up.

"Congratulations," said Nancy.

To Claire, the woman seemed surprised but happy.

The others were silent. Conversing in any way beyond a brief introduction was becoming strained, she realized. She understood now what Simon had meant about the vibe of the office. These lackluster people, as bland as the battleship grey carpets, were just serving their time in this public office – until retirement, presumably.

"Will we get fast-tracked?" Claire asked, hoping a joke

would break the awkwardness. "I mean for our marriage license?"

"We can't do that," said Bob, frowning and pushing his horn-rimmed glasses farther up the bridge of his nose. He looked at Claire as if she had proposed a bank robbery or mass murder. "That wouldn't be legal."

"She's kidding, aren't you, Claire?" said Simon, who now seemed anxious to leave.

He was worried that Brian might squeeze in some more jabs, Claire realized. Anyway, the task had been accomplished: The girlfriend assignment was complete, so they were now free to leave.

"Nice to meet you all," she said, as the two spun around and walked swiftly down the hall to the nearest exit – not even the main one.

She grabbed Simon's arm affectionately and slowed down his pace, so they would appear more leisurely and relaxed.

When the two erupted out of the building and into bright sunshine, the metal door slamming loudly behind them, they unlocked their arms and burst into fits of laughter.

The brilliance of the summer day contrasted sharply with the drabness of City Hall – so much so, that it suddenly made the office visit seem unfathomably distant.

Claire could see that for Simon, it was as if an escape valve had been released, the stress dissipating almost instantly. A wave of affection washed over her and inexplicably tightened her throat. She noticed that Simon's laughter had morphed into tears, which he blinked away, not wanting her to see.

Taking her cue from him, she pretended to be mesmerized by the sky, glancing up as if the afternoon had offered her a celestial vision of sorts. This also gave her the chance to push aside the pang of sadness, near despair, that resonated in her body. She suddenly felt ashamed for the lack of careful planning, the levity with which she had approached this pantomime, when it clearly wasn't a game for Simon.

The two walked up to Dundas, arm in arm, then across University Avenue to a tiny French restaurant with a secluded backyard.

After they were seated, Claire asked about Simon's real love life. It was time to stop pretending, after all.

"I'm a romantic," Simon confessed. He seemed to want to talk. The two had ordered a carafe of white wine – as per the French setting – and likely the alcohol had facilitated his candor, as well as the fact that they were alone in the backyard, ensuring privacy, with neither of them needing to return to work.

Whatever the impetus, Claire appreciated his new openness, especially since he never shared his thoughts in group therapy, which continued to frustrate her. What's the point of this new therapy experiment if you're not going to participate? At least he had opened up to the group at the Sir Nicholas. That was something.

"I believe in the office, in marriage, I mean," he said.

Claire knew that legal marriage would never be possible for someone like Simon.

"I have one love of my life," he continued. "It's my place in Cabbagetown. It's barely a house, I should preface. More like a cottage. Built around 1880. I looked up the records. I don't know much about renovating. I'm a complete novice. But I'm redoing the floors, renovating the microscopically small kitchen and living room from the ground up," he said, painting a picture for Claire. "It's a long process."

"A labour of love," she said, smiling. She enjoyed seeing him so animated.

"Well … yes, you could say that," he said. "I've also had some assistance from a blond-haired, blue-eyed neighbour."

"Do tell."

"It's not romantic," he clarified. "Jann's been assisting me, here and there. It started one day, a few months back, when he helped me carry the flooring in from the delivery van to the front steps. I couldn't have managed it by myself. He's also been a sounding board for other ideas. He knows a lot about construction and renovation.

"I've been seeking his advice every second or third day. Trying not to be too obvious. When I see him in the street, for example, I'll saunter over, as if by accident, to ask him about floor stains, baseboards, or crown mouldings."

Claire nodded, taking it in.

"Jann's in a long-distance relationship with a painter who's studying in Montréal under some surrealist …" he continued. "But that might not be forever."

Simon told Claire that he had sensed a possible split from the painter, the distance proving too much for the couple, and he wanted to be there, on the scene, when the inevitable happened. He would need to be patient, and not push things, he said.

"My God," Claire exclaimed, "you're shy!"

"This is true. But I'm also afraid of starting a relationship.

Life as a gay man isn't without its challenges. Trudeau may have made gay partnerships legal, but the two worlds will never intermingle."

"What do you mean?"

"Case in point. Do you know the St. Charles Tavern on Yonge between College and Bloor? A major gay hangout. A female impersonations revue. Drag queen culture at the tavern focuses on Halloween but continues year-round. This is, for most Torontonians, the face of the gay world. Which is, to Mr. and Mrs. Joe Q. Public, grotesque, obscene. Something they want to hide from their kids."

He described to Claire how redneck drivers on Yonge, with their drunken passengers in tow, would throw bottles and eggs at the patrons of the St. Charles. It was a regular occurrence in all seasons, no matter what the weather – rain, snow, sleet.

"Naturally, patrons started using the back door to avoid being seen. Same with the bathhouses. Consistently raided by the cops. That's a given."

"So, basically, to meet someone you need to do it in secret," Claire said.

"Jann says some things are changing. He's much more of an optimist than me. A friend of his is actually planning to open a gay bookstore in the city. Can you imagine?"

"That's a first."

"Plus, there's a gay picnic planned on the Toronto Islands, Hanlan's Point, later this summer. I might ask Jann if he's interested … What do you think?" Simon queried.

Claire could see that he genuinely sought her opinion. There was a hint of trepidation in his question. She was both surprised and touched that her views seemed to matter a great deal to him.

"I definitely think you should woo him away from his Montréal painter," she said.

"Everybody has to eat, right? Picnics are picnics," he said, smiling. "It would be like inviting someone to lunch, right?"

Claire had an idea as to the importance of the picnic, a sense that things in the gay community could, under the right conditions, become more public. "That's a big deal, isn't it?" she asked.

"It will be quite a feat, given Toronto. The city's a reflection of our square mayor. A through-and-through WASP. You know he's a member of the Orange Order? Talk about old-fashioned."

Simon described how he often saw the mayor at work, "marking his territory like a silverback gorilla," marching around, looking official, catching everyone off guard.

"The man shows up for work at 8:00 am, without fail. Believes in 'big P' progress. Do you want to know what that means? Development. A major shopping centre in the city core and an expressway down Spadina that would cut right through Kensington Market and Chinatown."

"Really?" Claire made a mental note to read more about municipal politics. She had no idea about the expressway. It didn't seem right to wreck these old neighbourhoods.

"The mayor sets the tone for City Hall, for how daily operations and decision-making take place. He always sides with the Council's old guard and criticizes hippies in particular. He says they're deserters from the US military. Untrue.

"He also hates arts groups. He was embroiled in a controversy around the Henry Moore sculpture – *The Archer*, have you seen it? He says it doesn't belong in a public space. He went so far as to say, outright, that the people of Toronto wouldn't want this sculpture in a public space. What arrogance, speaking for the whole of Toronto!"

"What about social issues, women's rights, free love or, well, loving who you want to love?"

"You mean being gay? No, being homosexual clashes with his worldview. The topic isn't even on the table, not on the perimeter, the very edges of possibility."

Claire suddenly realized Simon's dual realities, the fine line that he negotiated every day: On one hand, he was playing the role of a straight man working for the City with his crisp black suit and, as of today, a status quo girlfriend with nest-building plans – a safe persona that Claire had now reinforced.

On the other hand, there was the truth: He was a homosexual man, developing strong feelings for another man, and increasingly aware of a new kind of consciousness and political activism in the gay community, albeit not without hazards.

These diametrically opposed personas coexisted in Simon, and likely would for the foreseeable future. But how does a person live like that? she wondered.

11

There was more to the story than Simon had revealed to Claire over lunch. He appreciated her gesture, pretending to be his girlfriend, and her desire to carve out a renewed friendship, a space where they could grow beyond their shared hospital experience. But there was a limit to what she could truly understand. He didn't mean this in a condescending way – quite the contrary. Instead, he wanted to shield her from the harsher realities of being a gay man in 1971 – mainly, the hatred that ran under the surface of things. The first gay picnic on Hanlan's Point was intended, after all, to mark the anniversary of the Stonewall Riots in Greenwich Village two years ago.

That said, he knew that events in mild-mannered Toronto didn't usually escalate to violence. Police targeted gay magazines and bathhouses, but the mood of the rare public gay events in this city had been largely celebratory. It was an accomplishment just to be walking the streets, openly telling the world you're attracted to a member of the same sex. That alone, was a victory.

The idea that freedom – and freedom from shame, in particular – was possible, this was something that Simon thought a great deal about, having not yet attended any of the demonstrations or marches. He was an observer, to date, far from the front lines. The public aspect of it was the largest hurdle for him. In this way, he knew that the picnic would be a watershed moment in his own personal history. His parents' disapproval had, by now, evolved into a near-complete estrangement. This rejection had left its mark on Simon, like a scar that still held within it the memory of great pain.

After his lunch with Claire, and throughout the evening, he considered what it would be like with his City Hall coworkers the next day. Would they ease up on the taunting now that they knew he was slated to be married, that he had a steady girlfriend, and that he was "normal" just like everyone else in the office?

He headed to work the next day with a renewed sense of optimism. Lunch with Claire had been a much-needed shot in the arm. He reminded himself to call her and say thanks.

The morning went along like any other in the Marriage Licensing Office. Simon's coworkers acted customarily toward him, and so he relaxed. He even caught himself whistling a pop tune, which, he had to admit, seemed uncharacteristically cheerful.

This mood ended swiftly, however. At the midmorning break, he headed to the washroom. Here, he found himself staring at a set of block letters directly above the middle urinal, scratched aggressively into the wall with something sharp like a nail or screwdriver: *YOU ARE DEAD SIMON FAG!*

He instantly twisted around to see if he was alone in the washroom: Yes, the room appeared to be empty. He checked under the stalls. His hands were shaking; his mind reeling. There was no doubt this was a message from the mailroom gang, a direct threat.

Being identified by name was particularly searing. Almost everyone in the office would read this, at least all of the men who used the washroom on this floor, which numbered around thirty by Simon's hasty calculation. And most likely half of them had already seen it.

He wondered if he could clean it off or conceal it. If it had been done with a pen or magic marker, he could have easily coloured over the message but, due to the tools the perpetrator had used, coverage of this kind would be impossible. He considered whether a section of the wall could be replaced, then bitterly laughed at the notion of going to Maintenance to explain the situation. The custodians knew his name. This incident would be the butt of their jokes for the rest of the summer.

He locked the washroom door, giving himself more time to think. "Fuck, fuck, fuck," he whispered under his breath as he paced around the room. He was sweating and starting to hyperventilate.

One of the stalls suddenly creaked open. Brian emerged, having hidden himself by perching on a toilet seat. He stood, looking almost sheepish in the centre of the room.

"How long have you been there?!" Simon yelled, hysterically. "I suppose this is your handiwork?"

"Look," Brian said, putting his hands up in a disarming gesture, "you gotta know nobody buys your little story."

"What story? What are you talking about?"

"The girlfriend."

"Jesus! What is this, fucking high school?"

"The guys, they …"

"– They what? Don't have anything better to do with their lives in the goddamned mailroom?" Simon was on a roll, unable to stop the rush of adrenalin once it had been released and was coursing through his veins. "I should report you to HR! Or the police! What d'you think about that?"

Simon knew this route would be fruitless, but he was throwing everything he could think of at Brian. Perhaps this would scare the bully because it could, possibly, put his job on the line. Doubtful, but it was worth a try. Without the safety of the others, perhaps Brian could be taken down – not physically, but through some other type of threat. Simon knew that he had the intellectual edge on the man. That was certain.

"The guys, they get going … egg each other on. You know how guys are … I can't … I can't do anything," Brian said.

Simon thought it was odd that the man seemed to be struggling to find words. Was this the first time he had actually spoken to him one-on-one? he wondered.

"But you're the fucking leader! What are you talking about?!" Simon yelled.

"They expect me to … to say things and such … You know, it's kind of a game. For fun," Brian said, lowering his voice.

He seemed to be afraid that their conversation could be heard on the other side of the washroom door.

"Fun at my expense," Simon said with a sigh, sensing that the imminent threat was fading. He felt exhausted, all of a sudden, by the brief exchange.

"Unlock the door. This'll look weird," Brian said, almost begging. Again, the apprehension of someone coming into the room was making him very uneasy.

"Alright," Simon agreed and unlocked the door. "But you need to fix that," he said pointing to the wall. "I don't care how. Just do it."

"Okay," Brian said, bolting for the door. As he passed very near to Simon, almost shoulder-to-shoulder, he mumbled, "Sorry."

Simon remained alone in the washroom, stunned by what had just transpired. He composed himself as much as he could, then headed out the door and back to his desk. What else could he do? He desperately wanted to go home but realized it would look bad, suspicious even. The rest of the day was a blur; he was irrevocably distracted, reliving the bathroom exchange over and over again in his mind. For the remainder of the time, he processed marriage licenses without looking up from his desk. He skipped lunch and let someone else take the front desk. He felt unable to face all of the excitable soon-to-be newlyweds, unwilling to face the public.

At the end of the day, when he was sure that the majority of his coworkers had left the building, Simon snuck back into the washroom with a magic marker, hoping to somehow cover the graffiti or at least revisit the scene for a closer inspection.

He stopped in his tracks. The wall had been smashed in. There was a huge hole, an ominous perforation, the size of Brian's fist, above the urinal.

12

Paul was increasingly desperate to see the kids. But it seemed impossible to get Cynthia on the telephone to set up a visitation. He understood, in part. With two children under six it would be hard to come to the phone – what with dinner, bath, and bed staged within two short hours. She probably didn't even hear the phone ringing. There was only one telephone in the kitchen, and the bathroom and bedrooms were far away from it, at the back of the house.

So, he called her at work. Not a good idea. She seemed angry, starting the conversation in her neutral business tone, then turning sour when she realized who was calling. By the time he finished "Hey, Cyn" he could almost hear her eyes rolling.

She began by complaining about the kids. Jason had been fighting a wicked cold, and the babysitter, a woman down the street who took care of the kids when Cynthia was at work, wasn't pulling her weight.

"Why not call me, Cyn, honestly?" Paul suggested. He would love to have the boys over to his new place, as long as John and Larry were behaving themselves and Rachel's naked lovers weren't loafing around.

He suspected that Cynthia would fail to answer this question. She had a habit of changing the subject when it came to him taking the kids. However, on this particular occasion, the gods must have been smiling. Cynthia's voice softened a little as she said, "Actually, Paul, it would be a big help." Evan was deemed valid for release, on Sunday, as he had not contracted Jason's cold and was well enough for a jaunt with his father. Finally, success at setting up a visit with at least one of his children!

Picking Evan up at the old house felt strange to Paul. Cynthia didn't want him to step beyond the threshold of the doorway. How she conveyed this new code of behaviour, he wasn't even sure, but he knew it to be the case. She seemed angry, even at a distance. Or was she melancholic? He wondered if, in the past, he had misconstrued sadness as antagonism.

He stood on the doormat, waiting for Evan to collect his bicycle with training wheels and tie his shoelaces, both of which took an eternity. During this time, Paul peered down the hall that led straight into the kitchen, smelled the rich scent of coffee wafting down the corridor and mixing with the familiar, wood-timbre smells of his former home. This was a place where he had once belonged.

An intense wave of nostalgia hit him like a jolt to the heart that radiated up from his esophagus and settled – a vice grip – in his throat, rendering speech an impossibility.

"C'mon," he croaked in Evan's general direction.

He held his son's soft, tiny hand as the two headed into High Park. It was awkward because Evan had insisted on taking his bicycle so he could show his dad the progress he had made in mastering the vehicle. This meant that Paul was, with one hand, steering the tiny bike from one of its handlebars and, with the other, clinging on to Evan's hand to prevent him from straying into traffic.

They decided to go to the zoo, Evan's favourite. They headed to Deer Pen Road. His son seemed to be mustering up the courage to ride his bike. Perhaps the progress was not as swift as he had initially boasted.

Once in the zoo, they positioned themselves in front of the yak pen – again, Evan's favourite. He was fascinated and a little frightened by the animal's snorting nose and snake-like black tongue. When the yak sneezed, which happened frequently, he couldn't stop laughing.

They sat down on a bench that faced the pen. The two animals were inside a flimsy-looking wooden structure, seeking shade. It seemed as though visitors to the park had also taken refuge from the tremendous heat of the day. The park wasn't as full as usual. Paul and Evan were alone in the zoo.

Paul had brought some grapes, to Evan's delight, and the two awaited a potential yak sighting while they ate the fruit.

"Mommy had a sleep over," Evan said as he picked an invisible piece of fluff off one of the grapes.

Paul could feel his heart sinking to the pit of his stomach.

"What do you mean?" he asked, trying to sound casual.

"A man came over."

"Who was he?"

"I can't remember."

"A friend of Mommy's?" Stupid question.

Evan nodded. "They let me watch cartoons."

"Was he nice?" Paul asked, again trying to keep it breezy. This was the only question he could rightfully ask his son, although he really wanted to know one thing: if this man was fucking Mommy. His throat started to tighten once again. He felt as if he might cry, right here on the bench in front of the yak pen.

Evan didn't respond to his question. He was looking at his father with renewed intensity.

"Daddy, your face is so red!"

"When do you think Mister Yak will come out?" Paul asked, attempting to distract his son, pointing in the direction of the pen. "I think I saw some movement in there," he lied. "What do you think?"

Evan stood up and walked cautiously toward the chain link fence to get a closer look.

Paul took a deep breath, trying to collect himself, not wanting to lose it in front of his son.

"There's a Mr. and a Mrs. Two of them," said Evan, correcting his father.

"Oh, I didn't realize," Paul said, stammering. "I thought they were … friends or brothers."

"No. They're married," said Evan in a matter-of-fact kind of voice as he peered into the den.

Paul could feel his heart tearing slowly. Was it possible his son was drawing an analogy with the yak's marital status?

Finding a parallel to his parents' situation? Did Evan really know what was going on? It was very hard for Paul to figure out how his son's young mind was processing things.

"How're you doing Evan?" he asked, cautiously gauging the situation, hoping his voice could maintain a light-hearted quality. "I mean, how's your summer going? Are you looking forward to Grade 1 in the fall? That's pretty big-time, isn't it?"

"When summer's done will you come home?" Evan asked. "'Cause you said."

Paul's mind frantically ran through any possible conversations he or Cynthia might have had with Evan to lead him to believe this was a possibility. Had his wife promised, or hoped for, a reunion? This did not make any sense, since she had clearly welcomed some man, some unknown man – to Paul at least – into her bed.

Evan was looking directly at him, waiting for an answer. His back to the yak den, he stood with his scrawny legs, chubby cheeks, Cool-Aid-stained t-shirt, and big boy haircut that made him look like a shrunken man with a disproportionately large head.

"Well," Paul said, looking down at the pavement that had been upturned by the serpentine roots of the old trees that lined Deer Pen Road, trying to respectfully answer his son. He knew he needed to choose the right words. "Mommy and I aren't really sure what's going to happen next."

Evan nodded.

"We're still a family. The four of us. I'm always going to be your Daddy, and Mommy's always your Mommy. That will never change, even if I live somewhere else."

"Okay," said Evan, appearing slightly relieved.

Just then one of the yaks came out for a drink from the large metal cylinder in the middle of the pen.

Evan heard the commotion and ran back to the fence.

Thank God for the beast, Paul thought.

Evan had got one thing partially right: When Paul moved out, he was thinking that the situation would be temporary. Perhaps he had said something to Evan along these lines at the time. If that were the case, he was genuinely remorseful. He shouldn't have bolstered his son's expectations like that.

As he walked Evan home a few hours later, Paul wondered about the possibility of getting back together with Cynthia. Would he want to get back with her, if he had any say in the matter? But how could that be remotely possible, given the state of things? He had learned, in one fleeting but intense conversation with his five-year-old son, that his old life was dissolving even more quickly than anticipated.

Then there was Claire. Sleeping with her certainly complicated things, he had to admit. In truth, Paul had been thinking of her with increasing frequency and in a way that was impossible to predict or control. Sometimes, he wondered what she was doing at a particular moment or imagined her at work, in her publishing house, editing quietly beside a banker's lamp with a spare pencil lodged in her hair. (He had fabricated a detailed workplace scene for her in his mind.) At other times, he remembered the night they slept together. The shape of her, the feel of her skin, the smell of her hair had left a kind of resonance inside of him. It was difficult to keep these memories at bay, to set them aside when, for him, they were akin to an ongoing narrative, as if the two of them were still rolling around in the cool sheets. He caught himself smiling more than once and realized that he needed to put a stop to this. It was, after all, just one alcohol-infused night. And when Paul had awoken the next morning, she was gone. He might have thought that the night was a dream, but a mind-shattering headache had brought it back to him without mercy, in fragments.

He wondered how Claire was feeling about it. He really wanted to talk with her but wasn't sure what to say. Was she cool with a one-night stand between friends? And were they friends, after everything? How could their relationship be classified? Surely it wasn't merely clinical? He wasn't even a qualified social worker anyway. He hoped it wouldn't be awkward at the next group therapy session but his anxiety over this was mounting.

13

A few days after group therapy and the extracurricular jaunt to the Sir Nicholas Tavern, Beata received a second letter from her son.

Dear Ma,

I know you are hurt because we left for the States. But we needed to go. And if we had told you in advance, you would have tried to stop us.

Things are different without Dad. It's hard to explain, but we need to reconnect with old friends.

We are staying with my friend Sal, on the south side near the Stateway Gardens high rise. He is cool about it, and he has the space.

Aisha and I both found work. She's doing an office temp job and I'm at a record store closer to the downtown. Not exactly a career, but it's a gig. So we're able to contribute to food.

I don't know how long we will stay here with Sal. He has been squatting in this space for three and a half years and the City hasn't caught him yet, so it seems okay.

It's good to be back. We don't really see the war to be reason enough to stay away. That was your issue, yours and Dad's.

As I tried to say, we don't think the way you are thinking about Dad is healthy. Your talking to him, I mean. You probably didn't realize that we know about this, but we do. Aisha figured it out first. We think you need help, from a doctor.

Aisha's madder about this than I am, and she would probably kill me if she knew I was writing to you.

I'm not sure when we'll see you. But I knew you'd need to know that we're okay. Don't worry about us.

Love, Etienne

"No return address!" Beata said, imploringly.

"What will you do now?" Jafari asked. He was sitting across from her in the living room, wearing the same red and green sweater as always.

"I don't know. Wait for something to change."

"That's not in your nature, m'dear," he teased.

"Very funny."

"What worries you the most?"

"Safety. How can they be squatters?! I mean, honestly! What kind of stability is that? Being on the wrong side of the law."

"It's not unheard of in Chicago these days. If Sal's been doing it for years, they're probably safe. And if they were in a slumlord set-up, arson would be a threat."

"I should be reassured by this?!" She had read in the newspaper that slumlords sometimes committed arson to claim insurance. "I wish that the neighbourhood wasn't so dicey."

"True. Gentrification is a way's away."

"Do you have to speak like an academic all the time?!"

"I'm just looking at it objectively."

"How can you do that when there's nothing objective about this? These are our children, Jaf. I've been following things this spring and summer. The upheaval's captured a lot of headlines, none of which are favourable."

"Yes. That section of Chicago's lost a fair chunk of its population. Young folks getting educated, moving out. The concentration of poor families ..."

"Every time we drove through the area, Jaf, it was scary. It had a ghost-town feeling. The roads were littered with trash. The streetlights had been shot out. Don't you remember how bad things were?"

"A kind of lawlessness, yes, I do recall. But you have to let them go a little, try to live with the situation. It's beyond your control. You have to accept that."

She knew he was right. She wanted everyone in her family to be happy and settled, to want for nothing, but often, the more she tried to achieve this, the worst things became. She was aware of this cyclical tendency. She also knew that she was spinning out of kilter. This was part of what drove the kids away. Etienne's letter had made it clear.

"I have an idea for you to consider," Jafari said, changing the subject. "A rainy day sort of thing ..."

"Yes?" She was intrigued that he might have thought of a different way. She leaned forward and studied his face, eager for a lifeline.

"Let's take off for a while. Come away with me. I could show you Nairobi, the neighbourhood where I was born. Or maybe London. I still know it like the back of my hand."

She sat back in her chair, stunned by his suggestion. This could be a true escape, she slowly realized. It was a brilliant proposal, given everything that was transpiring.

"Isn't Kenya in turmoil?" She had read about the Ugandan refugees pouring across the border. Roughly twenty thousand people had fled the country in the last two months.

"The refugees are being absorbed. But I take your point," he said. "London then?"

"London," she said, smiling.

He always knew the right thing to say. She should have guessed that over time, over their many conversations, Jafari would have come up with a solution. He always did. She felt giddy with relief.

"Let's plan things soon," she said, suddenly realizing that she needed to leave the apartment for a gallery opening. The Crafters' Guild was launching a new show on a popular basket weaver.

She left her apartment with the idea of London still turning over in her mind.

* * *

Two hours later, Beata was staring at her reflection in the dimly lit washroom in the basement of the Guild, inspecting her wrinkles as she bent over the sink washing wine glasses.

"You could help, you know," she said to Jafari who was perched on the back of the toilet seat, keeping her company.

He smiled and dipped his fingers into the soapy water. "I'll wash all the dishes in London."

Directly above the bathroom, on the main floor of the Guild, the collective buzz of voices intermingled with the sounds of light jazz. Beata could hear, and feel, the floor creaking under the weight of so many visitors.

The opening was a success, it seemed. The baskets were mounted on the wall and hanging from the ceiling like vines. It was an ingenious way of displaying the work, Beata thought. The resulting environment felt organic and forest-like. This was enhanced by the fact that the basket weaver fashioned the pieces out of roots, retaining even the thinnest, hair-like tendrils. Walking through the gallery, earlier in the week while the show was being installed, Beata felt as if she had been transported into a rabbit warren.

For the opening, the curator had set up spotlights that illuminated the root baskets in such a way that the space took on an even more magical, otherworldly quality. These lights also heated up the gallery, which the curator had not anticipated. And now, with so many visitors, the room quickly became an inferno.

Beata was relieved to spend some time in the cool basement at the makeshift dishwashing station.

The Guild had rented one hundred wine glasses for the evening. The wine was donated by one of the wealthier patrons. Three high school students, dressed in white shirts and black pants, were circulating trays of cheese and grapes. The Guild had, at the last staff meeting, voted on the cheese type. Camembert was deemed too elitist, so they opted for Gouda. It seemed more down-to-earth, the president had said. Visitors were offered napkins, rather than plates, which saved on renting dishes.

This hypervigilance over the budget seemed a bit heavy handed to Beata when she first joined the Guild, but over time she realized it was necessary. Money was extremely tight. Each paycheck, distributed by hand at staff meetings, was accompanied by the supposition that it might be the last.

Surprisingly to Beata, employees were not running for the hills and seeking other, less precarious jobs. Instead, they stayed put, despite the wage freezes. This was an ardent group that profoundly identified with their work, Beata realized. They honestly believed in the rise of the crafters' movement with a fervour that wasn't dissimilar to that of the British craft movement in the 1840s. To this lot, crafts would, in time, take over the world. Seriously.

Ella Fitzgerald's sultry voice seeped through the gallery floor to the washroom below, as Beata finished the batch of glasses. The lemony scent of dishwashing soap perfumed the air. Steam from the dishwashing had fogged the mirror, despite the fact that Beata had been using cool water – a necessity for such a warm evening. The atmosphere in the basement had become increasingly sauna-like, thick with humidity.

Jafari picked up a hand towel and started drying the glasses, carefully stacking them back into the boxes from the rental company, upside down. When he filled the last box, she picked up the container and headed for the stairs. The glasses would then be set up, on the gallery's main desk, ready for the next round of drinks. Beata's shift was over. It was time for the next person's dishwashing duties to begin.

She stopped halfway up the stairs, taking an impromptu break. Her body was aching from having bent over the sink. She sat down in the darkened stairwell and rubbed her lower back, content to sit unnoticed.

Someone had propped open the rear door of the gallery. The rich, earthy smell of summer wafted down the stairs to Beata. She sat very still, just thinking.

Jafari leaned up against the stairwell. "You were always sentimental about summer," he said as if he sensed her melancholy.

She remained seated for a few more minutes, listening to the muffled sounds of the crowd, appreciating the moment of calm. She resisted going back to the main-floor gallery, back to the real world. Instead, she would rather have stayed with Jafari, remained inside of their intimate and unending dialogue. This was her security blanket. Sometimes, very rarely, she felt she was teetering on the edge of both worlds.

"– There you are!" said a voice from above. It was Claire!

Beata was genuinely surprised. She collected herself, suddenly feeling self-conscious, worried that Claire may have overheard her conversation with Jafari.

"My goodness," she said, her voice giving away her astonishment, "how nice of you to come!"

On the bus ride to the Sir Nicholas Tavern, Beata had mentioned the gallery opening in passing – extended an invitation to everyone – but never imagined that anyone would take her up on it.

Claire walked halfway down the stairs to give Beata a little hug while balancing a wine glass.

"We take turns doing the dishes," Beata said. She realized that it must have looked odd, her sitting in the stairwell with a box of wine glasses in the middle of an opening. "I'm on a break."

"Love the baskets," said Claire as the two headed up to the gallery.

Beata was, once again, struck by the exhibition space illuminated by honey-white spotlights drawing the viewers' eyes to the tendrils dangling from the ceiling.

The music was very loud in the gallery. A tenor sax solo blared over the roar of numerous, impassioned conversations.

With the crowd, the noise, and the heat, Beata suddenly felt overcome by the kindness of Claire's gesture, showing up like this, as if it was no big deal. She could not find words to express this, so the two women simply circulated the room, investigating the dangling baskets, taking in the scene.

She wondered if Claire was as desperate as she was for a friend, a good friend, someone she could really talk to.

14

This was a precise attack; every word was carefully selected for maximum impact. "You are a passable editor," Maron said before Claire could even reach the guest seat in her boss's office.

It felt, to Claire, like she had never left this room, as if this were part of an endless and irresolvable confrontation.

She took her seat, five feet in front of her nemesis. Having learned from her last encounter, she pivoted around to shut the office door, preventing others from hearing, whether they wanted to or not, what was sure to be another marathon chew-out session. The annual review, part two.

The rewrite of the Milgram experiment was still a fresh emotional wound. The physical lesion, however, was on the mend. Claire's palm had already shed a deep scab. Fresh pink skin was now the only evidence of the self-inflicted wound.

This time around, Claire was slightly better prepared for battle although the idea of speaking up, of fighting back, was still something she would need to carefully consider before doing so. The discussion at the last group therapy with Paul had resonated with her. She knew that she had to do something, but she was biding her time as to the optimal moment.

She decided to sit on her hands to prevent a possible reenactment of the injury. She wondered if it would be bearable to absorb Maron's criticisms without the tried-and-true mechanism, the transfer of pain.

"… But a poor writer," Maron said, closing the thought, like two book ends: You're bad at one task, but worse at another. Nice.

Maron didn't seem to be affected by saying these sorts of things, right to a person's face. Normal people would couch these criticisms; they would soften the blow. Not Maron. She stared directly at Claire as she spoke. Her black hair was, as always, tied in a tight bun. She appeared more severe than ever.

Claire didn't know how to respond. Was there a question in this statement? Was there a particular section of a manuscript to which Maron was referring? There was nothing in her boss's statement that Claire could grab hold of. The insult was non-specific. That was classic Maron. This way, a person could not improve, could not move on. Both parties were stuck in perpetual disappointment.

Again, Claire thought about group therapy. She wondered what Paul would suggest at this very moment. Was there something she could be doing, right now, to stop the inevitable?

And then it happened: She froze. She stopped processing, at least on the surface. Internally, she was thinking things through, assessing from all sides, but a sweeping sense of incredulousness numbed the process. How does Maron get away with speaking to people like this? To what end is this kind of one-sided conversation?

"I have taken time out of my busy day – actually, I wrote this in my personal time on Sunday night," Maron said as she thumbed a piece of correspondence.

Was Claire supposed to feel thankful that her boss had carved out some time for her over the weekend?

Maron picked up the correspondence and held it just out of Claire's reach. "I'm giving it to HR this afternoon."

"What's the content? What are you going to say to HR?" Claire's hands had found each other, the right thumbnail resting in the palm of the left hand, starting to press along the lifeline.

"It's adding to an existing file, Claire," Maron said as if stating the obvious. "Explaining your deficiencies. If you're planning to continue working here, at this publishing house, you'll need to improve."

"Can you explain?" Claire asked, floundering. "I mean, I'm having trouble putting this into context. My authors, my academics, are happy with my work. I know that."

Claire prided herself on being a vigilant editor and arch grammarian. Never in two years had she failed to deliver a manuscript to Production that was in any way approaching late or over budget. In fact, she was customarily a few days early with her submissions, and the cost of photographs and other permission items usually came in under the estimate.

"Your authors can't dig you out of this. They like everybody. They're just happy that somebody chose their work for publication. Don't kid yourself."

Claire knew this statement was untrue. There were, in reality, many difficult and perpetually unhappy authors, some of whom she had won over in time. Sure, they were happy to be on the road to publication because it often guaranteed tenure, which, in turn, determined their future trajectory as academics, but there were many challenges that accompanied the road to publication and a positive experience with an editor was not, by any means, a sure thing.

Claire's authors were loyal to her – of this, she was certain. She gave them all of her time and consideration because she was passionate about books, the ideas themselves. As a result of this diligence, many academics were on exceedingly friendly terms with her – and this, in particular, seemed to irk Maron. Even more so, after the Milgram incident. It was clear that her boss was incapable of sharing in the success of others or championing one of her own.

"As I told you before, in the first part of this review, I've been talking with others about you," Maron said. "And the consensus is … well … not good. But you know this already."

If this were the type of information that Maron was feeding to HR, then Claire knew it would soon be on record. The content of HR files became the official truth. Claire's biggest nightmare was actually happening: Her boss was papering her file to fire her.

As was often the case, the conversation ended abruptly. Maron was called away to a production meeting before their discussion could reach a conclusion. The threat of continuation was raised, yet again. This pattern was too striking to ignore: Maron repeatedly dumped on subordinates, then left things hanging to avoid rebuttal or confrontation. These inconclusive dialogues haunted Claire; they loomed. In fact, it was their unfinished nature that posed the biggest threat because, again, nothing concrete was on the table, nothing constructive from which to make improvements or facilitate a fresh start. In this way, Claire's situation felt hopeless.

She wondered if Maron were Machiavellian at birth or if she had evolved to be like this over time. Determining this nuance could help her to think of Maron as pure or not-so-pure evil. But in this area, Claire struggled. Her access to Maron was limited to these office chew-out sessions from which she could glean very little points of understanding.

After she left Maron's office, she went straight to the women's washroom and emptied her palm. This cut was not as deep as the one that had just healed, and it was on the opposite hand. She washed the blood away and brushed off a tear that had escaped the moment she arrived in the washroom.

Thankful to be alone, she went into a stall, locked the door, sat on the toilet seat, and thought about her next move. She considered calling Simon but decided against it. She wondered if his day were going any better than hers, and how the girlfriend ruse had affected things at the Marriage Licensing Office.

After ten minutes, she walked back to her desk, pretending that nothing had transpired.

She revisited her conversation with Maron, off and on throughout the day. Powering through a crime and deviance manuscript proved to be a semi-sufficient distraction.

Death and depravity made her situation seem comparatively lighter.

By the early afternoon, however, she suddenly realized that the correspondence about her disappointing performance must be back on Maron's desk, face up for the world to see. In her inability to process the information that Maron was unloading, Claire had failed to take what was, she assumed, her own copy of the dreaded paperwork. Why else would Maron have floated it in front of her nose?

Ten or twenty people likely went through Maron's office every day, dropping items into her IN box, Claire calculated. With this line of reasoning, many people would have had the opportunity to read or glance over the paperwork. Soon everyone would know about her shortcomings, Claire realized in horror. Her reputation as an academic editor would be in ruins.

After three or four minutes of sheer panic, during which time Claire felt as if she were going to throw up, she realized that she had no other option than to return to Maron's desk. But when? She needed to develop a plan.

"Get your shit together," she said to herself. "Fucking get it together."

She stood up in her cubicle to get the lay of the land. Everyone in her area seemed perplexingly upbeat and chatty, hovering around the water cooler. Then she remembered why: The company's summer cruise was slated for the late afternoon and evening.

"Bloody hell," she said under her breath. She hated this annual event where the publisher rented a tall ship and, together with all staff, cruised around the Toronto harbour.

Most employees loved it, she had to admit. They always stayed late into the night, eating and drinking, and listening to a local band that provided passable covers of Crosby, Stills, Nash, and Young, and the likes. Staff particularly enjoyed the free booze, all part of the package that was supposed to be a thank-you from management for another successful year. The event also served to pump staffers up for the fast-approaching fall sales season.

Claire saw through the theatrics. She dreaded the event. However, she realized that she would have to attend the cruise and appear happy, given the circumstances. There was no escape, she bitterly surmised. So she left her cubicle, interacted with her peers, smiled, and joked with her fellow editors as if everything was normal.

She surprised herself with her ability to switch gears and present an almost extroverted version of herself: breezy, fun Claire. No one would ever have imagined what had transpired earlier in Maron's office. This was how Claire wanted to keep it.

Claire wanted to be the upbeat, non-anxious woman she presented to her coworkers. As false as it was, it actually worked on the surface. It allowed her to function, to reintegrate into the workplace, after a nasty confrontation with Maron, on her own terms.

More than anything, she wanted to bury one unshakable emotion: shame – not because she had messed up (she knew, deep down, that Maron's version of reality was skewed), but because she, an intelligent person and dedicated editor, had allowed this to happen. And worse yet, she couldn't figure out a solution. This would continue. It was like watching an avalanche or tsunami – some kind of natural disaster – in slow motion and being unable to stop the path of destruction.

By the water cooler, Claire overheard that Maron had already gone down to the Toronto harbour, to help set up on the tall ship – more like get an early start on the free bar. She seized her moment and slipped back into her boss's office to retrieve the correspondence.

She snuck into Maron's office, closed the door, and snatched the paperwork. As she did this, however, she knocked a paperclip holder onto the floor between the chair and desk.

"Shit," she said under her breath, crouching down to retrieve the small magnetic box.

From this stooped angle, she heard the unthinkable: Maron's voice. Her boss was rapidly approaching.

"– Forgot my keys!" Maron bellowed, her hand jiggling the doorknob.

The telephone began ringing just as she opened the door.

Maron's imminent arrival, combined with the terror that was overtaking Claire's mind, forced the editor to make a sudden decision. Instead of fleeing past Maron, which would have been insurmountably suspicious, she remained in a crouched position, tucking herself completely under the large desk like a burrowing animal, her arms tightly wrapped around her knees. She held her breath when she heard her boss enter the room.

Maron snatched the receiver from across the desk. Claire heard the tinkling of keys, deducing that her boss must have discovered them somewhere on the surface of the desk.

"Hello?" Maron barked into the telephone receiver, sounding slightly out of breath.

On the other end of the phone, Claire could make out a child's voice, high and animated although muffled. Maron has children?! The idea seemed unfathomable. Don't spiders eat their young?

"You know you're supposed to be taking care of your sister," Maron said as she sat down on the surface of the desk, inches above Claire's head. "You have, once again, managed to screw up."

Barely audible response, sounding close to tears.

"Oh, this was your fault then."

Muted noises.

"I don't care who spilled the cereal."

Stifled answer; a small peeping noise.

"Can't you do anything right? I mean, really –"

Definite tears on the other end.

"Where's your father? Not that he's in any way helpful –"

Pause in crying, then a mumbled reply.

"Well, that's just stupid. Don't you think, for one second, before you do these stupid things?"

Silence. Maron slammed the phone down and left the office, grabbing her keys. "Jesus Christ, when does it end?" she said under her breath as she closed the door.

Claire remained under the desk for a few minutes, possibly as many as ten or fifteen, trying to control her racing heart.

* * *

She was thinking of the Lakeshore Psychiatric Hospital, remembering her first interactions. And in her mind, she was back. Why this particular memory sprang into her consciousness at this moment was a mystery. Was she worried that she might need to go back into the hospital if group therapy didn't work out? That would be, admittedly, the worst-case scenario. But the stakes were high with Maron, and the similarities between what had initially brought Claire to the hospital (Alice, the first dreaded boss) and what was happening now, with Maron, were striking.

She recalled her first appointment at the hospital. This memory was vivid. While she sat crumpled under her boss's desk, it seemed as if she were reliving it.

Claire had felt scared and vulnerable at this appointment. She wasn't sure how she would describe her feelings to the doctors. She waited outside of the patient intake room on a row of chairs with cool metal backs, along with other possible residents of the hospital, who largely kept to themselves.

There were no niceties, or how-do-you-dos, as Claire imagined there would be in another kind of healthcare facility like an OBGYN's office with all the happy pregnant people. No, the patients here were stoic, as if they were saving their output for the professionals.

She couldn't have described any of her fellow patients. They were ghost-like entities, crushed by one thing or another, waiting to be put back together again.

It was winter, early 1968, and the weather that year was exceptionally cold. Outside, Claire could hear the wind howling around the large old compound, hugging the corners, and breaking into wind tunnels in the wide-open spaces between buildings.

The hospital grounds had a frozen-in-time kind of quality, she had noticed when she walked in from the bus stop that first day. It was like the land that time forgot. The snow only seemed to reinforce this idea of separateness from the rest of society. She knew she would be a part of this disconnected world, if she received a doctor's recommendation to stay.

Claire had taken a medical leave from her job at this point in time. The so-called back injury. Leaving work was another sign of leaving society. She wasn't exactly sure how she felt about it. The shift away from normal life was scary due to its possible permanence. How long would she be living in this place? What if she never got out, or it took years to unravel her problems? This was the great unknown that added to her anxiety by providing a whole new set of things to fret about. That was the irony: While trying to help herself, she was digging deeper into despair.

On the other hand, the idea of leaving society and going into the psych hospital offered Claire a fresh start where others would take care of her, where she could truly fall apart, put the mess of everything out into the open, and pass the burden to the doctors. It would mean a tremendous relinquishing of control, which, to an editor and a highstrung person, seemed like an impossible task. How could she truly let go and put her future into the hands of others? Was this even possible for someone like her?

The door opened. A patient exited. The medical secretary called Claire's name.

Claire had been investigating the scars on her palm, which had begun to clear up since she started the medical leave. She jerked up when her name was called and found herself drifting into the doctor's office, past the secretary, whose horn-rimmed glasses magnified the red edges of her eyes. The woman looked tired, Claire could still recall, as if it were yesterday.

Three doctors attended – or rather, one doctor and two med students. She was invited to sit down, so she removed her thick wool coat, hung it on the back of the chair along with her purse, and sat down.

Her chair faced the row of men. To Claire, the trio felt more like a panel of judges, which made her uncomfortable.

As the psychiatrist spoke, introducing himself (Dr. Williams) and the earnest-looking students, Claire tried to place him. He was young and thin with short-cropped black hair. He seemed familiar. By his third sentence, she had figured it out: Intro Psych at U of T. They were classmates seven or eight years ago.

He evidently didn't remember her or was pretending not to recall. She had sat behind him all year, and the only reason she remembered him was because he had asked a great deal of questions – to the point of being annoying. During class, he had rarely turned around – why would he when the professor was in front? – so, there was no reason why he should remember Claire, who always sat in the back of the class.

In any case, recognizing the man made her feel uneasy. Should she say something? She considered this, but decided against it. Still, this discomfort only added to her growing apprehension. Was she actually checking herself into a psych hospital? Was this really the right thing to do?

Instead of worrying about her former classmate, she concentrated on the two underlings. One young man had particularly kind eyes. Claire imagined that these two students were probably keen on helping people – not yet jaded by compromises to patient care or administrative duties. She appreciated this.

A funny thing happened when Dr. Williams asked the first question. Claire, a natural writer who unpacked ideas and described all aspects of complex phenomena, could not find her words. She was silent – processing, but unable to vocalize or articulate her situation.

More specifically, she could not find a suitable beginning point to start talking about how her world had been destroyed. The conundrum was, on a certain level, simple: to stay or go in a toxic work environment. People face this kind of problem every day, so why couldn't she handle it like normal folks?

In truth, she knew that her dilemma was complicated and messy, and it involved deep-down meanness on the part of her boss – that horrid Alice, seeking to claw her way to the top by crushing others, women in particular – that she needed to articulate. And yet, to recount the incidences, one by one, seemed like airing dirty laundry. Each case in isolation seemed to be petty, but it was the accumulation of incidences that had led her to this hospital.

Claire had been, as she was now, stumped by the viciousness of her boss. Why would someone tear a strip off another? The excessiveness of this, the gravity, was what paralyzed her, and it was the most difficult to share, to discuss frankly and honestly.

When she opened her mouth to answer the question, she ended up crying. After about five minutes, she pushed through and spoke. Disappointing herself, she presented her case badly, through a mismatched and non-chronological history where outrageous injustices intermingled with silly, inconsequential details. She wasn't even sure if she were coherent when speaking to the medical team.

However, when Dr. Williams determined that she was eligible to stay at the psych hospital, Claire felt hugely relieved. Even now, years later, she could still feel that physical response – what it felt like to let go and start healing. The idea that the doctor believed her (if not her garbled story, then certainly the feelings behind it), that this team of people could help her, was overwhelming. This was mercy. Unadulterated compassion. It made her want to cry with relief.

A few weeks into her hospital stay, she ran into Dr. Williams. He took her aside and said, "Claire, forgive me. I didn't recognize you at first. I believe we went to U of T at the same time." He didn't mention it was in an Intro Psych class, sidestepping the issue with sensitivity. "How are you? Is our program helping?"

She nodded, at a loss for words, once again struck by his kindness. Some people truly are benevolent to the core. She realized that her experience with Alice had eroded that faith in human nature.

* * *

As she hunched under Maron's desk, Claire wondered if she would ever need to go back to the hospital, to wait once again on the cool metal chairs outside of the admission office.

She thought about Paul and the group. Despite her compromising position in Maron's office, she was not the same person as she had been when she went into the hospital. After all, she had recovered then, and today she was gaining strength from group therapy.

She got up, feeling confident enough to open the door, cautiously peeking out to ensure that no one was watching. She grabbed the correspondence from Maron's desk and headed out. When she exited her boss's office, she was pleased to discover that most of her coworkers had already left the building and begun the trek to the harbour.

Although she had planned to travel with a few editors, the group must have gone without her. She wasn't offended. It had been a casual invitation. In fact, she was thankful not to have to make small talk any earlier than was necessary.

She travelled by subway to Union Station, then walked to Queens Quay. The tall ship was moored at one of the docks near the Redpath Sugar plant in an underdeveloped area of the city.

It was six o'clock when she started walking to the ship. The sun was still blazing. Sweat oozed from every pore in her body.

She soon caught sight of the tall ship, *Pathfinder*. It was massive. It dominated the waterfront with a mainmast height of nearly sixty feet. The bright white hull was broad but streamlined. She knew that this large ship could host one hundred passengers with ease.

The ship's cream-coloured sails were up, but motionless. The sheer height of these sails was impressive. She couldn't imagine someone brave enough to climb to the top.

From a block away, Claire spotted her coworkers spread across the deck, drinks in hand, most smoking up a storm and gazing to the south, the Toronto Islands. She could also hear the band, warming up with a Stevie Wonder tune, having evidently added some brass this year.

As she stepped onto the gangway and carefully began her ascent to the ship, she heard Maron's voice, shrill and animated above the music. She realized that she could not avoid a small gathering of women, clustered by the gangway, its individuals encircling Maron like disciples. She braced for impact.

"Claire! So glad you could join us. I was just saying that I hoped you were coming this aft," Maron said.

"Yup," said Claire, confused but playing along. Maron always did this: engaged in this game where they were best mates in public while she tore a strip off her in private. It was perverse.

Claire was accepted into the fold. She let herself relax a little, lit a cigarette, grabbed a beer and, like everyone else, peered south into the thick of trees on Ward's Island.

Soon after, the tall ship launched.

Two hours later, when the band was in full swing, Claire noticed Maron off to one side of the bow, draped over one of the execs. Her boss's arms were around the shoulders of the senior bean counter who appeared equally drunk. When the inevitable sloppy grope and messy kiss happened, it was no surprise.

Realizing that Maron was out of commission, Claire took in the scene and tried to relax. As the sun set over Hanlan's Point, casting long shadows across the deck, the light transformed into a golden hue and the temperature lowered. The sun, mirrored in the water, created a twinkling light that reflected up into the ship's sails.

People were clustered in small groups around the deck. The band was playing Marvin Gaye after a short dip into reggae and calypso, looping back to Crosby, Stills, Nash, and Young as expected.

Claire sat in a wooden seat by the stern, smoking a cigarette and nursing her third beer. She didn't see Maron's approach until it was too late.

"You know, I do things for a reason," her boss said, slurring her words. "But I like you Claire, I really do. Don't think I'm picking on you. 'Cause I'm not. Not really. You'd know if I was picking on you."

"Okay," said Claire, hoping Maron's statement would hang in the air and no further words would be necessary; the conversation would be, luckily, over.

"I know you're a good writer," Maron whispered in a conspiratorial fashion. She was leaning down into Claire's face, her right arm supported by the back of the chair. Her breath smelled like cheap red wine. Her lips and teeth had been stained a bright crimson. When she smiled, she looked like a vampire after a particularly gruesome kill.

Claire gazed squarely into her boss's face, assessing the level of drunkenness. When she was sure that Maron's eyes were not focusing consistently – instead, their attention drifted in and out, as the woman seemed easily distracted by unseen things in the water and trees – Claire stood up, flicked her cigarette off the side of the deck, and walked away.

From her pocket, she pulled out the correspondence that she had covertly extracted from Maron's office and began ripping it into tiny pieces, which she threw overboard. It didn't matter. She had already memorized the content.

Memo to: Rose Granger, Director, Human Resources

Rose:

It has come to my attention that Claire is falling behind in her responsibilities. She has never been a top performer in the Higher Education Division. She struggles to keep up. Important deadlines have been missed this season. Errors have been noted.

Given my many years in academic publishing, and speaking from experience, I feel that Claire does not understand the job well enough to succeed. Too much time has passed during which she has failed to retain the fundamentals, despite my mentoring and guidance. She is a slow learner, someone for whom grammar is a particular weakness.

Her authors are equally dissatisfied with her work. For this reason, above my own concerns, I believe there is no solution other than putting her on probation until the year's end. Additionally, at year's end, I recommend that the company withhold the standard of living wage increase that is our existing policy for all staff.

Cordially, Maron

It felt good, therapeutic even, to rip the correspondence into a million tiny pieces. Claire watched the bits of paper slowly float away. Of course, she knew that there would be another copy of this letter on its way to HR, if it weren't already there. It just felt satisfying to destroy a small portion of Maron's toxicity.

As the evening wore on, Claire became bored with the small talk of her increasingly inebriated coworkers. As everyone seemed to be having a grand time, she became evermore disengaged. Her face simply could not support more forced smiles or fake laughter. She was drinking, but the alcohol didn't seem to have an effect on her. Regrettably, she felt stone cold sober. By nine o'clock, she very much wanted off the ship, looking wistfully at the twinkly Toronto shoreline as dusk approached.

The party, it seemed, had a shelf life after which things got exponentially worse. One secretary threw up, her torso dangling, unladylike, over the handrail of the tall ship. Her friends were holding her hair back but missing a few strands that subsequently leaked vomit down the woman's blouse and skirt (it seemed that no one had the heart to mention it). The woman's friends were fawning over her and patting her back, all the while clutching their own dresses and purses to ensure nothing would get splattered.

There was a long line-up for the only washroom on the ship. The queue, which wrapped around the deck, was more than two dozen people deep at one point. With the vast consumption of alcohol by nearly all passengers, and a few cases of motion sickness, the need was pressing. Judging from the look on these people's faces, Claire couldn't tell if they needed to urinate, defecate, vomit, or all of the above. Either way, it was going to be very bad. She could well imagine the state of the solitary washroom.

In her sobriety, Claire reasoned that there must be another washroom. It seemed impossible that there was only one on this vast ship. She set about finding another below deck.

She was surprised to discover that the lower level of the ship was empty. Perhaps this area was reserved for the crew, she considered, half expecting someone in uniform to redirect her back upstairs.

All the lights were off on the lower level. It was comparatively cool. Claire could make out four or five wingback chairs randomly scattered around the room. They looked very comfortable, unlike the wooden seats on deck. She plunked herself down, sunk into the chair, and lit a cigarette. The washroom search could wait. She was content killing time, listening to the muted music from upstairs, the muffled conversation interspersed with a few roars of laughter.

Just then she heard a toilet flush from the far side of the room. So there was a washroom down here after all!

She got up to make her move but stopped, mid-track. She heard whispers, slurred nonsensical mutterings – one male, one female – from behind the bathroom door. She retreated to her seat, safely hidden from view as the chair faced away from the washroom. She considered leaving, heading back upstairs so as not to embarrass the culprits, but had no way of knowing when they would emerge from the washroom.

After a few more minutes, curiosity overcame her and she peeked around the back of the chair.

Suddenly, the door snapped open. A ray of light spilled into the larger room. Claire saw, as clear as day, Maron stumbling half out of the small room, her hair dishevelled, having been sprung from its usual knot, her blouse unbuttoned down to her waist.

On the threshold of the doorway, Maron's ankle twisted out of her high-heeled sandal, and she erupted into giggles. She looked backwards into the washroom for reassurance, but the man offered nothing.

Maron fixed her shoe while bracing against the doorframe, buttoned her shirt up, and smoothed her hair down. As if gathering strength, she inhaled deeply then headed for the stairs.

Claire froze. She wasn't sure if she was visible from her boss's perspective. Only her head peeked around the armchair, and the room itself was dark.

Maron walked right past Claire's chair, completely unaware as to her subordinate's presence. She then ventured up the stairs, grabbing the railing to keep from toppling over, as if the ship were battling great whitecaps on the open ocean when, in fact, the surface of Lake Ontario was as smooth as glass.

What now? Claire asked herself. She knew the man was still in the washroom. There was no other way for him to exit the space, so she remained half-concealed and waited for him to leave.

The senior accountant exited the washroom after a few minutes. He didn't appear to be drunk at all. He walked out of the washroom and across the room as if nothing had happened.

15

It was going to be a good day. Beata loved venturing into the countryside to document crafts for her liturgical project. She adored doing her "fieldwork" as she liked to call it. Today, she had rented a green AMC Gremlin from the car lot on Bloor to drive out and hit three churches.

Participation in the project was voluntary on the part of the religious establishments. Beata had sent a letter of inquiry at the beginning of the spring to set the wheels in motion.

Not surprisingly, many churches were ecstatic to have been given the opportunity to showcase, in their shy way, the talents of local artisans. The work of many quilting bees, for example, was put forth with great pride.

Despite her firmly rooted atheism, Beata was moved by these pieces. They reminded her of the way Etienne or Aisha would bring home a painting from art class. There was something terribly poignant about presenting a created object to the world as a proxy for the self as if to say: "This is me" or "This is who we are." It made her throat tighten with a kind of primordial affection.

On the drive today, she wanted to talk with Jafari again, about Etienne's letter and the idea of going to London.

"Do you think it's a problem, our talking like this?" she asked, glancing out the car window. The rolling hills around Caledon unfolded in a mesmerizing way that made her unwind more and more as the city grew farther and farther away. They had left Toronto at sunrise.

"Is there a problem?" she queried again. "When we talk?"

"Was there a problem when we spoke like this when we were together?" Jafari asked. He was ribbing her, as he always did. He had a way of making her feel better about everything.

"I mean, the kids think this is weird," she said, pressing him. "That's what Etienne's letter implied."

"Since when do we worry about what others think?"

"They're not others. They're our children."

He had wound down the window and his right hand was palming the warm winds. He looked very relaxed, half reclined in the passenger seat.

"They'll come back to you, Bea," he said, patting her shoulder.

No one but Jafari called her Bea. She hadn't heard this nickname since his passing, she suddenly realized. How could she have forgotten this? The idea that she was losing the memory of certain mannerisms, unique to Jafari, deeply upset her. But she refused to dwell on it. Not today, on such a beautiful morning.

"We need to start thinking about London," he said. "Just the two of us, getting away from everything. I'll show you all my old haunts."

She agreed; the idea had taken root. She had, in fact, thought about little else since he proposed the idea.

Making good headway, they now approached the first destination: a Catholic Church in Caledon. For the liturgical project, it offered two huge banners, fashioned by the local sewing group; a chalice made by an elderly goldsmith fifty years ago; and seven stained glass windows by a British-born artist, including a giant rose window depicting Christ descending in a gorgeous red robe with a robin's-egg-blue background. Beata had admired this piece and its unique colour combination when she first spotted it in a magazine article.

"Let me do the talking," she joked as she turned off the road and parked the car in the lot adjacent to the church. They got out, stretched their legs, and headed toward the entry.

"I'll mind my Ps and Qs," Jafari teased. He stopped and gave her shoulders a squeeze.

She turned to face him, straightened his collar, and removed a random hair from his cheek. "You know I love you, right?" she said, surprising herself with the question.

He smiled and nodded in a way that was so typically Jaf – a little bit cocky, a little bit teddy bearish.

From out of the corner of her eye, she caught a glimpse of curtains fluttering in the upper window of the nearby clergy house. Had someone witnessed her conversation with Jafari? She stepped away from her husband and headed, once again, toward the portal.

The church was empty. The sound of the large wooden door opening broke the ambient silence. The unadorned creak echoed through the narthex and nave.

The interior was dim – no lights had been turned on yet – but the morning sunshine spilled into the building through the upper windows, illuminating the space with a delicate silvery light. Beata was struck by the sense of peace.

The church smelled like wood and wax. She had realized the sameness of these eighty-year-old buildings. United, Presbyterian, Anglican, Roman Catholic, they all smelled the same. Not dissimilar from libraries, she thought, because there was an unmistakable scent of dust that mingled with the wood and wax. She could understand how this aroma brought comfort to parishioners. Even she was becoming accustomed to it.

A large painting hung to the left of the entryway, a replica of St. Francis feeding the birds, from the life cycle of the religious leader painted by Giotto. She stepped closer and inspected the tranquil scene, entranced by the delicate foliage of the trees and the gracefulness of the mendicant as he bent down to feed the sparrows.

While she examined the artwork, a priest appeared from out of nowhere. He stood, wordlessly, holding a card with the prayer of St. Francis embossed onto the surface in gold lettering. It was almost spooky.

Then he said plainly: "It's good that you talk with him."

"Who?" she asked. Was he referring to God? she wondered. Did he think she was praying? I'm not superstitious or looking for indoctrination, she reminded herself.

He smiled and then turned on his heel.

Beata was dumbfounded. Could he see Jafari too?! Had the priest witnessed her conversation with her husband outside the church? Her heart was racing.

"Our meeting will be in the antechamber," the priest said over his shoulder. "We are humbled that you would select the artifacts of our parish for your project."

She could tell, by his gentle tone and the particular way that he shepherded her to the meeting room, that he was not intending to discuss this any further. The moment was gone.

As she followed the priest, she caught a glimpse of Jafari, high up in the clerestory by the stained glass windows, laughing his ass off.

16

Having tossed and turned for hours, unable to sleep, Paul got up to read in the wee hours of the morning. He turned on his bedside lamp and pulled out a gem of a book that he had found in a discount bin at a bookstore down Roncesvalles. Hours later, likely around seven o'clock, he was thoroughly engrossed in American psychologist Carl Rogers' client-centred therapy and his nineteen propositions, established in 1953.

The book was almost twenty years old, Paul readily admitted, but the humanist theory that Rogers was proposing still held up in today's modern era. Moreover, Rogers had updated his core idea in 1961 with the notion of the fully functional person – that is, someone who would have a growing openness to experience; someone who was living each moment fully. Paul wondered if this were possible. In particular, he was drawn to Principle No. 18: "When the individual perceives and accepts into one consistent and integrated system all their sensory and visceral experiences, then they are necessarily more understanding of others and more accepting of others as separate individuals."

He was wondering how he could weave this idea into the next group therapy session, when suddenly, a commotion erupted outside of his bedroom.

Footsteps clambered down the hall. John burst into his room. "Crack down. It's happening!" he yelled.

Paul sat straight up. It was uncharacteristic for John to be so alarmist. But before Paul had the chance to ask what the "happening" entailed, John had fled the scene, leaving the door ajar.

Larry, clad in pyjama bottoms, clearly having been awoken in a manner similar to Paul, stuck his head in the doorway.

"Hey, man," he said. "The despot's comin'."

"What does that mean?"

"The Mother. The fuzz," said Larry who was, for some reason, clutching a stack of *Science* magazines. It looked as if he had been told to evacuate with one prized possession, and he'd made his decision. It dawned on Paul that the publications must belong to Larry.

"John's mom? So what?" Paul asked, increasingly confused.

"You've never met her, have you?"

"I get that she's the real landlord, not John, but so what if she visits?"

"She might have questions."

"What kind of questions?"

Larry darted down the hall, heading for the kitchen, without answering.

Paul decided to ignore the two of them. He wasn't giving in to the panic of some kind of inspection. He had nothing to fear.

Feeling tired and exasperated with the silly goings-on of his flatmates, he closed his book, turned off the lamp, rolled over, and went to sleep.

He arose hours later, well rested, and headed for the shower, fumbling with the arms of his thin blue housecoat as he walked.

"So, you've finally decided to grace us with your presence?" a steely female voice bellowed from the kitchen.

Paul wondered who this annoying woman was talking to as he continued on his way to the bathroom. Then he remembered the pending visit of John's mother.

"Don't walk away from me, young man," she continued.

Paul chuckled at the idea of John being on the receiving end of these orders. Ah, families, he sighed, walking into the bathroom and closing the door with his foot.

The washroom door suddenly slammed open, and the woman's voice filled the small space, echoing mercilessly as Paul struggled to close the flap on his pyjamas.

"– What the fuck?" he said angrily, staring at the big-boned woman who had planted herself in the middle of the doorway, hands on hips.

"Don't use foul language with me, young man," she shrieked at close range. "Not when you've got so much explaining to do."

"What're you talking about?" he yelled back, flushing the toilet defiantly. "You know I live here, right?"

"Of course I do. The lads have told me everything."

"What do you mean?"

"I think we need to have a little chat."

Paul followed her into the kitchen where he found John and Larry sitting obediently at the table, which, incidentally, looked very clean. The room was, in fact, spotless. He had never seen it like this. At last, he thought, his flatmates were now taking chores seriously! The dream of the commune had taken some kind of leap forward.

John and Larry didn't make eye contact with him. Rachel was probably hiding in a closet with some new musician in tow.

"Would someone mind telling me what the fuck is going on?" Paul asked his two flatmates.

"I know about the Maree-who-annah," John's mother said, looking at Paul in a way that he assumed was an attempt to penetrate his soul, but failed to do so.

"The marijuana? Okay, so?" he shrugged. "It's a free country."

"Do you know it's against the law?"

"I am aware of the law." He stifled a laugh, adding, "What's your point?"

"My point is: You are corrupting my son and his dear and very impressionable friend, Larry."

"How am I doing that?" Paul said, snickering. "I think they were corrupt before I got here."

"By forcing them to grow it, of course! Insisting on illegally using the backyard – my backyard, I'll add – as a veritable growing field. Against their will." She glared at him, then dramatically swung around to gaze out the back window in the direction of the illegal plantation.

John shot a look at Paul. "PLEASE," he mouthed silently.

Larry was harder to read. Paul couldn't tell if he were about to cry or laugh. His flatmate clutched his magazines as if he had been violated and stared down at the floor.

Paul suddenly realized that John and Larry had conspired and determined that he was to be the fall guy, but he thought quickly on his feet. "Legally, this is your property, lady. You're the one breaking the law."

She was silent.

"I pay month to month," Paul mused aloud. "I could walk away from this joke of a setup any time," he said directly to John. Paul had suspected for quite a while that he was the only person in the house who could actually make rent. John and his mother needed him, not vice versa.

"This communal living doesn't work optimally when you're living with … well, these two …" he said as he swept his hand in the direction of John and Larry.

"Are you a Communist?!" she shrieked.

"Well, yes," he said. "I'm trying my hardest."

"John, you are well aware I don't allow Communists or hippies in this house."

"I didn't know, Mum," John said. He faked astonishment pretty well. "I'll get rid of him."

When his mother turned again to look at the crops, he mouthed to Paul: "I'M SORRY."

"Nice," said Paul sarcastically, "get rid of me like a roach. Bloody hell."

"Watch your language, young man."

"Look, I'm not a young man. I'm a grown man, in fact.

I have a steady job, well, sort of. It's more like a project. But I have the rent money. Christ, I have a family, responsibilities. I vote. I'm the best goddamned tenant you'll have. Or at least that you have at the moment. You'll never find anyone else to put up with these two shitheads."

It was uncharacteristic of Paul to swear so profusely, to a total stranger, but in this case, it felt good right down to the bone.

"No offense," he said, turning to Larry and John. He didn't intend to insult Larry. John, however, was a different story. He was pretty much a spineless toad in Paul's mind at this point.

"None taken," Larry said, winking at him.

"Language!"

"Holy. Fucking. Shit," Paul said right to her face. "Shall I call the cops on your pot farm, lady?! How'd that be?" he threatened, knowing full well that he would sooner relocate than work with the police on this type of incrimination.

The kitchen fell silent. John's mother looked as if she were going to have a stroke. Her face was flushed, and she was out of breath.

"Haven't we, as a society, moved beyond this kind of repressive authoritarian thinking?" Paul asked, not caring for a response. "Of all the shit that's going on in the world today, all the poverty and war, why hang your hat on marijuana? I mean, honestly. Shouldn't the stuff be legal anyway? What's the harm?"

John's mother grabbed her purse and left the house in a huff.

"You're my fucking hero, man," Larry said to Paul.

Feeling as if the day was almost wholly ruined before noon, Paul ventured out of the house shortly after John's mother left. He needed to get away from his flatmates for a while.

He decided to wander around Roncesvalles. Maybe he would buy a treat for the kids. There was a possibility that he might have them again soon, if Cynthia deemed it viable. He headed to the green grocers.

Although shaded, the fruit and vegetables at the grocers on the corner of Garden and Roncesvalles were looking particularly wilted. The heat of the morning had proven too much for them.

Paul found himself staring at the lot, suddenly overcome by the decision between mangos or peaches, tomatoes or corn on the cob. There were no grapes.

"I'd go with the peaches."

He turned around to see who had made this suggestion. He was very pleased, relieved even, to find Claire.

"Hi Paul," she said smiling.

"Good to see you. How've you been?" he asked, wondering if she were actually fine with the other night, their drunken sexual encounter. Perhaps it was best not to say anything. Just play it cool. They were both adults, right?

"Survival mode at work, but well, you know ..." She waved off the gravity of her own situation. "How're you?"

He sighed and shrugged. "Not great," he admitted.

"Want to grab a pop and sit in the park for a while?" she suggested. "I'm not doing anything today."

They bought two 7Ups from the grocers, each pressing

the cool dewy surface of the bottles up to their foreheads as they headed into High Park.

"My life is, as I've mentioned, kind of complicated, right now. The separation and all," he said as they sat on the stone wall by the duck pond at the southern end of the park. Here, the willows provided some measure of relief from the blazing sun.

She nodded thoughtfully.

"I'm also living in a mad house. I realize this now," he continued.

"Your place on Indian Road? It seemed fine to me." Her first reference to their having slept together. She said it in a matter-of-fact sort of way.

"Communal living with three strangers."

"Not what you were expecting?"

"I thought it would be more … Communist."

"More like sharing things, you mean? More authentic to Marxist theory?"

He snorted. "The guys I live with are pretty much the antithesis of theoretical. Evidently, Marx never left instructions for who takes out the garbage, cuts the grass, does the dishes, buys the groceries …"

It felt good to joke about the situation, to let off some steam. He found himself laughing, genuinely laughing, with Claire. He realized it must have been a long time since he had done so.

He looked at Claire, studying her for perhaps the first time – by day, at least. She was sitting cross-legged, as was her tendency, on the stone wall. The sun was in her eyes, making her tear up and blink a bit. Strands of her wavy ginger hair fell out of her ponytail each time she spoke with animation. Her cotton shirt, with strings around the collar, billowed in the slightest breeze. Her shorts were frayed at the edges.

She appeared to be amused by the stories of his crazy living situation, so he elaborated. By the time he had worked his way up to the dead raccoon story, the two were both howling.

In recounting this anecdote, he absentmindedly touched her knee, for emphasis. He felt the resonating warmth of her flesh for a split second, then quickly removed his fingers.

He remembered how soft the skin at the small of her back was – the memory came back to him instantly. The sensation stormed through his body.

She, on the contrary, didn't seem to notice his touch. She had moved on to watching the ducks. She really did seem cool about everything. He wondered if he would be able to follow suit.

17

"Shit, shit, shit," Simon cursed under his breath. He was running out of time, and he didn't want to be delayed for group therapy. Working late at City Hall meant any time after 4:01 pm. It was now 4:25 pm, and the place was like a ghost town, the overheads half dimmed in a new initiative to save energy.

Hunching over his desk lamp, Simon was now most likely the sole employee in the entirety of the New City Hall.

His typewriter had jammed late in the day, and when he popped down to Supplies, this department had neither a technician who could help nor a secondary machine that he could borrow, so he had to walk to Central in the Old City Hall across Bay Street, pick up another machine, haul it back across Bay, unpack it from its cumbersome suitcase, plug it in, and start his work over again. When all was said and done, he was woefully behind in the day's processing of marriage licenses. Powering through the daunting stack, he made a fifth cup of coffee and settled in. Typing at warp speed, he worked steadily, keeping a highly regimented focus. The only sound that broke the silence of the office was the soft but consistent clacking of his typewriter.

He finished the stack of processing at exactly 6:05 pm, switched off the Smith Corona, and gently set the plastic cover over the typewriter. Grabbing his briefcase, he headed toward the elevators.

The moment he left the building, Simon felt uneasy. He had the distinct feeling of being watched. Then he heard laughter – the unmistakable male drunken kind of guffawing that could only mean trouble. He hastened his pace but didn't turn around to see if anyone was intentionally following him.

He decided to walk up Chestnut Street, which looked empty – a questionable move, but he figured he would hop on a streetcar heading to the University line within minutes.

"There he is!" someone yelled. "The puff who's supposed to be getting married!"

Simon could tell by the cacophony of footsteps that the person was not alone. This group was surely the mailroom gang: Bob, Willy, Doug, and Brian. They often hung out after work, drinking copious amounts of alcohol.

Simon kept walking, even more swiftly, still refusing to turn around to catch anyone's eye, which would only serve to further engage the aggressors. Instead, he sought to join the crowds along Dundas as quickly as possible. Again, if he could only jump on a streetcar, he would be fine.

Suddenly, Simon was knocked to the ground. A blow from Bob had landed him on the pavement flat against his right ear, which led to an instant and persistent ringing sensation that left him disoriented. He struggled to his feet.

The second strike, from Willy, was so swift and violent that Simon suddenly found himself, by some strange and unexplainable journey, on the hot brown asphalt of Chestnut Street once again.

Then time expanded; he felt as if he were dreaming the slow-motion course of events in a dispassionate, disconnected sort of way. He was only vaguely aware of his arms instinctively held up to defend against the blows or his cries that echoed down Chestnut Street. He could not consciously control his own body; it was working automatically. As a result, he felt no pain. It was as if he had left his body and was floating up and out of the scene for a bird's eye view of the beating. He was hazily aware that Brian was standing back from the group, watching, and smoking a cigarette.

The next fist-to-jaw connection, this one from Doug, brought Simon back to the here-and-now, but left him in an awkward position, sprawled on the pavement like a turtle that had been turned upside down, unable to right itself, legs scrambling in the air. He knew that he would have to get himself out of this vulnerable position, and fast.

Then Brian stepped forward, gesturing to the others to move aside. They obeyed, and his plum-coloured face advanced at a rapid speed into Simon's airspace, as if the man had some juicy insult to hurl.

"You made me do this," he said with clenched jaws. Ham-fisted, he grabbed Simon's lapel with his left hand and clenched his right fist in a tight ball beside his temple, as if ready to spring.

Simon could smell stale beer and cigarettes on his breath. He could see that Brian's hands were shaking. He looked directly into Brian's eyes – the only real act of defiance he could muster from this defenseless position – and noticed that the man was tearing up. Brian looked as if he were about to cry.

A gathering of secretaries turned the corner about a block north from the scene, suddenly interrupting the altercation. Simon could see them out of the corner of his eye. The women stopped in their tracks, instantly aware of what was in progress. Then someone screamed. It was bloodcurdling.

For a second, all of the men involved in the beating froze – each party acutely aware of the other. Then, swiftly, the attackers fled in the opposite direction.

As soon as it was safe, the women ran to help Simon, offering tissues for his face. He realized his cheek had erupted with blood, which was now indiscreetly dripping onto his crisp white shirt.

The women insisted on calling the police.

Confident that Brian and his cronies were gone, Simon brushed off the secretaries' alarm, politely telling them that he was fine and that he had to be somewhere else very soon. He got up and caught the next streetcar.

All of the human kindness and empathy from the women evaporated on the streetcar. Simon sat by himself at the back of the vehicle. People stared at him as he mopped up his bloodied face with Kleenex. Anyone – male or female – who subsequently got on the streetcar avoided sitting beside him. Clearly, he meant trouble.

In time, he was confident that he had soaked up the majority of blood. He tucked the Kleenex inside of his briefcase, which still had splatters of blood here and there, and took a deep cleansing breath as if to say to himself, you're okay, let's move on.

He then ignored everyone on the streetcar, gazed out of the window into the setting sun, and opened the window full way to catch any available breeze. He needed to feel something cool on his face. The air, however, offered little comfort. He felt the skin around his eyes and cheeks swelling and pulsing with every heartbeat. By now, the pain was undeniable.

He was, however, not going to let this stop him. He was anxious to get to the group therapy session, hoping Paul, Claire, and Beata would wait for him to arrive. He felt, at long last, ready to talk.

18

July 19. The ninth group therapy session. Paul arrived early to the church for the meeting, hoping to catch Claire before the others. He was still and increasingly unsure about how to deal with things after he and Claire had slept together. Was it strange that they hadn't talked directly about it? He didn't mention it the other day in the park with her, nor had he raised the issue in subsequent group therapy meetings – in private, of course – but it was bothering him more and more as time went on.

Luckily, Claire was already at the church, sitting on the front steps, reading a loose-leaf manuscript, her pencil dangling from her hair. The minute he saw her, even at a distance, crumpled over the stack of paper, immersed in her editorial task, he felt a wave of emotion, a kind of longing, rush over him. His heart raced a little bit faster.

She looked up and smiled as he approached, tucking the manuscript into her tote bag and standing up to greet him.

"Hey," he said, stopping short of hugging her.

"Nice running into you down Roncy."

"Listen, Claire, I – I should've said something earlier. This was weeks ago … But I hope things aren't going to be weird for us after –"

"After we slept together? No, we're solid."

"Good, that's good," he said nodding, as if to convince himself that he, too, could be this rational about things.

"I shouldn't have –"

"– Paul, you're overthinking this. The evening was fun and all … but nothing heavy," she said as she repositioned her bag over her shoulder and looked at him, squinting. "We're both adults. Free agents," she added, tilting her head, as if to make sure he understood.

"Nothing heavy, yeah," he agreed.

He almost adjusted the strand of hair that kept falling into her face but reminded himself that he shouldn't touch her. He really needed to put everything into the past. No, what happened that night was a one-off, he told himself. They needed to go back to how it was before everything took a romantic turn.

He was glad, relieved even, that she was so comfortable with everything, so unbothered, although it perplexed him a little bit. Most women would have been possessive, defensive, or even embarrassed, he thought, then realized how sexist this line of thinking was – his presumption about how she might feel simply because she was a woman.

They walked into the church and down the stairs, an easy silence between them. It dawned on him, as he approached the session, that all of Claire's anxiety was related to her work. By contrast, her life outside of work, her personal life, wasn't something she stressed about at all. And he had not factored that into the mix. She had more or less forgotten about that night after the Sir Nicholas Tavern, it seemed. She had compartmentalized things, whereas he clearly had not.

Beata arrived, and the three waited for Simon, casually catching up on their week. There was a really nice rapport in the group now, Paul thought. They had bonded over the past two months.

After ten minutes, he decided to start without Simon. He must be working late, Paul figured.

"Welcome to the ninth group therapy session," Paul began.

Beata and Claire nodded in approval. Everyone agreed that time was flying.

"Why don't we go around our circle, starting with Beata."

She began without hesitation. "I received a letter from my son, explaining things in a little more depth. He knows, as does Aisha, that I'm going through a lot."

"How are you feeling about … or, dealing with Jafari's death?" Paul asked.

"I feel he's not very far from me. I had an interesting conversation with a priest recently. I felt we made a connection. I might visit him again."

"Like religious counselling?" Claire asked.

"No, this was for work, a special project. And I am not a religious person. I don't believe in God," Beata said. "Counselling? I'm not sure. But he made me feel like I was doing something right. He seemed to understand me instantly. It was uncanny."

"Sounds like a healthy support for you," Paul said.

"That's all from my end," she concluded. "I'm thinking of a big change, but I'll share that with you in the future. I'm ironing out the details."

She was clearly holding something major back, but Paul didn't want to force her. Perhaps he would return to her at the end of the session.

"Claire, how are you coping with that challenging boss of yours?" he asked. "Can you give us an update? How's your week starting?"

"It never begins well. Sunday nights are the worst."

"How so?"

"It's a slippery slope: On Fridays, I feel like an accomplished professional, overseeing the work of senior academics across the country – deans, research directors, and the like. But this feeling starts to fade by Sunday. It's as if something goes terribly wrong between 5 pm on Friday and 9 am on Monday."

"Your confidence erodes," Beata said.

"I go over confrontations with Maron, replaying them as I fall asleep – so much so, that I dream about imagined train-wreck conversations. I wake up drenched in sweat, unable to convince myself, for several minutes, that the confrontations never happened."

Paul wondered if Claire had left his house that night, unable to sleep. Maybe that was why she left.

"Five minutes into work on Monday usually breaks the spell," Claire continued. "But the moment I lock eyes on the boss or see her, even at a distance, like when she pulls up in the parking lot in her brown Buick Skylark, the cycle begins again."

"Do you think your boss inspires that kind of fear in everyone?" Paul asked.

"No, some people really like her."

"How do you know?" Beata queried.

"Today's a good example: We had a meeting of the MOFT committee. It's short for 'Mapping our Future Together' – I know, a fucking insipid name. Pardon my French. And woefully ironic: The person who made up the acronym was let go in last year's redundancies."

Paul snorted. This sounded like something out of the social workers' playbook.

"Anyway, the committee meets once a month, and provides information for staffers on HR policies and publishing templates for processing manuscripts.

"The so-called benefit of the committee is that folks are supposed to be able to speak frankly because no senior managers attend the meetings."

"That's bullshit," Paul said.

"Today's meeting was a real eye-opener. The subject was annual assessments. My favourite topic," she said sarcastically. "I arrived early to the meeting, had a cigarette, took in the view. A bunch of Canada geese have taken up residence under the maples.

"Rose from HR arrived next, as chipper as always. Is it mandated to be so fucking cheerful? She said, 'Looks like another hot one,' or something equally meaningless."

The others, all women, had filed into the room over the

next three minutes. Everyone was young, Claire reported, some clearly in their first few years of work after university or college. "This makes me feel old. I always wish that there were some mid-career folks, editors like me, on this committee."

"A friendly face," Beata said.

"Rose began the meeting with something ridiculous like 'Annual reviews can be worrisome, but management here is understanding. Progressive, in fact.' Can you imagine? Then a few others chimed in, saying that their review was as easy as pie."

"How's that possible, given your boss?" Paul asked.

"Jane, a junior editor, even said that Maron's her mentor. She described her as sweet-natured! I swear, I just about choked on my cigarette!"

"What did you do?" Beata asked. "I mean, how did you react?"

"I excused myself from the group and went into the back stairwell in the warehouse, where no one can hear you scream."

The primal scream! thought Paul. At last, an application! He decided not to mention it, however, for fear of breaking the flow of Claire's story.

"I don't understand why her experience is so different from the others," Beata said, reaching over to touch her friend's hand. "Why's her boss bullying her and no one else?"

Paul was equally confounded.

"The letter that the boss is sending to HR is probably beginning to make its way through the process," Claire said.

"What process?" asked Beata.

"I don't know. HR systems. Maron's papering my file. I don't know how long it will take for me to get fired."

"That must be adding to your anxiety," Paul said sympathetically.

"Right now, it's at the core of it, to be honest."

"Have you thought about going to HR to have a confidential chat?"

"That's a good idea," said Beata. "You could check on the status of the letter too."

"I don't know if I trust Rose."

"Gaining clarity on your status in the company from another, more objective, party could help you deal with your mounting anxiety," Paul suggested. "Having that knowledge could make you feel more in control."

Claire considered this option. "Meeting with HR would be confidential, right?"

"Yes. HR's supposed to be there for the worker."

"I think I can do that," Claire said, sounding ambivalent.

Paul watched as her demeanour changed slightly, sensing she was finished reporting for this week. He knew that she would need to mull the idea over. He also sensed that she would need to be backed into a corner before she would willingly challenge authority. But wasn't she already at that point? What would it take for her to fight?

He suggested the group take a break. In truth, he was finding it difficult to concentrate. His mind had started playing tricks on him. Flashbacks of his evening with Claire popped into his brain in short, sharp recollections – details that he had not remembered, until now: the soft goose bumps on her hips, the curve of her shoulders in the pale moonlight that trickled in through the curtains.

As he headed to the washroom to splash water on his face, he realized that he had crossed a line with Claire that night. No, he hadn't merely crossed the line, he had ventured far beyond the line and into another territory altogether. He could well imagine what his MA supervisor, Vladimir, would think. "Too close to the subject," he could practically hear the man saying.

All of Paul's ruminations evaporated, however, when he set foot in the washroom. He could not have prepared himself for what he saw: Simon was sitting on the floor in the corner, his face badly beaten.

"Good lord, man!" Paul said, stammering. "A – are you alright?"

"I'm okay," said Simon, not convincingly. "It's a story. I finally have a story for this group."

"Let's get some cool paper towel on that cheek," Paul said as he violently yanked at the dispenser on the wall, folded the towel into a small square, and ran cool water over it.

"Sit down on the chair," he instructed. Then Paul gingerly placed the wet pack onto Simon's left cheek just below the eye socket.

Simon closed his eyes in a wince with each painful application. "The coolness helps," he admitted.

Paul noticed Simon's body relax a little bit. He held the towel in place, tipping Simon's head back so the water would run away from his face.

"Thanks," Simon said quietly.

Even though he didn't know Simon very well – the man had hardly said ten words in weeks of group therapy – Paul could tell that he was deeply touched by his caring for him. It was as if this unexpected brush of kindness was, itself, overwhelming.

After a few moments, the two men left the washroom, heading to the main room. With the additional light in the hallway, Paul could almost see the purple-yellow coloration slowly spreading across Simon's features.

Claire's face had a look of horror when she saw Simon. "Oh my God. What happened?!"

"I fell on a paperclip," he said wryly.

"That's not funny. Who did this to you?" she demanded, grabbing him by the shoulders.

"I believe you've met my coworkers."

"You've been to Simon's work?" Paul interrupted. "Why?"

"They beat you up in City Hall?" Claire asked, ignoring Paul.

"Don't be ridiculous. It was extracurricular," Simon quipped.

Claire led him to one of the small chairs, holding him by the arm. "I'm so sorry. We shouldn't have done the happy couple routine. Do you think that made things worse?"

"Wait – what?" Paul asked, trying to follow.

"There's no way you can connect those two things. It was a random encounter after work. Brian seized the moment."

"No," Claire persisted. "Look at the consequences."

"You were only trying to help. And I'm going to talk tonight. It's time," Simon said to Claire.

"Do you feel ready?" Paul asked. He didn't want to press, but, at the same time, this was clearly not something that could be swept under the rug.

Simon took a deep breath and glanced at Claire.

She nodded by way of encouragement.

"Okay then," he began. "I'll start with the elephant in the room, second only to these bruises. You could say they're definitely connected.

"I'm gay," he said plainly. "I trust you're not going to try to fix or cure me, Paul?"

"You're not broken," Paul said. He was proud of Simon, imagining how difficult this would be for him.

"I do, however, get beat up on occasion. This time, it was my coworkers, which kind of threw me. I knew they were getting increasingly hostile, but I suppose the work environment, during nine-to-five, protected me. When we ran into each other outside of work, tonight, they just let loose."

"Unforgivable," said Beata. She didn't seem surprised by Simon's confession of being homosexual, Paul noted. Perhaps she had guessed, as he had, when they went out to the tavern and Simon mentioned "someone" in an earlier relationship.

"I visited Simon's work, pretending to be his girlfriend," Claire explained. "To get them off his back. It seemed like a good idea at the time."

Paul took in this news, now understanding the sequence of events that may have triggered the attack. He suspected that Claire's visit, although well intended, may have exacerbated things, but refrained from voicing his thoughts to spare her feelings. It was clear that she and Simon had a strong friendship, and he didn't want to do anything to weaken that bond, especially now when Simon clearly needed support.

"If it's okay with you, I don't really want to concentrate on this one violent incident," said Simon, turning to Paul for permission.

"You can talk about anything," Paul said. "You can start with the everyday." He looked at Simon, trying to determine whether he genuinely wanted to talk. Yes, it seemed as if he was bursting to speak.

"Well, as you know, I'm renovating a Victorian cottage," Simon began, as he lit a cigarette.

Claire and Paul also lit up. The mood seemed cozy and intimate all of a sudden.

"Aren't you getting some help with your renovation?" Claire asked, prodding Simon to continue.

"Ah, you mean Jann?" he said smiling.

This was the first time that Simon had divulged his feelings at any length in group therapy. It was a genuine breakthrough, Paul believed. In nine weeks, he had never seen Simon smile so readily – this, in spite of a mangled face, which still looked painful.

Paul sat back and listened to the story of Simon and Jann. He had not forgotten what it felt like to fall in love. In fact, in hearing Simon's account, Paul realized that this was precisely what was getting him into trouble with Claire.

19

Eager to clear his head after the session, Paul decided to walk home from the church. It was a decent night, after all. The heat of the day had subsided and what remained was a comfortable, cloudless evening.

He was pleased that Simon had turned a corner and begun opening up to the group, but the beating had left Paul's mind reeling. The juxtaposition of Simon's obvious happiness in talking about his relationship with the neighbour, alongside the state of his face, still haunted him. Clearly, such a thrashing was never outside of the realm of possibilities for a gay man in Toronto. Simon had acted as though sooner or later it was inevitable. Paul found this shocking. He questioned his own sheltered life. How could he have been so unaware? Weren't the '60s supposed to be all about love and liberation?

By the time he reached Roncesvalles, he felt emotionally exhausted. The trek had failed to clear his head.

His house looked welcoming. The lights were on in the living room. Unfortunately, this meant that someone was home. He prayed it was not all three of his housemates. The thought of John, Rachel, and Larry, all together, was disheartening. Would he ever get used to living with these people? Would he ever truly think of this place as his home?

As he walked up the cobbled path to the house, he heard sitar music. Loud. He realized that all the windows on the main floor were open. The music spilled out into the summer night.

When he entered the living room, he quickly spotted Larry seated on the floor, legs crossed, eyes closed. An issue of *Science* magazine was balanced, open-face, on his knee.

Upon closer inspection, he suddenly noticed that Larry was wearing his butterfly shirt. There was no mistaking it – this was his own shirt! The shampoo thief had moved on to stealing clothes. He could feel the anger rising in his body, the blood thumping at his temples, but he decided not to take the issue up with Larry. Maybe later. (He forced himself not to think of how this must have transpired: Larry, sauntering into Paul's room, opening his closet, and peering around for a fresh-looking shirt …) Instead, he stomped his foot on the floor so as to alert his flatmate of his presence. He was too tired to yell over the music.

Larry's eyes popped open. "Hey, man," he said, appearing happy to see Paul. "How's it goin'?"

"Where are the others?"

"Rachel's got a gig and John's out with Monster Mom."

This news lightened Paul's spirits considerably. "What's the music?" he asked.

"Ravi Shankar."

"Never heard of him."

"He taught George Harrison to play sitar. They just did a huge concert for Bangladesh in New York. A fundraiser. It was in all the papers."

"Hmm," Paul said, nodding. He sat down on the sofa, lit a cigarette, and began running his fingers through his hair.

"You look like shit," said Larry.

"Thanks for noticing."

"What's up, brother?" Larry asked after lowering the volume on the record player and sitting down beside Paul.

"This group therapy thing."

"What about it?"

"The problems people have ... they're ... Well, things are more complicated, more dire, than I realized."

"You can't fix people, man. Let them be who they're going to be. Just exist," Larry said, helping himself to one of Paul's cigarettes.

"I slept with a woman in the group," Paul suddenly confessed. He needed to tell someone.

"Oh, that's who she was."

"How do you know?"

"I was in the living room. That night. You both walked right past me, although I couldn't really see anything. It was dark and the lights were off. I was trying to come down from a bad trip. You two looked pretty wasted."

"She's actually really great." Paul sighed.

"You know what your problem is, man?"

"You're going to tell me, aren't you?"

"You're taking this way too fucking seriously."

"Taking what?"

"Everything," Larry said, throwing up his arms. "Jesus, you're the most serious person I've ever met. The most intense. You look like a hippie, but you think like an old man. You really need to get stoned."

Paul considered it. "What strain?"

"I believe this calls for 'Fuck You Up.'"

Why not? thought Paul. He had nothing to lose.

They went to the backyard, pulled out the folding chairs, and smoked an industrial-sized joint. "This is the salvaged batch after the incident," Larry said, referencing the raccoon overdose, with which he still seemed to be struggling.

Paul sat on the opposite lawn chair, glancing from time to time at the marijuana crop that had been ploughed under by a team of landscapers hired by John's mother. He peered up at the maple tree as they passed the joint back and forth, then sat back in his chair, waiting for the drug to take effect. Ravi Shankar was still on in the living room.

"I don't feel anything," he said after five minutes. "How old is the stuff?"

"Wait for it," said Larry, grinning like a Cheshire cat. "It's got an unexpected kick."

"I really don't think I'm feeling anything," Paul insisted.

There was, however, a particular sensation of floating that had swept in like a fog, hitherto unnoticed. Paul's arms were now resting on unseen pillows. Marshmallow pillows. They were all around him like clouds; his body was encased in a giant fluffy embrace.

He looked at his arms and was pleasantly surprised by the fact that he could see the molecules rising up from out of his limbs like tiny bubbles. How had he not noticed this before? The human body is a miraculous thing. So many tricks it can do!

"You can see your molecules if you really try," he attempted to tell Larry, to inform him of this miracle, using mind power alone.

He watched the molecules float up to the maple tree and perch on the branches like birds on a wire. The moonlight caught their shimmery surfaces, which made them appear like the bubbles of dishwashing detergent. Green and purple swirls that Paul could not tear his eyes away from. He simply could not look away.

Paul felt strangely proud that these tiny cells were able to do this; they were like his children, leaving the nest. "I love you little guys," he whispered to them, becoming surprisingly emotional.

In time, he shifted his gaze to Larry, noticing for the first time this evening that his flatmate had not shaved. But it was more than that: He appeared increasingly hairy. Thick whiskers had sprouted from his cheeks. Second by second, the hair on his head was transforming to a pale grey, growing around his face, and spreading down to his arms, like a film in fast motion, soon covering all exposed skin. Black banding around the eyes interrupted the splash of white fur on his face. His eyes became smaller and receded into his skull where they resided like curious small dots. Conversely, his nose grew out from his face, protruding to a pointy black button with a streamlined jaw that supported the snout. His ears, now furry even on the inside, rested naturally on the top of his head.

Larry, still fully clothed, had transformed into a

human-sized raccoon. The butterfly shirt had, under the tremendous volume of fur, expanded to the point of bursting.

Paul observed as Larry glanced at his watch, wrapped around his furry wrist. His flatmate's paw had delicate bony fingers and sleek black claws. He watched intently as Larry said: "You're right, man. Maybe the stuff's too old."

20

The bruise on Simon's cheek had mutated into a soft mustard hue after a few days. But Jann spotted the evidence of his friend's violent encounter from a distance, as the two met on Harbour Street the morning of the gay picnic. They would have travelled down together, but Jann had to submit a renovation quote at the crack of dawn.

"Long story." Simon waived it off, determined not to let the incident mar their first official date.

But Jann was having none of it. "You're not getting away that easily," he warned as he grabbed Simon's hand and the two walked southward toward the docks.

This unexpected display of affection, from a man whom Simon had secretly adored for quite some time, both surprised and overwhelmed him. He suddenly realized that being beat up had taken a monstrous toll on him. It was as if Jann's single act of caring, so spontaneous and natural, had triggered a flash of insight for Simon as to how far he may have fallen into despair.

This glimpse, in turn, offered a new sense of optimism. It broke the spell of hopelessness that Simon was not willing to admit, even to himself, before today. His emotions very nearly overcame him. His eyes started to quiver, but he put on his sunglasses to disguise the effect of Jann's simple gesture.

A thin but steady stream of people flowed to the waterfront from Union Station. Everyone was headed to Hanlan's Point – men and women, gay and lesbian couples, families with small children in strollers, and some overly excited dogs. Then, within minutes, before Simon and Jann were able to board the ferry, the crowd swelled. Simon quickly estimated it to be a few hundred in number.

The posters had instructed picnickers to bring food, and many had taken it to heart. People showed up with coolers stuffed with sandwiches, potato salad, cheese, and fruit. Doubtlessly, there were bottles inside the coolers, Simon considered, but the officials working at the docks never searched anyone's belongings.

Jann had said he would supply lunch because Simon had invited him on this date – another gentlemanly act, Simon thought.

The mood at the waterfront was exuberant. The crowd seemed enlivened by the notion of being able to embrace or kiss their partner without fear of reprisal. It was all about solidarity, and sharing an upbeat, family-based event with loved ones for perhaps the first time in public, Simon realized.

They caught the ferry around 9:30 am. The unhurried speed of the boat, and the distance between the harbour and

Hanlan's Point – a broad arch to the southwest – made for a leisurely journey.

"It feels like a vacation, doesn't it?" Simon said as the city grew smaller and smaller.

The two peered over the rail on the upper deck, Simon mesmerized by the churning waters below, which emitted a pungent fish scent, and the approaching horizon of the islands. The inundating purplish silhouette of trees along the shoreline combined with the rising sun, hovering low in the sky like an enormous coral-coloured orb, created an ethereal scene.

Jann set his knapsack down and put his hand over Simon's on the railing as the two gazed at what promised to be a stunning summer day.

A pair of seagulls followed the boat, circling closely for snacks, like bread or popcorn, frequently tossed by passengers. The birds could catch these giveaways midair, which provided a great source of entertainment for everyone. The gulls' sharp cries punctuated the hum of the ferry's engine.

"Are you going to tell me what happened to your face?" Jann asked after a few moments.

"I was jumped by some coworkers." No point delaying the discussion. "After work, I mean."

This wasn't unknown territory to Jann, Simon knew.

"They're Neanderthals," he continued. "I could sense they had it out for me."

"Look, I know that going to HR or a superior is career suicide. Being fired for your sexual identity isn't unheard of. What kind of a place is your work?"

"City Hall? Bureaucracy of the highest order. Mediocrity, conservatism. An old boy's club in many ways."

"Clearly, they're not the right sort of boys," Jann said, joking.

Simon smiled, relieved to speak with someone who knew the drill. It was refreshing not having to explain anything. There was an easy shorthand between the two. Although he appreciated the support from Claire, Paul, and Beata, they didn't truly understand his predicament. Not in the same way that Jann did.

"Why don't you leave City Hall?" Jann suggested. "What's your job title?"

"Office Admin."

"Education?"

"MA in Commerce and Business Administration."

"Impressive. You know you can take that anywhere. Why are you working in such a straight-laced environment? No pun intended. Everyone needs business managers and office administrators, right? Why stay at City Hall … or in government for that matter?"

"Because I've been there for a while. Because change is bad."

"That's where you're wrong. Change is good. Take a chance. You deserve to be happy."

"You? Your schooling?" Simon asked, wanting to know more about Jann and change the subject at the same time.

"George Brown."

"That's new, isn't it?"

"Opened in '67. The Kensington Market Campus was overcrowded so they launched a second one on Davenport, and another on College."

"Furniture design?" Simon guessed.

"Woodwork," Jann said holding up his hands. "Slivers to prove it."

"What's a typical job for you?"

"High-end custom work in Rosedale and Lawrence Park, mainly. Like the one I quoted on this morning."

This made sense in Simon's mind. No wonder Jann seemed so capable with the floors, so knowledgeable when discussing renovations.

He wondered about Jann's history, his family. Did he have siblings? Where were his parents? Was he originally from Toronto? He knew there would be time to gain a more complete picture of his life, but he found himself wanting to know everything right away. He told himself to wind down a bit. Play it cool.

He admired Jann for the freedom with which he conducted himself. This man was out of the closet, living his life. He appeared to be at peace. Calling his own shots.

The shoreline approached. The boatmen prepared to dock, readying the thick mooring lines to wrap around the bollards and stabilize the vessel.

"I could get used to this," Simon said, more to himself than Jann.

"To what?"

"Well … you," Simon admitted, a little flustered.

Jann laughed.

When they disembarked from the ferry, along with a hundred others, the sunburned terrain of Hanlan's Point unfolded in front of them with willows and tall grasses on either side of the pathway. A team of cicadas started, in tandem, as if to announce it's going to be a hot one.

Signs with arrows were posted on every fifth tree: "This way to Toronto's gay picnic!" The well-documented path led to one of the beaches on the western-most side of Hanlan's Point.

The large group of people, with kids, dogs, and coolers in tow, walked leisurely along the path and eventually joined with a few early birds – picnickers who had already set up at the beach or maybe even slept over the night before. The space was sheltered by more willows, under which many folks had moved picnic tables. In the open areas, away from the trees, they had also set up hibachis and installed a make-shift volleyball net. The smell of charcoal mingled with the sweet scent of coconut tanning oil.

It didn't take Simon and Jann long to select an ideal location a little farther away from the action, which centred around the volleyball net.

From his knapsack, Jann extracted a blue-and-white beach blanket, which he promptly spread over the patch of land. He sat down on the blanket, urged Simon to do the same, and withdrew from his knapsack a small bottle of vodka, an even smaller bottle of vermouth, two martini glasses, a jar of stuffed olives, and a package of tiny skewers for the olives.

"After all," he joked, "we're not animals."

"Is this breakfast?" Simon asked, laughing.

"Why not? Aren't we on vacation, after all? Pretend we're in Spain. It would be cocktail hour by now."

"You've been to Spain?" Simon asked, awestruck. Jann

seemed so worldly. Simon, by contrast, had never travelled across the Atlantic. Europe seemed distinctly inaccessible.

"Yes, I have, and I'll take you someday," Jann said mixing the drinks, then passing one to Simon.

"What's it like?" Simon asked, sipping his martini and glancing around at all the people. He noticed that someone had brought a guitar and was starting up nicely with Cat Stevens.

"Sunny all the time, palm trees, great food, fabulous music and dancing, old architecture, beautiful sandy beaches … Not in any way like dreary old Toronto."

"No offence to this lovely beach here," Simon added, kidding.

"No, you're right. At this moment, Hanlan's Point is the very best beach in the world."

Simon wanted to remember every second of this day, this moment. Things had never looked brighter for him, he could say without an ounce of hesitation.

21

Time to bite the bullet. On Paul's advice, and the consensus of the group at their last session, Claire made an appointment with Rose in HR. Here, she would discuss the letter that Maron had submitted – a document ultimately aimed at Claire's termination.

It was simple enough for Claire to make the appointment with HR, but her sense of dread was mounting as the meeting date grew closer. The night before, she tossed and turned, unable to settle.

When sleep came, disturbing dreams interrupted it. She dreamt that she reported Maron's extracurricular activities on the boat cruise to the head of HR – something she would never do. As tempting as it was to offload that juicy nugget, to do so would be sinking to Maron's level. No, instead, she would stick to the workplace atrocities, which were bad enough.

She knew that going to HR was a sound and reasonable course of action, but she feared the execution. It was causing her anxiety to rise considerably, and once it had ascended to a certain point, it was impossible to quell the feeling, to step down from the cliff.

After a fitful sleep, she woke up before the alarm clock. It was a cool, almost fall-like morning, she noticed glancing out the bedroom window and opening it a crack.

She got dressed quickly, with shaking hands, imagining these are the clothes in which she could be fired. Too nervous for breakfast, she managed one cup of coffee before she headed out the door.

She made it to work on auto-pilot. Once there, the idea that she could be fired on the spot or escorted out of the building with her personal belongings in a cardboard box became a very real drama that was unfolding in her mind. She went so far as to fetch a box from the warehouse, which she figured could accommodate her belongings – a few photographs, two plants, and an art nouveau tea tin that she used to hold paperclips. She even tested the box's ability to carry these random things and determined that it was an appropriate size and strength. She would be able to pack up in under three minutes, if necessary.

Thankfully, as she had arrived early, Claire encountered very few people in the office. She was struck by the utter silence of the place as the sun rose and, through the floor-to-ceiling windows on the eastern side of the building, it cast a radiant glow over the space.

She realized how much she would miss this office, her professional home for more than two years. She loved her manuscripts; her authors, scattered throughout Canada's finest universities; and the academic rigour of it all.

It was a shame that it was going to end in such a disgraceful way, she thought. How would her authors be told that she had been fired? Most likely a phone call from Maron, and Claire could well imagine what her boss would say about the way things had ended.

Heading out for a quick cigarette, she passed the mail slots and noticed something in her IN box, a thin envelope. She ripped it open immediately.

It was a carbon copy of an addendum to Maron's HR letter, to inform Claire of the update. It read:

Furthermore, I would like to take the opportunity to address how much Claire is costing the company per annum. In addition to her salary of $6,588, I have added real estate costs, dividing the building among all of our staff and determining exactly how much, in mortgage installments, we are paying for Claire's presence in the building or more specifically, in the 7-x-5-foot cubicle she occupies. This adds up to $15.32 per year.

Similarly, I have calculated heating ($33.60) and electricity ($27.76) associated with Claire. Pens and paper add up to $15.67 and photocopying is $207.65. Finally, plumbing costs, again calculated by dividing the overall costs among all personnel to estimate the sum of Claire's use of the facilities. This comes to $14.45. The grand total is $6,902.45 – nearly $7,000.

I propose we hold Claire accountable. To facilitate this, I have taken the liberty of creating a table for her to complete each day to document how she is using her time. It is divided by 15-minute allotments for greater accuracy.

Jesus Christ. Could it get any worse?

Claire went out for a cigarette, sitting on one of the picnic tables on the small patch of grass beside the parking lot. She glanced around the industrial park, resigned to her fate.

Remnant feathers and down from the abandoned nests of Canada geese that had settled in the spring still drifted around the area, mingling with milkweed seeds. Today, these elements added a surreal quality to the scene as the wisps of down drifted slowly around in the air like the contents of a snow globe.

Claire thought about Rose, who was likely now preparing for the imminent HR appointment. This woman, a little vapid, always seemed happy, which naturally made Claire suspicious. Was it possible to be this blissful, consistently? Would this woman be cheerful even while firing an employee? Would she have a smile on her face when she rubberstamped the termination?

Claire steadied her emotions and headed to HR. She sat outside of Rose's door, her hands locked together, her right thumbnail already starting to press into her left palm along the crease of the lifeline.

Rose's door snapped open, which made Claire jump.

"Oh, I didn't mean to scare you!" Rose said, laughing. "Come in! Make yourself at home."

Claire obeyed.

"What can I do for you today?" Rose asked, urging Claire to sit down and closing the door. She returned to her desk, folded her hands together on the surface like a schoolgirl, and cocked her head slightly to the left in a bird-like fashion. Claire wondered if this kind of body language was part of HR training: Appear as if you are engaged and empathetic by tilting your head to one side.

"Well," Claire began. She was unsure how to start the conversation and cursed herself for not having anticipated this hurdle. How could she have failed to plan for this particular moment?

Should she inquire as to when she would be fired? And what, exactly, were the ramifications of Maron's letter documenting her failings? After all, the correspondence, and its killer addendum, were surely lurking somewhere in Rose's steel blue file cabinets, which formed a military-looking wall in the small office.

"I – I guess I'd like to know about my file," Claire said, sussing out Rose's reaction.

"Your file?" Rose asked, appearing confused. "Anything in particular?"

"How it will be handled … I mean, the steps to be taken."

As her thumbnail dug deeper into her palm, Claire could feel herself shrinking in the chair. It was as if the floor was sucking her down into a vortex.

"How what will be handled?"

"The letter, the documentation Maron submitted."

"I'll have to check. Why don't I pull your file now," said Rose. She evidently knew the location of everyone's records by heart. She found the manila folder with Claire's name on it immediately. "Let's see …" she said as she began flipping through the pages, which, from Claire's perspective across the desk, seemed to number under ten.

"I was hoping we could establish a kind of trial period, a grace period, where I might be able to preemptively set up new systems," Claire said, getting her thoughts in order. But without a clear idea of her specific failings – other than their being all-encompassing, according to Maron – she didn't know what kind of revised systems would make sense. She was trying to save her job. She was on the verge of begging.

She felt her thumbnail cutting into the skin of her palm as she squirmed in her seat. This was getting worse by the minute.

Rose looked up from her paperwork.

"Listen," Claire said, stammering, "I know my wages are to be frozen, in terms of the standard of living increase … and I can live with that, I suppose, as long as this is confidential –"

"Your wages aren't frozen. That's against policy. We give all employees a standard of living increase at their annual assessment. At the very least."

Claire stared back, feeling unable to process this new information.

"Where on Earth did you hear your wages were frozen?"

"It's based on performance. And I – I made a mistake in editing or rewriting a chapter of a psychology book this spring … The Milgram experiment …"

"Well, there's a letter in your file from a psych professor," Rose said, extracting the correspondence.

"You mean a letter from Maron," Claire corrected Rose.

"No. It's written on university letterhead and it's from the professor." Rose slid the letter across the desk.

Claire could see that the correspondence was from the academic whose chapter she had rewritten. It was a thank you note for fixing the Milgram experiment and for helping his book to be published. It was addressed to Maron, praising Claire's editorial skills.

"Didn't Maron show you this letter?" Rose asked. "It's quite exceptional. Doesn't happen every day."

"But where's Maron's letter?!" Claire strained to see the contents of the file, frustrated by Rose's inability to address the question at hand. All she wanted to know was how to keep from being fired.

"Why yes, there's a note from Maron here, too," Rose said as she extracted a one-pager. "It's your assessment for this year."

Here we go, thought Claire, the axe was about to fall. "That's what I'm talking about."

"I can't address it because it hasn't been processed," Rose said, drawing the paper ever so slightly closer to her chest, making it clear that she could not share the contents with Claire.

"We process all assessments at the same time. Next week, I believe I have you pencilled in for Thursday," she said as she leaned over the enormous desk calendar to check the date.

"I – I don't want to interfere with your HR process," Claire said, close to tears. "I just need to plan ... Look, Rose, I'm a practical person. I need to know ... I mean, I realize people have been talking with Maron and there's ... well, disappointment. I know it's written in the file. I've seen the assessment. Maron showed it to me."

Rose reached out with a look of grave concern on her face. "I think you're mistaken, Claire."

"No, please be honest."

"Maron's recommending a raise due to your stellar performance – her words," Rose said, pointing to the assessment. "It's written here in black and white."

Claire impulsively reached out to grab the piece of paper, eager to prove Rose wrong in some perverse way. With this sudden gesture, a pool of blood from her palm splattered, in large dollops, on Rose's desk and quickly oozed across the woman's calendar. In an instant, it formed a bright red shape that looked like an island with an ever-expanding coastline.

"Oh my God!" Rose stood up, by reflex alone, then quickly grabbed a Kleenex from the box of tissues beside the telephone. "Are you alright?" Within seconds, she was on the other side of the desk, pressing the Kleenex into Claire's hand.

For Claire, it felt as if this were happening in a dream. She wondered if she were back in bed, tossing and turning in the small hours of the morning. She peered at Rose, inspecting the look of genuine concern on the woman's face, and asked herself if perhaps she had mistakenly pegged the HR lady as superficial.

She mouthed the words "I'M OKAY." She felt the comforting vibration of her vocal cords, but she couldn't hear any sound. Instead, there was a rushing noise in her head like a waterfall. It felt as if she were going to faint.

Her instincts were still switched on, however. When Rose ran out of the office to find the first aid kit in the warehouse (where most accidents occurred), Claire didn't hesitate to open the HR file, now bloodied, and read Maron's actual assessment. She needed to see it with her own eyes.

Rose was correct. It was a favourable review. Maron had given her a rating of "above expectations." A raise, not the anticipated wage freeze, and certainly not dismissal from the company, would accompany this rating.

Claire set the paperwork back on the desk the way she had found it, even though this meant that it would surely absorb more blood. She walked out of the office, heading to the front door. The tissues fell on the floor like red and white petals leading out of the office, but she didn't care.

She circled around to the back of the building, lit a cigarette, and reclaimed her earlier position on the picnic table. The parking lot had filled to capacity since her last visit about an hour ago. The asphalt, combined with the heat of the day – steadily rising – now made the outdoor space oven-like, but Claire was content to remain. She decided to lie down on the surface of the picnic table and concentrate on the cloud formations that were gently easing their way across the surface of the sky very high up in the stratosphere. She tried to calm herself.

After a few minutes, Rose tracked her down. She walked toward the picnic table, slightly breathless. She looked very concerned. She sat down, took a cigarette from Claire's pack, and lit it.

The two women remained at the picnic table for several minutes before talking.

"What's really going on?" Rose broke the silence.

Being outside the physical confines of work made Claire feel as if it were a safe place to talk to Rose. Off the books. She wondered what Paul would think of this turn of events and wished she could call him. He had given his phone number out, after the group therapy session where Simon had shown up with his battered face, impressing on each of them that they could call him at any time, day or night, if they ever needed someone to talk to. A pang of something close to sadness or regret swept over her. She realized that she missed him. It was not unlike a feeling of homesickness.

"What's up, Claire?" Rose repeated.

Realizing there was nothing to do but tell the truth, Claire told Rose without holding back any details. She was finished with dancing around things.

When she went to her desk, thankful to be doing something routine to steady her nerves, she had no idea what Rose would do with this new and damning information. But she was too exhausted to consider the woman's reaction. She wanted to get lost in a fresh manuscript and forget what had just transpired

HR acted swiftly, however. Within the hour, via the overhead speakers, Maron was summoned to Rose's office.

Driven by overwhelming and unstoppable curiosity, Claire followed her boss to HR, being careful not to be detected. As soon as Maron closed the door to Rose's office, Claire leaned up against it, cupping her ear on the cool surface. She didn't care if anyone witnessed this shameless eavesdropping. Thankfully, no one was around. Summertime staff in HR was always skeletal.

She could hear the conversation clearly.

"It has come to my attention that you have, once again, been threatening your staff," Rose said in an unvarnished fashion.

What did she mean by "once again?" Claire wondered. This was a bombshell. Had Maron been bullying others too?

"Now, Rose, you and I are seasoned professionals. We've both been in this business for a long while. You know that the mentoring process can be challenging."

Maron was attempting to placate Rose, this was obvious. The woman was so clearly two-faced. But would Rose fall for it?

"This is beyond mentoring," Rose shot back.

"Now, I value your expert input above all –"

"You are conducting yourself in an unprofessional –"

"We both know that staff are like children. They need to be kept in line. I'm sure you realize this, Rose. Don't they teach you that in HR school?" Maron laughed gently, still attempting to turn things around.

This statement made Claire's blood boil. She remembered overhearing how Maron spoke to her children. How could anyone equate outright cruelty with learning or guidance?

"I don't agree with that philosophy and it's incongruous with our Code of Ethics," Rose stated.

"We have a Code of Ethics?" Maron was becoming increasingly agitated.

"Of course we do."

"That's a bit of a joke, isn't it?" Maron spat. "Nobody pays attention to these sorts of bureaucratic things. We're here to make books, to make money, plain and simple. My goodness, look at you, with all of your silly HR rules."

"I'm going to give you a choice, Maron: Quit on your own accord, although you'll receive no references from this publishing house, or be fired."

Whoa, the gloves were off.

"You're bullshitting me."

"You're mistaken. Pack your belongings. We don't tolerate this behaviour."

Claire felt like crying. She was overwhelmed that Rose would stick up for her, and so vehemently.

"Who the hell have you been talking to? Emily? Jane? Frederick?!" Maron yelled.

Claire backed away from the door, fearing her boss might erupt from the office at any moment in search of the culprits. But inquisitiveness got the better of her, and she returned.

"It doesn't matter," Rose said.

"No, I'll bet it was Claire, that nervous little shit! This is about the addendum, isn't it? That was a stroke of genius. Did she come and report it? No, she wouldn't have the balls to talk to you. She's a nut case, you know. It was actually fun planting the seed on that one."

Claire was incensed.

"Fun?" Rose's voice raised. "You told Claire you were papering her file! This is simply not true. She's an excellent editor and you, yourself, have given her a positive review. What kind of game are you playing, Maron?"

"Ya, the woman's totally crazy. Such a perfectionist! What a nerd. I wanted to see what would happen if she fucked up."

"But she didn't."

"I know. That's the beauty of it!"

Claire turned on her heel having heard enough. Maron had incriminated herself without recourse. It was clear, now, that she had not passed on any of the negative documentation about Claire to HR. It was all an elaborate ruse.

Fifteen minutes later, Claire watched from the window of the second-floor boardroom as Maron was escorted out of the building. Rose had been brutally efficient, Claire realized.

Maron yelled something at Rose, who must have been standing by the exit door, out of range from Claire's perspective, and gave her the finger as she sped away in her shit-coloured Buick Skylark.

The announcement, released that afternoon, said that Maron had resigned to pursue other ventures, but everyone knew the truth. Water cooler conversation confirmed that no one had liked her, that many had felt victimized by Maron, but everyone had been too afraid to say something, not even in the stupid MOFT meetings, Claire realized. Two junior copyeditors were crying with the relief of it all.

People were curious about what triggered the firing, but Claire said nothing. She was more stunned than anything. She had never imagined Rose could be so forthright. Clearly, she had underestimated the woman.

That night, sitting on her balcony, while a warm breeze drifted through the surrounding trees, Claire let the news sink in. This was a fresh start, a new beginning, she thought. There could be no mistake. What that actually meant, or how things would change from this point forward, in the coming weeks, months, and years, were not important.

For the first time in a long while, Claire felt as if she might be on her way to getting better, to fixing herself. She couldn't wait to tell the others.

22

This was heaven. Beata was standing under a chuppah, mesmerized by the ornate stitching. The particular way the light shone through the fabric from high above the synagogue's domed ceiling was otherworldly.

She had brought her camera to document this liturgical piece as part of her ongoing project. She was alone in the synagogue. The administrator had let her in and allowed her free rein of the place for the afternoon.

Beata was still thinking about the priest she had encountered at the last church. How did he know that she spoke with Jafari? Was there an aura around her? She was considering going back to Caledon, under the guise of the liturgical project, and gaining more information. Not in any formal way and certainly not in a religious fashion, but more like a one-on-one conversation of two equals. She could tell he, a near stranger, was sympathetic to her in a way that no one else in her life was. And was this the reason she felt drawn to him? She couldn't shake the feeling that he had some kind of understanding about the big questions in life. Was there something to religion after all?

Jafari had made himself comfortable on the cushioned benches midway back. But today, she didn't feel like talking. She was still processing the idea of moving to London. It had thrown her for a loop. On one hand, the notion of starting again with Jafari in a new place, just the two of them, was very attractive. She wanted to leave Toronto, all of a sudden, it seemed. What was left for her here, after all, now that the kids were gone?

But again, she had a gnawing sense that there was something wrong, incongruent, with the way she was living. Were her children right? Somewhere along the line there had been a disconnect. She realized this, but she couldn't tease apart the unique strands of it. Things were overlapping, crisscrossing, intersecting.

It was slowly dawning on her that there were, indeed, two separate realities that she was dipping into, spending time in, as if they were, merely, different sides of the same coin. But the analogy of the coin, in truth, was not holding up. Beata had to admit it was weakening, the two sides incompatible.

Some days, she felt as if she were dreaming, living another person's life. She went through her hours, filling time at the Guild, going through the motions, while deep down she had disengaged. Her mind, her spirit, was elsewhere.

She connected best with birds, with the sky, with High Park because these things seemed to be speaking the same language as her, to be on the same frequency.

As she photographed the chuppah, she thought about group therapy and how she had, to date, represented her life in this forum. She was the grieving widow, a role that she had more or less assumed, both internally and externally, because this way, she could properly grieve. And her loss, her pain, brought with it a tremendous heaviness. It cut to the marrow. But she hadn't been completely honest with Paul's group. She could sense that Paul knew there was more to her story but didn't want to press her.

She forced herself to return to what was really import-ant. She was happiest, most alive and in love, when she and Jafari were together, there was no doubt. Everything paled by comparison; nothing was more real. When she spoke with him, sitting quietly in the kitchen nook or driving on a country road, a slice of that happiness was returned to her as if by magic. It was accessible again, down to the smallest detail, but was it real? she dared to ask herself. Or was it more like a mirror, a copy of what had been; a ghostly resi-due that was, or became over time, more real or valid than the original? To answer this question would be to admit that the two Jafaris, the dead and the living, were not, in fact, identical.

Can a person, by determination alone, create a world that they wished existed? she wondered. But this was to assume that willpower, or the rational part of the mind, was doing the heavy lifting, which was untrue. Instead, Beata knew that she was tapping into something truly mystic, profoundly beautiful.

For her, this kind of beauty was only possible at the most barren moments, within the deepest feelings of despair and hopelessness. It appeared, without her conscious inter-jection, like a delicate flower blooming out of asphalt – an utter impossibility.

The kids were another issue that she dwelled on as she photographed the chuppah. She missed them tremen-dously, worried about their safety, and sought to be reunited with them soon, but she couldn't imagine how that would happen. Their judgment of her was a barrier that seemed to be strengthening daily. Their overt dislike of her conver-sations with Jafari, their own father, was one of the mech-anisms that built and reinforced that bulwark. She hoped that she could work through this with Jafari, that their conversations could help.

"Let's talk about your London idea," she said, sitting down beside him. "Tell me about your favourite places."

"I gravitated around LSE, which is in Westminster between Covent Garden and Holborn. It's central London. Lincoln's Inn Fields, behind the university, is a charming small park that you'd like."

"I'd love the green spaces."

"There are so many gardens in London: Hyde, Regent's, St. James, Green Park … It's like having ten High Parks in one city."

This was music to Beata's ears. The idea of these green spaces made her want to move right away.

"Where would we live?" she asked. "It would need to be big enough for the kids to visit."

"I lived in one of the residences, back then. Maybe we could do the same."

"Because you're an alumnus?"

"I'm sure we could get a good deal," he said confidently. "A place that has plenty of room for the kids, of course."

"Maybe I could get a job at the university," she suggested.

"Not just LSE, there are many. University College, Imperial College, King's College, Queen Mary, University of London, Royal Holloway … You could work anywhere, Bea."

"I could get good references. I suppose I should get on that right now," she said, thinking aloud. "With September almost here, that would be the best time to head over. If I'm not able to find work in the fall, they'd hire again in the new year, right?"

"The sooner, the better, I think."

"We really could start again, couldn't we, Jaf?" The idea had, by now, cemented in her mind. Beata was becoming more fully committed to London. The notion that had felt so out of the blue, just a few days ago, now seemed like the most logical, almost predictable, decision in Beata's mind. Why not go to the city of Jafari's past, where he first set down his academic roots, the city with so much green space? This was the lifeline she needed. Through this decision alone, she gave herself permission to be happy again. It was time to take radical steps.

23

Getting stoned with Larry was not the stroke of genius Paul had intended. It solved nothing. His head was residually foggy, and he had a niggling suspicion that he may have shared a little too much personal information with Larry. Furthermore, he was still worried about group therapy.

Making matters worse, he had scheduled a discussion with Cynthia later in the afternoon – or rather, she had granted him speaking time, telephone privileges. He wanted to make it clear that he knew about the man situation, the bloke his wife was apparently seeing. Evan's innocuous comment in the park, with the yaks, had left him wondering: Who is this person? Was he attempting to co-parent the kids, my children? How was this man's sudden interjection into their lives going to affect them?

It was early morning and, having stewed about these things for some time, all Paul wanted to do was put these worries aside for a moment, have a quiet coffee and cigarette out back, sit peacefully on one of the lawn chairs, and listen to the chorus of birds as the sun began its life-affirming ascent.

John approached, destroying any sense of peace. "Mother wants you to be the new landlord," he said, standing in front of Paul, blocking the sunshine.

"Bloody hell, why? She's the landlord. Or you are, right?"

It was nine o'clock in the morning, for Christ's sake, he thought. A moment's peace from this madhouse would do him a world of good. Moreover, the landlord question struck him as acutely irrelevant. He stared back at John, who seemed to feel no urgency in answering his question.

"Mother actually likes you," John finally said. "Trusts you not to let the place go to rat shit."

"Well, that's high praise. At our last encounter, you'll recall, I was the corruptor of youth. I thought her next move would be hemlock."

John looked confused. "This isn't about locks or security. It's maintenance and upkeep. Maybe you're not understanding what I'm saying."

Sweet Jesus, thought Paul, is this guy a total moron? "Look, I've got enough on my plate," he said. "I can't do it."

Larry stumbled out of the house letting the screen door slam behind him. He pulled out the second collapsible lawn chair leaning against the house, sprung it open, plunked himself down beside Paul, and lit a joint.

"Good morning, my brothers," he said after taking a drag.

"My mother wants him to be landlord," John pointed to Paul as he explained to Larry.

"And I've declined. I have no interest … and other, more important things are going on right now," Paul said feeling frustrated. His quiet morning had been completely usurped.

"He's having trouble with the wife," Larry explained to John.

Paul shot him a look of incredulousness.

"Thin walls, my friend," Larry said, as if eavesdropping was unavoidable and he was just as much a victim as anyone. "And, to be frank, I'd be more upset by the fact that someone's screwing my wife."

Paul suddenly remembered telling Larry about this when they were stoned. *What was I thinking?!* he cursed himself. Perhaps Larry's raccoon persona had morphed into a kind of therapist in Paul's mind.

"Someone's screwing your wife?" John asked.

"Although you've seen some action with the ladies," Larry said to Paul. "Let's just put that out there."

"No, let's not!" said Paul, infuriated.

"Wait, why's he upset?" John was confused.

"Stay with us, man," Larry explained. "He's upset about his kids being influenced by this new dude. Their potential new dad."

"That's it! We're not talking about my private life. This is not happening!" Paul said as he violently extinguished his cigarette in the grass and headed back into the house.

"Do you still love your wife?" Larry asked. "Because I'd be more worried about that."

"Well, you don't have a wife, do you?!" Paul shot back as the door slammed.

"Jeez, what's got his goat?" Paul heard John ask Larry as he headed to his room.

He kicked the bedroom door closed, lay down, and picked up the Maslow book he had been fitfully reading. He was determined to plough through the volume, but it was proving an excruciatingly dry read.

Suddenly, he put the book aside. "He's fucking right," he said out loud. It hit him like a ton of bricks. Sidestepping the irksome detail that Larry seemed to know everything about his personal life through numerous invasions of privacy as well as the few times when Paul may have let his guard down, one fact remained: The drug-addled shampoo-stealer was actually correct on this point. Paul was, in fact, more concerned about his sons than his wife. Something had changed in his thinking.

When he had first heard from Evan that Cynthia was dating, he was consumed by the idea of another man sleeping with his wife, another man taking his old spot on the left side of the creaky bed that they had purchased five years ago – the first piece of furniture they bought as a couple. Another man having coffee, reading the newspaper on the comfy sofa in the living room, his living room, on a lazy Sunday morning. Another man grocery shopping with his wife down Roncesvalles, hosting dinner parties with friends – not that he and Cynthia had done this in years, but the idea was there. Another man replacing him, in his own life, in every sense.

So, what changed? He slowly realized that perhaps he didn't want to be that man planning dinner parties with Cynthia or sleeping in the creaky bed with her or reading the paper beside her on weekends.

He had to admit that Larry raised a very interesting point. His flatmate had cut to the chase.

By noon, Paul had gathered his thoughts in preparation for his conversation with Cynthia. He decided that he would not lead with an enquiry about the new man. Instead, he would take the high road and focus on the kids. He was determined to arrange his next visit with them.

He considered whether there would come a time when he and Cynthia would be able to talk about this more naturally, like friends, without a mountain of angst embedded in the conversation. After all, wasn't this era of liberation supposed to unchain people from convention and expectations? There was a good side to her. It was just that he hadn't engaged with this side for a long while.

Paul prepared for the conversation in the kitchen. As fate would have it, both John and Larry were out, and Rachel failed to come home last night – a new boyfriend, a boisterous drummer, according to Larry, was on the scene. All of this meant that Paul was, mercifully, alone in the house, and privacy was more or less guaranteed.

He dialled his old phone number, then hung up, abruptly deciding that he needed a glass of wine and a cigarette. He poured himself a generous amount of red wine in a coffee mug, lit up, and retied the elastic in his hair to more firmly yank it away from the base of his neck, anticipating a profusion of sweat during the conversation. He removed his sandals, tossing them to the corner of the kitchen, and paced around the room, steadying his nerves as if he were about to wrestle with an opponent of gargantuan proportions.

The phone rang three times before Cynthia picked up. "Hello?" She sounded agitated. How was that possible, Paul asked himself, from one word?

He suppressed the knee-jerk opener: "I hear you're fucking someone," and instead said, "Hey, Cyn. It's Paul."

"Oh." Clearly nonplussed, but slightly softening.

"I thought we should chat." He tried to sound upbeat, as if this phone call caused him no consternation whatsoever.

"I suppose so," she said. "Do you want the kids this weekend?"

Curious, he thought. She seemed all of a sudden willing to relinquish the boys. This must be related to the new man.

"Well, sure."

"You can come and collect them," she said, sounding more distracted than angry.

"Do you have any plans?" he asked, not wanting the conversation to end. "I mean, how're you doing, Cyn, honestly?"

"Jesus, Paul," she said, "I really don't have time to talk about this shit with you now."

He suddenly remembered how much she disliked discussing her feelings. How could he have forgotten this overarching quality deeply embedded in the woman's personality? On more than a few occasions, mainly in the middle of a barnburner of an argument, she had accused him of talking too much about his feelings.

How could he have failed to see this before? He was beginning to imagine the veritable time bomb that their relationship had been. In this light, it seemed a miracle that the two had stayed together as long as they had. Was it the boys that held the marriage together?

He tried to remember what it was like when he first met Cynthia – the euphoria of falling in love; the saucy, super-hot sex where you can't keep your hands off each other; the dizzying rush of adoration that rapidly builds when you're fascinated with every detail of this new person. You're entranced by their stories, their individual histories – so much so, Paul realized, that the day this person enters your world becomes a new starting point in your own life. You are permanently changed.

At the start of a new relationship, you like yourself, partially because you've seized the opportunity to recreate a newer, better version of yourself in the eyes of your love interest. You can edit your life, present your history perhaps more interestingly, omitting the sour elements, any cringe-worthy moments of selfishness or malice. You show the happy, balanced ideal of yourself, which isn't a lie altogether, but it's a version of the truth. You reconnect with a kinder, more generous account of yourself. At this stage, Paul mused, you're thoughtful – buying flowers, planning romantic walks, cooking special dinners, and generally maintaining a level of intensity that comes with falling in love. Life is exciting, urgent, and vibrant. Everything seems remarkable.

Then come the first elements of the long haul: You move in together – since things are still great, you may have rushed into this phase. You meet each other's friends and family, still carefully maintaining the better version of yourself, hosting dinner parties and potlucks, barbecues and birthdays with the sets of new people that get folded into your life slowly over lingering glasses of wine and long conversations. Most of these people, Paul found, were genuinely nice. He enjoyed this process.

Next, the first pregnancy, which was a bit of a surprise to Paul and Cynthia. It occurred very early in the relationship, but they managed to keep their heads above water. That said, Paul sensed a shift in Cynthia. She seemed increasingly exacerbated by him. There was an undertone not dissimilar to regret. She didn't take delight in the kids as Paul did. He could see this. By the second child, she seemed outright peeved, as if life had taken a turn from which there was no escape. He could see she was floundering.

By the time the long haul had descended, like a dark cloud, it seemed as though both Paul and Cynthia were not sure that this was what they had wanted after all. The varnish of adoration had thinned to the point of nonexistence. There was no lovemaking, no walks in High Park, no special dinners. To Paul, it seemed as though they were living like awkward, slightly disgruntled roommates, waiting for something to change or get better.

"Okay, another time," he said, realizing the phone conversation with Cynthia would be short.

"Look," she said sighing heavily into the receiver, "I'm sorry, Paul. I'm just tired."

That was a change. She never apologized.

"No problem," he said, letting her off the hook. He sensed they may never have that heart-to-heart discussion that he so needed.

After he hung up the phone, it surprised Paul to real-ize that he had fallen out of love with his wife. Complete awareness of this was scary at first, like having the rug pulled out from under him. He caught himself feeling wist-ful, pining – once again – for a meaningful conversation with Cynthia, this one to retrace their relationship. Like attending a funeral for an old friend, such a conversation could be a chance to recount a life that no longer existed, as a sign of respect. But there was none of that. Cynthia would surely have rolled her eyes if he were to suggest such an introspective re-examination of their history. She hated that sort of melancholic thinking.

If he were a gambling sort of person, Paul probably would have bet that he and Cynthia would never get back together. Not now. This moment may just be, he figured, the lowest point in their relationship. The absolute lowest. It really was over. When you can't even be bothered to talk about it, it's dead.

24

Today marked the six-month anniversary of Simon and Jann's first meeting: the fateful encounter where Jann offered to help Simon carry the floorboards from the delivery truck to the living room.

They decided to make the most of it. Simon took care of the arrangements, so when they left his Cabbagetown house at 6 pm, heading westward as the sun was just beginning to tickle the treetops, Jann had no idea as to the venue. Simon had booked a table at his partner's favourite restaurant: Barbarian's Steakhouse on Elm Street, one of the most exclusive restaurants in the city.

"What have you got there?" Jann pointed to the grocery bag Simon was carrying.

Simon refused to reveal anything about the mystery, including the contents of the bag.

They walked through Cabbagetown, studying the potential of a few random cottages, some of which were in a near-dilapidated state. They fantasized about how they would renovate these small homes, starting with the front porch, for curb appeal, and then moving into the gardens, many of which could be quickly restored with a bit of raking and a few well-positioned hostas to brighten things up.

As they approached Yonge and turned on to Elm, Jann said, "No. You didn't."

"Yes. And you'd better put these on." Simon pulled a blazer and tie out of the bag. "There's a strict dress code, you know."

The two stood outside of the dining establishment fumbling with their ties, fully realizing how ridiculous it must look to passersby. Simon then folded and tucked the bag neatly into his breast pocket, as they stepped into the restaurant with heads held high.

To walk into Barbarian's from a sunny street was like venturing into a rabbit's warren from a bright meadow. It took a while for their eyes to adjust to the darkness. The ceilings were low, and the series of wood-panelled rooms were dimly lit. The restaurant offered a multitude of Group of Seven paintings, but Jann said he preferred the grander European artworks around the place, which depicted ships navigating treacherous waters and the like. These paintings, he believed, infused the restaurant with a feeling of Old Britain, of Empire, which blended well with the plush furnishings and the tangible elegance.

In time, as their eyes adjusted, Simon and Jann could make out a series of round tables, with crisp white tablecloths and a few booths with comfy-looking benches.

Simon inhaled as the host, dressed in a smart-looking tuxedo, met the two men. The scent of the place was always the same: roast beef and Yorkshire puddings, mingled with cigar smoke.

"Good evening, sirs," said the host. He stood at attention as if he were waiting just for them. "How may I help you this evening?"

"Table for two," Simon said as he gazed around the environment. "I made a reservation."

They followed the host down a narrow hallway from the bar. This led to a larger room. Here, they were seated in the corner, which provided an excellent vantage point for the entire room.

The restaurant was busy. Many conversations were in full swing, threatening to drown out the classical music piped in through unseen speakers somewhere close to the ceiling.

Their waiter appeared not long after they sat down, lit the small candle in the centre of the table, and supplied them with drinks almost immediately. Simon knew there was no question as to Jann's order: a martini to start followed by a ridiculously large slab of prime rib with gravy and Yorkshire pudding. He followed suit.

"Your face is healing nicely," Jann said, touching Simon's cheek lightly enough so as not to attract attention. It seemed to Simon that Jann wasn't overly worried about perceptions here. This restaurant was gay-friendly, he had heard.

"Yes," said Simon, "I'll survive."

"It's not about survival. Although safety's an issue. And I'd hardly call it secure when your coworkers are lurking in the wings. You know that's a ridiculous way of looking at it."

"I wasn't focusing on my surroundings. I hadn't realized where Brian and the others could've gone after work ... I mean, usually I have a radar on them, to avoid a run-in. I'll be more prudent in the future."

"As I said at the picnic: You need to find another job, Simon. And it needs to be a supportive environment. You can't be looking over your shoulder all the time. That's not acceptable. Not in this day and age. It's 1971, for Christ's sake."

Dinner arrived and the two tucked into the meal with zeal, savouring the room, the music, the atmosphere as much as the food.

"The world's changing," Jann pressed in between bites. "The picnic was just the beginning."

"I'd like to believe you, but I can't imagine a time when I can walk down Bay Street or Yonge and Bloor, in the centre of the city, holding hands with you," Simon said as he lowered his voice. "I just can't see it."

"That day will come. We need to make sure of it. Get more politically active. Join some of the groups that are popping up. We met some people at the picnic, didn't we?"

It was true. They had enjoyed a lengthy conversation with one organizer at the end of the day-long event. To Simon, this man – who looked distractingly like the American swimming star Mark Spitz from the '67 Summer Olympics – was a little too ardent, but he could tell that Jann was fully engaged.

"You know I'm not a political animal," Simon said. "I like to keep my personal life separate."

"The personal is the political ... to quote Carol Hanisch."

"What have you been reading?!" Simon asked, laughing.

He had, over the past few days, begun to see Jann in a different light. Physical labour may characterize his job, but the man was intellectually curious – more so than Simon had originally realized. Each political conversation Simon had with Jann reinforced this growing realization. Jann was much more than the cute neighbour he had set his sights on months ago.

"Just the papers," Jann said, smiling. "I'm an active citizen. You could be too."

Being active was hard to imagine for Simon right now. The effort that his stomach was undertaking to process the overload of protein was making him feel sleepy and satisfied, like a snake having swallowed a large rodent.

They lounged at the table, nursing their drinks, killing a few cigarettes, admiring the paintings, and imagining the life stories of the other patrons for fun.

It was late when they left the restaurant. Simon was unsure as to the exact time, but the moon was already out. It was astonishingly vivid and, being close to the horizon, it appeared supersized. He could clearly make out many of the crevasses and craters on its golden surface, such was the size and visibility.

They walked straight up Yonge. Even from a distance, they could see that a commotion was brewing outside the St. Charles. Locals, driving by the gay hangout in their Camaros and Mustangs, were yelling obscenities at the patrons. Typical, thought Simon.

When he and Jann got closer, however, things suddenly changed. One of the cars stopped and five large men, who looked like footballers, sprung out, heading for the half dozen men who were milling around, like sitting ducks, just outside the doorway of the tavern.

Simon felt his stomach drop. He knew that someone would soon throw the first punch. This was going to turn violent.

Jann indicated to Simon that they should cross to the east side of Yonge and get out of the pending fray. The two picked up their step and headed over – a decision they instantly regretted, as two additional cars stopped and deposited more burly passengers into the street to hunt down the tavern's clientele. Simon quickly realized that this was an organized attack involving more than one carful of people.

They next did an about-face to run south on Yonge, when three police cars pulled up from out of nowhere, sirens blaring. The bright lights on the top of the cruisers cast fragments of illumination around the surrounding buildings like a disco ball.

"The fuzz!" someone yelled from the doorway of the tavern.

Six, fast-moving officers erupted from the vehicles. The first two had their sights set on Simon and Jann who were summarily tossed into the back seat of a cruiser within minutes. This occurred after a brief and somewhat confusing scuffle in which Jann attempted to explain that he and Simon were not involved in the altercation, nor were they patrons of the tavern.

The arresting officers, young and seemingly overwhelmed, weren't listening. It was clear that they were distracted by the mounting violence on the street.

From the rear seat of the car Simon and Jann watched the riot unfold.

Someone lit a piece of garbage and hurled it at the police – hardly a Molotov cocktail, but it did the trick. Backup arrived within seconds. The police began throwing as many of the thugs into their cars as they could manage.

"We need to get out of here. We're not part of this," Jann said to Simon. "I'm not about to be shoved in some lock up with these assholes – and neither are you."

"Look!" Simon said, opening the car door. "The cops must've forgotten to lock us in!" It seemed a miracle.

A few more cruisers had parked on the far side of the street closer to the commotion, and they blocked the road, which allowed Simon and Jann to escape without being seen. The two simply opened the right-side door; snuck out of the vehicle; and started walking, not running after Jann's instruction: "Take it slow!" effectively dampening Simon's primal urge to flat-out run.

Heading south on Yonge they left the scene, likely appearing only a little dishevelled to those who had gathered from farther afield to watch the escalating event. Surely no one would have guessed they had occupied the backseat of a police cruiser just moments ago.

By the time they hit Carleton, they were completely ignored by all curiosity seekers. Here, they broke into a run from sheer giddiness, their laughter echoing in the street.

At last, they entered run-down Cabbagetown. The moon was higher in the sky than before, but just as bright – much more luminescent than the yellowy streetlights in the area, half of which were burnt out.

The streets in this area were narrow, by comparison, and the branches of the trees flanking either side almost met in the middle. This cozy, forlorn neighbourhood smelled like soil, despite the lack of rain, and like overgrown gardens punctuated, on occasion, by the scent of late-blooming trees. This, thought Simon, was the best of summer.

They walked, in silence, in the centre of the street, simply because they could. Traffic was nonexistent in the small one-way streets and dead-end laneways. They sauntered a few feet apart from each other, still basking in the miracle of escape.

"We should move in together," said Jann all of a sudden. "What do you think?"

Simon stopped in his tracks. He was stunned. For the first time in a long while, just as he had on the Toronto Islands at the picnic, Simon felt as if his life were turning around on a large scale.

His answer was instantaneous.

25

Peace, at last. Paul lay on the ground in the backyard under the maple tree, looking up into the branches, mesmerized by the collective flow of the leaves in the moonlight. It was a beautiful night.

"What are you thinking, man?" Larry had followed him out, yet again. "You seem a thousand miles away."

"I'm thinking I don't really want to talk," Paul said, instantly regretting his bluntness. "Sorry, I'm just not up for a chat, I guess."

"I'm hearing your resistance, brother," Larry said as he extinguished a joint in the Coke bottle that rested precariously on the arm of the lawn chair. "For all life's big questions, you can always ask: What would the universe do?"

"Jesus, that's a cop out if I've ever heard one."

Larry went quiet for a few moments, and Paul felt badly for mocking his well-intentioned advice. Larry was, after all, trying to help, he realized.

"I meant the universe won't help me," Paul restated,

lighting a cigarette. "I don't believe in looking outward. I'd rather go inward."

"What if they're the same thing?"

"What does that mean?" Paul was confused by Larry's riddle-like query.

"What do you need help with my friend?" Larry started again.

"I'm disappointed, I suppose," Paul said, giving in.

"I can dig it."

"The final group therapy session's coming up on August 23 and I'm not sure I've been helpful at all."

"How many people in the group?"

"Four participants. One's quite lost, inaccessible, or more like living in another world that doesn't match reality. Another just started talking the other day, after a long silence. Weeks, in fact. And he only talked because he pretty much had to explain … He's grappling with a horrible work situation. As is the third person, really. Jesus, why are people so goddamned vicious?"

"Who's the fourth participant?"

"Did I say four? That's funny: Me, I guess!" he said, laughing. "It's nonhierarchical. I'm on equal footing with the others."

"Are you learning something in the process?"

"Yes, my incompetence. I can only hope that talking about their issues has helped them, that the effort itself has been positive."

"I'm sure it has been."

"I can't help thinking, if my own life weren't such a fucking mess, I might have been better at this group therapy thing."

"You and your wife are working out childcare plans, right?"

"Yes. Focusing on the kids."

"And your marriage? It's really over?"

"I can't imagine going back to what it was. This trial separation is permanent now, I suppose."

"What about the woman? The one you brought home, from your group."

"Oh yeah." Paul sighed. "She's great. But it was a one-off. We were both really drunk. We've talked about it … There are no expectations."

"I'm sensing you'd like expectations."

Paul let that sit for a while, then finally answered, "Claire's a free spirit. I think it would change, compromise her whole approach to life to be locked into a relationship. She's not looking for that. She's not like other women."

"You, my friend, have fallen hard," Larry said.

Paul was struck by Larry's demeanour. Perhaps he had underestimated him. He decided not to close down the conversation. Larry had won him over, to an extent.

"I've got to move on. Find a way. My inclination isn't to try to get my old life back, but to let it go," Paul said, then admitted, "I'm rather discombobulated. To be honest, living here has been … disruptive."

"Change is hard."

"I'm not sure this is working," Paul said, waving his arm around to indicate the entire environment.

"I hear you," Larry said. "And I counter it: We could have more potlucks."

"We've never had a potluck here."

"Okay, fondue?"

"Cheese won't help, Larry," Paul said, half laughing.

"Okay, more house meetings or social occasions to just shoot the shit."

"That's very kind of you." It wasn't a necessary or, in fact, an appropriate fix, but Paul figured it couldn't hurt. Was living here salvageable? he began to wonder.

"In your heart of hearts, man, what's something you would really want to accomplish? If there were no disruptions?" Larry asked, changing the subject away from women and family life. He seemed very earnest.

Paul knew the answer right away. "I'd go back to school. Get my PhD in psychology." The vehemence of his idea surprised him. He realized the notion had been floating around in his mind for a while, but he had not even admitted it to himself prior to Larry's prodding.

"Cool," said Larry as he lit up another joint and passed it to Paul. "I enjoyed my post-grad work."

Larry? Grad work? Paul wondered as he took a drag. How was that possible? The guy's too young and, let's face it, perpetually stoned.

Containing his surprise, he asked, "What's your field?"

"Astrophysics."

"No way." Paul was stunned.

"This is true, my brother." Larry settled back in the chair, seemingly content as he gazed into the night sky.

"Masters?"

"PhD."

"Holy shit. From where?"

"Cambridge."

"No. Fucking. Way. You have a PhD in astrophysics from the University of Cambridge … in the U.K.? How old are you?"

"Twenty-nine. I know: I look younger. And I was younger than my peers. I started Cambridge in physics, the Cavendish Laboratory, when I was fourteen. It was awkward with the ladies. No one wanted to jump into the sack with a pimply kid whose voice cracked."

"Why aren't you working?"

"I am. Got tenure at U of T five years ago. I'm on sabbatical now … Took the summer off. Let myself go a little, you could say." He pointed to the joint. "I'll start writing in September."

"Writing what?"

"I'm looking for evidence of black holes."

"What the heck's a black hole?"

"The gravitational collapse of a massive star. It's a theory. We can't prove it. There are a few researchers around the world who're on top of it."

"Why would a star collapse?" This sounded like science fiction to Paul.

"It's inevitable at the end of the star's life, when their energy runs out."

"I can relate," Paul said, joking. "So that's how you ended up here, in John's house? Looking for a place to write?"

"Yup. It's a decent crash pad. John's an okay cat as long as the mother's not around. And Rachel's rarely here anymore."

"I must say, I'm surprised," said Paul, feeling embarrassed for having grossly underestimated his flatmate.

"I could write you a letter of recommendation, in your

application, if you'd like," Larry offered. "Do you a solid."

"Well, that's nice of you." The idea would have struck Paul as preposterous twenty minutes ago. "I might take you up on that offer."

The two sat quietly, without talking, for some time.

What if, Paul supposed, he'd got it wrong all along? What if his beloved theories had, in a way, blinded him from learning from others, from actually listening to and extracting meaning from those around him? Not that books were all bad, as Cynthia loved to suggest, but perhaps they weren't everything. The art of reciprocity, having a certain generosity of spirit, had evaporated somewhere along the line for Paul. How had he become such a linear thinker, such a square? When did this error in thinking begin, and how could he turn it around?

Here was a case in point: Larry, whom Paul had pretty much written off as an unemployable stoner, was actually super bright. And he was trying to be a friend. The man had a good heart, Paul could tell. His intentions were thoroughly altruistic.

Maybe the universe really did have something to do with the orchestration of things, as Larry had suggested. Maybe Paul had been placed in this crazy house and in the group therapy setting at this particular point in his life for a different purpose altogether.

26

August 23. The final group therapy meeting. For Paul, this date seemed to have arrived too swiftly. He was still grappling with the idea that he hadn't accomplished anything. He felt he needed to work more with this trio but knew at the same time the experiment was coming to a natural ending.

It was another sweltering evening in which the sun's descent in no way brought relief from the heat of the day. Paul anticipated the coolness of the basement, feeling almost nostalgic about the musty smell that was infused into the fibre of the building.

He joined Beata and Claire, waiting for Simon. He stood by the apartment-sized piano, a new addition to the space. Claire was sitting cross-legged on the floor, picking at her freshly bandaged hand. Beata was seated on one of the tiny chairs placed in the familiar circle in anticipation of the meeting.

Simon skipped down the stairs so merrily that all three stopped and stared.

Paul said, "You're looking positively spry."

"I am, in fact. This is true," Simon said, uncharacteristically joining Claire on the floor.

He looked much more relaxed, compared to the last time, when he had shown up badly beaten. It was a remarkable transformation, Paul realized.

"Why don't you start, Simon."

"Jann and I are moving in together. He's coming to my place."

"Congratulations!" Claire reached over and gave him a quick hug. "I'm really happy for you."

"I'm happy too! We have a lot to do to finish the renovation of the main floor. It's pretty much a construction zone now. We're hoping he can move in the first week of September."

"Great news Simon," Beata said, chiming in, clearly enlivened by Simon's exuberance.

"Wonderful," Paul said. "And I see your injuries are healing nicely. How're things at work? Any more troubles from that guy in the mailroom? – Brian, wasn't it?"

"Nothing. He has steered clear of me. Maybe he thinks I'd report him. I'm not sure."

"I hope there can be some kind of agreement between you," Paul suggested. "Like a peace bond, but not so official."

"I might be able to offer a solution," Beata said. "I don't want to interrupt your time –"

"No, please, go ahead."

"Well," she began with some hesitation, "I've decided to move to the UK. Jafari's old stomping grounds. He went to the London School of Economics, you know. I am leaving this Saturday morning, bright and early. I too want to be settled by the beginning of September."

"That seems sudden," Claire said, looking concerned for her friend. "Have you ever lived in London before? Don't you need a work permit or something?"

"What about the kids?" Paul interrupted. They would definitely have a thing or two to say about this, based on what Beata had shared in previous meetings.

"Now, Paul, I have thought this through," said Beata. She clearly did not want to hear these protestations. She turned back to Simon, and said, "Here's how I might be able to help you: My position at the Crafters' Guild will be open. It's largely administrative, but quite interesting. I can brief you more, if you're keen. I'd be happy to put your name forward as a candidate."

Simon was visibly touched. "Thank you. This is unexpected, but yes. I don't know much about this line of work."

"I'll coach you. They're a little fanatical about crafts taking over the world. I think they'd be interested in your renovations."

"I'm planning to build a dining room table out of the old floorboards," Simon said. "Does that count?"

"That's perfect," she said.

"Tell us how you came to the decision to go to London, Beata," Paul asked as gently as possible. "Have you told the kids?"

"Not yet. But I received another letter from Etienne. This was the third. It was kinder than the last. I know he misses me. And Aisha seems to have weakened her resolve."

"Coming to terms with their father's death would have been very hard," Paul said. "You believed Aisha's anger towards you, which fuelled their leaving, was related to this, didn't you?"

"Yes, although I'm not sure exactly how."

"Anger's a secondary emotion. There's always something behind it."

Beata extracted a worn-looking piece of paper from her pocket. "I can read you the letter."

"Only what you feel comfortable sharing," Paul said, not wanting to pressure her.

"I'm among friends," she assured him and prepared to read the note aloud.

Paul noticed that she held the letter close to her chest as if shielding it from the gaze of others, as if it were a fragile script that would self-destruct under certain circumstances.

Dear Ma,

How are you? Chicago's okay, although we're having a hard time finding permanent lodgings. We were squatting in the first location. It wasn't a long-time situation. I think it's hard for Aisha to admit that her plans are anything less than perfect. You know her. But I think she's softening.

So we found a new place. Aisha has a lead on a better paying job at the library and I'm still working at the record store, so we could afford a three-bedroom place. It's large and there could be room for you too – Aisha's words, when we first saw the place. Maybe she's been hoping you would move back all the while? I would bet.

Would you ever consider this? We really miss you. I think Aisha was hard on you after dad died, too hard. She needs you. It's not just my idea. Maybe we could go into therapy? Like grief counselling. What do you think?

She doesn't know that I write to you every once in a while, although she probably suspects. You know how she always seems to figure everything out.

Love, Etienne

Now, in light of this letter, Paul was even more disturbed by Beata's decision to move to London. Here, her children were encouraging her to reconnect with them in a city where they had once lived together, and yet she was opting out, choosing instead to move across the ocean. What could possibly be pulling her to London, in direct opposition to her own children? It seemed completely irrational and contrary to her maternal nature. Paul could not shake the foreboding feeling that she was about to make a mistake that could have dire consequences.

"So," Beata said, putting the letter aside and surveying the room. "Sounds promising, in that they really want to reconnect with me." She folded the paper as it was originally pressed and set it down beside her on the next chair.

"Would you think of taking them up on their suggestion to return to Chicago, instead of going to London?" Simon asked. He seemed to share Paul's concerns.

"No. London's where I must go. It's the right thing to do. The kids can visit," she said.

The way she stated it, Paul knew that there was to be no

debate. He found it difficult to drop the subject but had to respect her decision.

"I'll miss you," Claire said so quietly that Paul barely heard. He realized that she had bonded with Beata over the past few months, and it seemed clear that the two had spent some time together outside of the group setting.

"Good luck," said Simon, still a little confused by her decision. "And thanks for the job tip. I'll pursue it."

"Well, I hope this move works out for you, Beata," Paul said. His hands were tied. He could not press her on anything, even though it was killing him.

"Claire, what's happening with you this week?" He changed his tack, hoping for some good news.

"I went to HR. To see my file and deal with the negative review my boss had submitted. Turns out, there was no file! She was making it up. Can you imagine?"

"That's seriously fucked up." Simon was shocked.

"I had to explain why I had called the meeting, which got sort of messy, but I forced myself to tell HR. My boss was fired the same day. The whole thing is surreal."

"Oh my God," Beata said, stunned.

"I'm really proud of you, Claire," Paul said. "You did it." His gaze was direct. In fact, he felt as if he might cry. Finally, something good had come of these therapy sessions! Claire may be the only one to truly survive, he thought, although Simon's future was also looking up. He still needed to get out of his workplace.

"Everyone's happy," Beata said, summing up.

This blanket statement made Paul worry even more about her. But he sensed that all of them, Simon, Claire, and Beata, felt as if their therapy session was up; the experiment was complete. It was time for everyone to go home and continue their lives. They had not really come today to dig any deeper into anything or to initiate another line of inquiry; they had come to wrap things up.

Realizing this, Paul thanked each of them for their contribution, their bravery in sharing their innermost struggles.

It was a hasty goodbye. Beata raced out of the meeting, eager to start packing. Simon also appeared to be in a great hurry, which left Paul and Claire alone in the church basement.

"I'm happy for you Claire, I really am," Paul said as the two walked up the stairs, slowly, lingering at the scene.

They exited onto Annette Street, relieved to discover that the heat had subsided.

Claire looked melancholic. "This really is the end, I suppose," she said as the two reached the curb. "How are you doing, Paul?" she asked, seeming to want to extend the conversation as they began walking eastward. "It's been a tough summer for you, too, I realize."

"A strange one, that's certain. I'm back into my books, re-reading *The Primal Scream*. I think it'll give me some insights … I've had a bit of a change in thinking related to a conversation I had with one of my flatmates, Larry," he said.

"Yes?"

"It turns out he's an astrophysicist. We were talking one night, and he got me thinking about a newish idea: getting my PhD in psych."

"That's brilliant, Paul," she said, squeezing his arm.

He realized that the one thing he most appreciated about Claire, above everything, was her capacity to partake in the happiness of others. This was genuine.

He looked at her intently. The two had stopped walking. They stood facing each other under the glow of the streetlight. It was dusk, now, and the pewter-coloured sky was gradually deepening in hue.

He couldn't help wondering what his relationship with Claire would have become if things had unfolded differently. Would they have been friends or lovers if they had met in another context?

"Will you stay at the house with your professor friend?" she asked. "This fall, I mean?"

"I don't know," he said.

If he were accepted as a PhD student, U of T would offer Paul something he could sink his teeth into for the fall and winter. He really did find solace in books. But he wasn't sure how he would pay for this education. He would need to get creative.

He suddenly wanted to be with his kids, as if the three-month experiment had been a crushing strain and he desperately needed to return to something elemental, and comparatively simple, like the love of his children. He missed Evan and Jason. Yesterday, after breakfast, there had been a hint of fall in the air, and it reminded him of the first day of "big boy school," Grade 1, which would be starting very soon for Evan.

Paul and Claire hugged goodbye. He embraced her more tightly than she did him, and he didn't let go for quite a while. Was this really the last time they would see each other? he wondered half panicking. But what could he do? There was nothing more to say.

When she walked away, she didn't look back. He wished she had. He observed her as she headed down the street, her hair illuminated under the streetlights, that ever-present pencil still poking out the top; the back of her shirt billowing slightly; her gait steady, determined, intrepid.

27

"We're looking for admin help in the Resource Department, the library," said the president of the Crafters' Guild to Simon. The two were seated, joined by others, for the interview.

The afternoon light filtered into the second storey of the old house through a small jungle of plants hanging from the bay windows. The sunlight was, in part, reflected off the windows of the Art Gallery of Ontario across the road.

"It sounds like fascinating work," Simon said, glancing around the small library, curious about the lightbox and the wall of cabinets.

In truth, the space looked as if it could use some serious reorganizing. Although the folders were housed in alphabetical order and easily identifiable with neatly typed labels, several large binders had been stuffed into each craftsperson's folder to the point of overflowing.

Above the cabinets, a display rack contained all the craft magazines published in Canada. It occurred to Simon that if there were a Crafters' Guild in Ontario, producing such written materials, then there must be counterparts across the country, also making magazines, newsletters, and journals. He noticed that many publications were devoted to a particular craft – metalwork, weaving, stoneware, and glass. He was surprised at the number of these publications. How did they subsist?

"Canada Council grants," the curator answered without prompting. "Everyone asks about the business model.

"Why don't you tell us about your current job and the skills that you could bring to this position?" the curator suggested. His assistant nodded as if to agree with the line of questioning.

Simon wondered why there needed to be so many people in the interview. It appeared as though the entire staff had shown up. Beata warned him that this could happen, as it had in her own interview, but she took this as a sign of their interest and compassion, and urged Simon to make the same assumption.

Beata had called Simon, the night before the interview, to offer some tips, warning him of the group's dogged adherence to the form-versus-function debate. These eclectic people meant well, she had emphasized, not wanting to turn him off the place.

During the course of the prep with Beata, Simon had gone so far as to select a craft to discuss with the group, as a demonstration of his affinity for or alignment with their interests. He even sought to weave into the conversation a few quotations from William Morris, British textile designer, poet, artist, and socialist associated with the British Arts and Crafts movement.

"I work as a senior administrator at the New City Hall in the Marriage License office."

"That must be fun," said the assistant curator. "Everyone likes a wedding."

"Well, it's a pleasure to connect with people," he said, calling to mind the friendlier clients, certainly not his coworkers.

"We have a similar filing system to yours, although there are no photos and there's no need for a lightbox. In fact, the filing system at City Hall is complex, having recorded marriages since before the turn of the century. Those that took place prior to 1900 were moved to the Ontario Archives a few years back."

The craft team looked tired. Simon wondered if he was boring them. Then he remembered Beata's advice. "I'm a crafter," he said. "Perhaps that's relevant?"

The curator perked up. "What is it that you do, Simon?" he asked.

"Well, to quote William Morris, I think everyone should have beautiful things around them, in their homes … functional things. I don't mean beautiful for the sake of being beautiful. Objects need to have purpose."

"'Have nothing in your house that you do not know to be useful,'" the curator quoted precisely. "You're a fan of Morris?"

"Why, yes. I'm an amateur woodworker, you could say. I've been restoring my home. It's a cottage that's perhaps the same vintage as this lovely house. I plan to build a table from the old floorboards."

The job was pretty much in the bag from this point onward. Simon could tell that their collective mind was made up. He left the interview thirty minutes later, feeling elated. He could sense a light at the end of the tunnel. His dreary existence at City Hall might be ending, with luck. It seemed a miracle. He had believed that he would live out his days within the confines of that veritable sarcophagus, avoiding his coworkers, and becoming increasingly cautious about his whereabouts so as not to find himself targeted. Jann was right: This wasn't living.

28

Beata was standing in the living room, surveying what was still to be packed for the move, when the telephone rang. Her daughter's voice brought her to her knees.

"Hi Ma," she said. It sounded as if she had been crying.

"How are you and Etienne?" Beata asked, her voice cracking. She wondered if Aisha knew that Etienne had written several times over the summer.

"We're fine." A pause, some hesitation.

"Thank you for calling. I've missed you."

"Me too. I know I can be stubborn."

"No, you?" Beata said, teasing. "How's Etienne?"

"Good. He's at work right now. We have a new apartment. It has three bedrooms."

"Sounds nice."

"We both found work," Aisha explained.

Beata pretended this was news to her. "You've landed on your feet. It's a great relief to hear."

"Ma," Aisha said, taking her time, "we got the third

bedroom, hoping you'd come back to Chicago."

Beata nodded silently, looking up to the ceiling, her throat tightening with emotion, her eyes welling up. It was true what Etienne had written about the third bedroom. They really did want her to move to Chicago to be with them.

"I know things have been hard for you. Losing Dad ..." Aisha continued.

"It hasn't been easy for you two either," Beata whispered.

"Things here have simmered down. Everyone knows the war's ending. It will happen. Soldiers are coming home."

"Really? Has the mood in Chicago changed that much?"

"Not overnight, but people seem to want to move on."

Beata knew, from the papers, that America was pulling out of Vietnam although the process was slow. There were increasing rumours of secret peace talks with the Nixon administration.

"Well, I've been thinking of the same thing. Your idea's serendipitous," Beata said.

"How so?" Aisha sounded excited.

"I've decided to move as well, to one of your dad's favourite places."

"Where?"

"London."

"England? Why?" Her daughter sounded genuinely confused.

"There's a connection. Your dad lived there, a long time ago."

"Oh my God, you're still talking to him, aren't you?" The tone of Aisha's voice changed.

"I'd love it if you could visit. Both of you kids."

"Is this planned and everything? Your mind's made up? This is insane, Ma." She seemed incredulous.

"I'm flying out this Saturday morning." Beata tried to sound confident and upbeat.

"You realize what you're doing, don't you?" Her daughter was on the edge of tears.

"I'm reconnecting." The image of the priest came to mind as Beata spoke the words. He would understand, she told herself.

"No, you're picking Dad over us … And he's dead! How can we compete with a dead person?"

"That's not true."

"If he were really here, he'd think you were crazy."

"Don't say that." Beata began to well up. "Please …"

"No, Ma. You think the person you talk to is Dad, but it's really your imagination. You're picturing what he'd be saying, or thinking, but it's not real! You've made up a phantom! You've wished him, or it, into being!"

"You don't understand," Beata said, pleading. The conversation was spiralling out of control.

"I do! You're sick and you need help. Jesus, I knew this was a bad idea but Etienne said I should try … If you really go, Ma … That'll be it, you know. We're checking out. I can't handle it, and it's really hard on Etienne. We'll never be in touch anymore. It's too hard watching you make these horrible decisions, living the way you do."

"Please let's not break contact, Aisha," Beata whispered. This was her worst nightmare, losing her children after having lost her husband. It would be too much to bear.

"You've already made your decision." Aisha hung up.

Beata collapsed onto the sofa in tears. How could her daughter have said such cruel words? Jafari was not a phantom! He was as real as Beata herself. She knew it in her bones. This was elemental. He had come back to her.

All of a sudden, she remembered him saying that the kids would eventually come around. She trusted his words as she looked over at him. He was sitting on the chair directly facing the sofa, silently. He had a sad look in his eyes.

She went to sleep that night with a heavy heart, but woke up very early, enlivened with the prospect of the big move. She had to put the conversation with Aisha behind her. She needed to let it go, but promised herself to pick things up once she resettled in England. She would win her children back.

The moment she fully awoke, she dressed, made a quick coffee, and then headed to the storage locker in the basement of the apartment building to pull out two large suitcases. She began packing her clothes, carefully selecting for all seasons. She put her toiletries into two plastic shopping bags, just in case the shampoo or moisturizer leaked on the flight.

She had decided to give the furniture and the rest of her belongings to charity. A truck would come tomorrow to collect all of this from her apartment.

The next twenty-four hours flew by. All the while, her conversations with Jafari intensified. With each passing hour, she became even more convinced that she was doing the right thing by moving to London.

The charity truck appeared on her doorstep at 8 am the next day, a cool morning with a hint of fall in the air. The workers seemed young but capable; they appeared to be strong. They packed up her furnishings with remarkable speed – three beds; an oak dining table and matching chairs; five bookshelves; two, tired-looking sofas; several rugs; two paintings; a coat rack; and about twenty boxes of odds and sods ranging from kitchen utensils to small lamps. They also took a few containers of clothes along with some of Jafari's belongings, seven pairs of shoes in paper grocery bags, three sets of very dusty curtains, and a few houseplants that Beata had nurtured for more than ten years.

Remarkably, they cleaned out the apartment in under an hour.

After she saw the charity truck off, from the street, watching it turn onto Annette and merge with traffic, she headed up for one last look at the apartment. Very soon, she would call a taxi to go to the airport.

This was the hard part, she knew. There was no way to pretend that every nook and corner of this apartment, where she had lived with Jafari and they had raised their children, did not hold special meaning for her.

She realized this was the last time she would witness the lemony morning sun shining through the bay window where she and Jafari had read the weekend papers together, over coffee, comfortable in their silence, for so many years. She tried to absorb every inch of it, capture the feeling of it one last time as if she could, by will alone, re-live a portion of its rich history. But it was too late, she realized. The space, having been stripped of the furniture, rugs, and curtains, was now filled with unfamiliar echoes. Where it had once retained the fuzzy remnant of lives lived, the ectoplasm of many holidays, birthdays, and anniversaries, this retention was crumbling. The velvety ghosts of the apartment were already fading, trickling beyond her reach. The only truth of place would be safely stored in her memory; this exquisite space would exist, from now on, in Beata's mind.

It was time to leave. The taxi had arrived. She heard two honks of the horn and knew this was her ride. She looked at her watch: 9:35 am. She left the apartment, tucked her boxes and suitcases on the landing for temporary safekeeping, locked the door, threw the keys into the mail slot, then headed to the taxi with her suitcases. She would have to come back for the boxes.

The cab driver helped Beata with her belongings, but not in a manner that was to her liking. She could tell he wanted to get to the airport as quickly as possible, and he could not start the taximeter until the vehicle was moving. She watched him manhandle her personal effects, wedging the suitcases into the trunk, forcing the boxes he picked up from outside of her apartment into the back of the vehicle. He was not treating these objects with the respect they deserved. These things that had once belonged to Jafari. Her eyes welled up as she watched the man's near-violent loading of the car. She glanced back at the apartment, then the tree-lined street where she had made her home, with her family, for so long. A wave of panic overcame her. Was she making a mistake? For a second, she almost aborted the mission, placing her hand on one of the suitcases just before the cab driver snatched it away. He didn't seem to notice her hesitation.

What choice was there, really? She had already sold and got rid of everything in the apartment, packed up her things for the UK, and even bought the plane ticket to London. Still, the unresolved rift with her children was like a heavy stone on her chest. The conversation with Aisha still lurked in the back of her mind. She hated to be upsetting her kids; she despised what the mourning process and, admittedly, her own poor coping methods, had done to her family. What if she'd been wrong all along?

*   *   *

Fifteen minutes later, Beata's cab arrived at the Toronto International Airport. She checked her bags at the Britannia Airways desk; waited at the gate for two hours; watched the comings and goings of the airport, the people, the families with kids in tow, the airline personnel transporting passengers in wheelchairs ... The commotion was a welcome distraction for her. She knew she had to maintain her focus on getting to London and not succumb to nagging self-doubt.

She boarded the plane and found her window seat well behind the wing, so, as she had predicted, her view of the land and sea wouldn't be obstructed. But as the other passengers clambered into the large airplane, it seemed the walls were coming in on her, as if the plane were shrinking. She stared out the window to calm herself, trying to focus on the activities of the air-traffic personnel on the ground, the folks who directed the planes with their cumbersome flashlights, and the airline staff, the luggage handlers, who also walked around the stationary airplanes. It worked to some extent, but she wondered, would it always be like this? Would she be pressing her anxiety down at every second? This would be impossible to maintain.

It took a half hour for all passengers to find their seats and get settled. During this time, the stewardesses helped three elderly people to find their seats and similarly assisted one young and frazzled-looking mother with an infant that wouldn't stop crying. Mercifully, the mother's seat was about ten rows ahead of Beata.

"Ladies and gentlemen. This is your captain speaking," a voice announced over the crackling PA system. "Welcome to Britannia Airways, Flight 558. We'll be taking off momentarily for Heathrow Airport. This is a direct flight. Please remain seated for take-off."

Beata looked out of the window, her hands folded on her lap. The person seated beside her, a middle-aged man with a tweed jacket and sandy-white hair, who had a very British look about him, was already scanning some business papers. He looked relaxed. He had probably made this trip a thousand times. He appeared almost bored with the idea of flying across the Atlantic Ocean.

The plane sat on the tarmac for forty-five minutes. The baby, who had calmed down at one point, started up again. People began to get fidgety, shifting in their seats and checking their watches impatiently. The man beside Beata asked the stewardess, in an upper-crust English accent that was similar to the Queen's, if there was a problem. She said there was a delay, an issue with a passenger, but she didn't know any details.

"Ladies and gentlemen. This is your captain." Again, the crackling PA system.

"Finally," the man beside Beata muttered under his breath.

"Apologies for the delay but we are looking for a passenger, and we've misplaced the flight manifest … Is there a Mrs. Bee … Atta … Car … Ann …?"

"– Karanja," Beata said, raising her hand. "It's Kenyan," she added defiantly.

All heads turned her way. Some people looked angry and scowled at her as if she posed a threat to their personal safety. But most were just curious.

"Would this person please identify themselves to one of the stewardesses," the captain continued, unaware that Beata had already made her presence known.

The stewardess nearest Beata approached her and said, "You'll have to return to the gate."

"Is there something wrong?" Beata asked, alarmed to be singled out like this.

Her heart was beating like a rabbit's. Her hands shook as she grabbed her purse, got up from her seat, and began walking down the aisle to the front of the plane, dutifully following the stewardess as if heading to the principal's office. She didn't lock eyes on any of the other passengers. Instead, she simply looked down at the carpet and followed.

The stewardess led her off the plane and to the gate where she had originally waited to board the plane.

There, at the now-empty gate, surrounded by Beata's luggage, stood a tearful Aisha.

"Let us help you, Ma," she said, pulling her mother forward to give her a hug. "You've already travelled a great distance without him."

29

The first whiff of fall hung in the air – a welcome indication as to the end of a blistering summer. Simon had left the windows open all night on the main floor of his cottage. A rich, autumnal smell had oozed in and taken over the modest space.

The sun, twinkling through the overgrown trees in the neighbourhood, had not yet ascended into the sky. In this dim and almost magical light, Simon stood in the centre of his living room, scratching his head, as if to wake up. He analyzed the half-completed floorboards.

Jann was fumbling around in the kitchen at the back of the house, searching for coffee.

"Please don't tell me you only have instant," he said, strolling into the living room with a half-empty jar of Chock full o'Nuts. "This is chock full o'chemicals. You know that, right?"

"I'll pick up some real coffee," Simon said, laughing. "As soon as the Dominion opens."

"The donut shop's fine for me. See how easy I am to please?"

Simon had decided to take the day off work as a reward for yesterday's interview at the Crafters' Guild. He was optimistic and felt good about how things had gone. Moreover, he wanted to finish the renovation so Jann could officially move in. He was in full-blown nest-building mode today, and he had a long list of things he wanted to accomplish, starting with a trek to the local hardware store to select a floor stain. If they worked all day, perhaps they could finish the living room floor and start to stain it. Then, at long last, the furnishings, currently mashed into the very small kitchen, could be moved back to their rightful places. It would be a rapid transformation that would turn the main floor from a construction zone to a real home again – and one that would now include Jann.

Simon quickly showered, then threw on an old t-shirt, an orange freebee from work that featured the New City Hall, and a haggard-looking pair of Adidas shorts – admittedly not his best look, but he wanted clothes that he could effectively ruin with the wood stain then discard. The municipal image seemed particularly appropriate. He could already imagine the slam-dunk into the trashcan.

He walked to the donut shop, which had just opened, and brought back two coffees and two Boston creams. He wasn't sure if Jann truly liked donuts – another detail of his boyfriend's life that he needed to learn, he thought, smiling.

They ate breakfast in the living room, sitting on the unfinished floor, as the sun rose. Neither had switched on the overhead lights, but the room gradually brightened.

Simon could tell by the look on Jann's face, his eyes cast down, that he was calculating how to best approach the floor. He wondered how long it would take, feeling eager to start.

The telephone rang. Simon had almost forgotten that it wasn't the weekend, and the working world was up and about. He raced into the kitchen to catch the phone.

"Good morning, Simon." He recognized the man's voice right away. It was the president of the Crafters' Guild.

"It's nice to hear from you," Simon said, holding his breath.

Jann walked into the kitchen, curious. He was looking intently at Simon.

"We'd like to offer you the job, starting the second week in September," the president said. "With the wages we discussed. I could send the paperwork over for you to sign today, if that's agreeable to you."

There was no question as to Simon's acceptance. Yes, it would be fine to have the papers sent to him, he assured the president.

"Congratulations!" Jann bellowed as soon as Simon hung up.

"You guessed, yes," he said beaming. "I got the job. I'm actually getting out of that hell hole."

"Goodbye, City Hall!" Jann said as he hugged his partner. "That's it: We're going to the grocery store. I'm making a celebratory dinner tonight."

The idea of leaving his job was something that Simon hadn't allowed himself the luxury to fully consider. It was hard to imagine that this kind of escape was truly possible. A wave of relief swept over him.

When Jann went upstairs to get dressed, Simon returned to the living room, taking stock of what this new job would actually mean. He wouldn't have to put up with Brian and his gang of thugs from the mailroom anymore, wouldn't have to sneak in and out of the building, trekking here and there only when he was certain that they weren't around. He realized, for the first time, how much he had altered his life to eliminate the possibility of another confrontation.

The beating had taken a toll on him and affected him, as well as his sense of freedom and security, much more than he had let himself believe. That day, in group therapy, he could see by the reaction on the faces of Beata, Paul, and especially Claire, that this had been an unacceptable act of aggression, but he had brushed it off, convincing others as much as himself that these things happen, that this was the price of being gay. The group's support meant a lot to him, but he knew that it was the influence of Jann, the presence of him, that gave him new hope for the idea of living freely, openly, in society. And the new job was a big part of this, a step in the right direction.

He closed his eyes, took a deep breath, and allowed himself to feel the full extent of relief. He had survived.

The rest of the day was hugely productive. Simon and Jann first did the grocery shopping at the Dominion down Parliament, then headed to the family-run hardware store, which had paints and stains in the back. After much deliberation, they selected a maple-coloured stain and headed home, each carrying two cans of the product.

As soon as they got back to the house, they set about finishing the floorboards. Jann cut the boards so precisely that they fit together like a puzzle, perfectly tucking in at the baseboards. Simon swept up quickly, then the two started the stain, working their way from the back to the front of the living room.

Realizing that they were trapped by the front door (and they couldn't walk over the living room floor to return to the kitchen, since this would surely ruin the floors), they had to traipse around the cottage to the back of the property and let themselves in through the kitchen. This confined them to the kitchen until the stain dried, but Jann seized the opportunity to start dinner. It was, after all, nearly eight o'clock. Both men were starving, having worked through lunch without stopping.

Jann whipped dinner up swiftly as Simon opened a bottle of red, turned on the radio, selected a classical station, and lit a candle that he'd rediscovered in one of the cupboards. When he switched off the kitchen overheads, the candle cast a lovely glow around the room.

"I'm working here!" Jann screeched in protest.

Simon switched the lights back on unceremoniously. "Only trying to offset the unsightly piles of furniture."

When the overhead lights were turned off, and the candlelight was the sole illumination, the slapdash piles took on a romantic quality. Without this, they looked like heaps of rubbish.

After dinner, as Simon washed the dishes, Jann tested the floors. "Still sticky," he reported. "We'd better go out for a bit."

"Drinks at that new place?" Simon suggested over his shoulder. A restaurant/dance club had just opened around

Church and Maitland. It was an Italian eatery six days a week (closed on Sundays, of course), but on Wednesday night, it opened its doors to the gay community, and morphed into a dance club.

Unable to venture upstairs to change their clothes – another unanticipated consequence of the floor staining – they popped over to Jann's house to grab more appropriate attire. Jann selected a tailored jean jacket. Simon borrowed a white blazer with wide lapels. It was a little large for him, so he rolled up the sleeves.

They left the house around 11 pm, in no particular hurry. Simon was in the mood to celebrate, still high from the job offer at the start of the day. The chill in the air had returned from the morning, and he was glad to have added the extra layer of clothing.

The new hot spot was tastefully decorated with a series of Tiffany lamps dangling in a row above the bar, and brown and orange wallpaper that looked like velvet. It was dimly lit, incredibly smoky, and packed to the gunnels with men of all shapes and sizes, stepping out on the dance floor or talking, in couples, along the edges of the large room. It smelled like sweat and Aramis cologne, the tell-tale scent used by gay men as a secret identifier as to their sexual predilections.

The music was bone-shakingly loud. Simon could feel the bass in his innards from the moment he set foot in the place. "Groove Me" by King Floyd morphed to "Chirpy Chirpy Cheep Cheep" by Mac and Katie Kissoon.

Simon and Jann squeezed through the crowd to the bar; ordered two beers, effectively yelling at the bartender to make themselves heard over the din; then gravitated to the dance floor, which seemed to be the epicentre of everything, to watch the crowd. They tried to talk a bit, but the music was so loud that they were forced to abandon any conversation.

The place was more of a pick-up joint, Simon realized, deciding not to stay much longer. He could tell by the expression on Jann's face – his crinkled nose – that the decision would be mutual. They would drink their beers, then head out. They could just as easily have opted for a nice glass of wine in the backyard. Who needs this circus? Simon thought.

He mimed to Jann that he was heading to the washroom on the second floor. Jann nodded back, pointing to the ground, indicating that he'd stay put until his partner's return.

Simon carved a path through the crowd and navigated up the narrow staircase to the washroom. Once upstairs, and fully aware of the layout of the building, he realized that it must be a turn-of-the-century mansion. The second floor was much quieter. It offered a reprieve from the music, which was so loud that it distorted by the time it reached the upper floor. Simon could no longer make out any of the lyrics. It was all bass and tinny rhythm.

He swung the door open. The room was built around a wall of mirrors above three sinks and a rusty-looking hand towel dispenser to the left of which was a "BROKEN" sign tacked up on the wall. At the far side, four men were standing at the urinals.

One particularly muscular man with short-cropped hair caught Simon's attention. There was something about the shape of the man's posture, the particular way he hunched a little to the left, that made the hair on the back of Simon's neck stand on end. It was an undeniably primal response in Simon that made him feel as if he were going to throw up, as if the walls were caving in and he was sinking into the floor, unable to move. His legs were cemented to the ground as the other three men at the urinal left the washroom, eager to rejoin the party.

Then Brian turned around. His expression changed from a dull glazed look to one of complete dismay the second he saw Simon.

The music downstairs stopped for a split second.

"Listen, I –" Brian began, then paused.

Simon realized that his coworker was formulating what to say. After all, the last time the two were within feet of each other, Brian's fist had been very nearly launched into Simon's face.

Simon's legs failed him.

The two men remained motionless until another person entered the washroom, accidentally pushing the door into Simon's back and nudging him farther into the centre of the room.

"Sorry mate," the young man said as he headed to the urinal, oblivious to the highly charged atmosphere.

This nudge, however, triggered Simon. The music started up again, and before he even realized he was out of the washroom, he found himself sprinting down the stairs, his hands barely making contact with the flimsy railing.

His whole body was convulsing. It was a miracle he didn't trip, but his legs now seemed to have a mind of their own. He pushed his way through the crowd to Jann – easy to spot with his great height. He grabbed his partner's hand and locked eyes with him as if to say, "We're leaving. This instant."

Jann had a look of confusion on his face as he set his beer down on a nearby table and raced toward the front door, following his partner.

The two fled into the near-empty street, crossing to the far side almost immediately.

Simon frantically looked up and down Church Street for a cab. There were barely any cars on the road, let alone taxis. It was a weeknight, after all.

"Take the back alley," he half yelled, breaking into an all-out run. He wanted to evaporate into the streets. Staying on the roads, on the sidewalks, would be too obvious. He knew that there were back alleys in this section of the city, where shop owners parked their cars and delivery trucks cut through in a pinch. These small laneways ran parallel to the main roads. Here, a person could easily travel vast distances, evading detection.

Simon knew that escape would be easier here, since the alleys tended to be lit sporadically. Every second streetlamp in the neighbourhood had burned out long ago, and the City was too backlogged to keep on top of light bulb replacement in such a low-priority area. Given this lack of light, the night would provide enhanced coverage.

"Are you going to tell me what happened?" Jann asked as he followed Simon into the nearest alley.

Once they had gone around the corner and were completely hidden from the street, Simon stopped and turned to him. "I saw Brian in the washroom."

"Brian ... the guy who beat you up?"

"Yes," Simon said, slightly exasperated.

"He's gay?" Jann asked. He seemed surprised.

"Evidently." Simon said as he started running again. "C'mon ..."

After they had covered a good amount of ground, Simon slowed down. He knew that Jann likely thought his pace was excessive but appreciated that his partner didn't mention it and simply followed his lead.

"That explains a lot," Jann said when the two slowed down. "If you think about it. Brian being gay, I mean."

Simon nodded. He was unable to prevent his heart from racing. It felt like he was having a heart attack.

They stopped behind one of the older buildings to take a break.

"You okay?" Jann asked, putting his hand on Simon's shoulder. "My God, you're shivering. I can feel it right through the jacket!" He hugged him.

Simon felt on the verge of complete exhaustion. He closed his eyes for a second, trying to relax, willing himself to calm down. When he opened them, however, there was no mistaking the identity of the shadowy figure under the next streetlamp.

The burly frame of Brian charged at Simon and Jann in an unstoppable vector.

Simon braced for the inevitable, but instinct took over and, in a last-ditch attempt at escape, he turned around and started to run out of the alley in the opposite direction, hoping Jann would follow. It felt as if he were running in mud or sand, as if everything was in slow motion and he was unable to gain traction.

With his back turned, it was so much worse not knowing how the attack would unfold, when the contact would occur, and how bad it would be. Yet strangely, within all of this, Simon took the time to scan the scene, the dark alley, the stars above the treetops, the backyards that flanked the alley on one side, the calmness in the foliage as a more distant streetlamp cast a pale glow on the uppermost leaves.

Jann's response, by contrast, was singular, blunt, and lacking any ambiguity. He looked angry as he stood his ground.

Simon hoped Jann was planning a defensive move.

But Brian flew past Jann and pounced on Simon like a tiger. He grabbed him by the back of the white jacket around his shoulder blades, hurling him forward at an accelerated pace – so much so, that Simon very nearly landed face-first in the gravel.

Simon's arms circled around, like the blades of a helicopter, in an attempt to control the violent projection. He landed on the ground with his palms, then knees, hitting the uneven surface, breaking the fall, and then rolled sideways once or twice, losing momentum quickly.

As he twisted around to face his attacker, he saw Jann swing a masterful right hook that landed squarely on Brian's left jaw, making a blunt thud sound.

Brian was shocked by the blow. But he seemed to bring himself back from the punch swiftly.

Simon, meanwhile, scrambled up, robotically swift. He knew that he couldn't remain down for long. "Can't you just leave us alone, Brian?" he said, exasperated. "This is a fucking stupid game we're playing!"

"I tried to tell you! In the can, at work, that day!" Brian roared.

Jann, confident that negotiation wasn't going to work, threw another punch, but this time Brian was ready for him, and he socked him right in the stomach.

Jann crumpled instantly. He gasped, attempting to force the air into his lungs as quickly as possible. "Don't you fucking touch Simon!" he wheezed as he struggled to stand up again.

With Jann incapacitated, Brian seized the opportunity. He punched Simon right in the stomach. It was the same street-fighter blow that the bully had administered to Jann, seconds earlier, but in this case, the thrust lingered as if Brian's fist were lodged in Simon's midriff.

Simon heard a very small clicking sound right before impact. It was as if the soundtrack didn't match the action as it sometimes happens in the movies. He fell to his knees.

Then Brian turned on his heels, wordlessly, and ran down the alley in the opposite direction.

Simon and Jann both watched him get smaller and smaller until he reached the end of the alley and exited onto Church Street.

Jann whooped for joy. "Goliath retreats!" he yelled, appearing very satisfied as he turned around to look at his partner.

Simon was flat on his back. He watched Jann approach with a profound sense of relief.

"You've got the wind knocked out of you. You'll be okay in a sec." Jann said. "Don't panic. The same thing happened to me just now. Let's get you up to a seated position," he added, grabbing Simon under the arms.

He stopped short. "What's that?" He stared at Simon's midriff with a curious look on his face.

"What?" Simon looked down and touched his stomach. It felt a little wet, but it was so dark in the alley that he couldn't see anything. Maybe he had rolled into a puddle, he thought, glancing around to see if the alley had any potholes or oily residue.

"Jesus! You're bleeding!" Jann shrieked.

Simon looked down again, this time rubbing the liquid between his fingers and realizing that it was, indeed, blood. He held his fingers to his nose. They smelled metallic. Yes, it was blood soaking through the white dinner jacket.

"I'm okay. It's just a little, honestly." He was not at all panicked – the amount was so small, after all. "I feel fine. We can slap a bandage on at home. Just help me up."

"You're staying right there," Jann said, removing his jacket and wrapping it tightly around Simon's waist. He also took off his shirt, folded it and stuffed it between Simon's stomach and the knot of the jacket. He then tightened the knot even more.

"The look on your face!" Simon said, laughing. "I'm fine. It's small. You're totally overreacting."

"I can't believe Brian stabbed you. Where was the knife? Was it a switchblade? I didn't see anything!" Jann said, sounding panicked.

"It must have been really small. I did hear a clicking sound," Simon recalled. "But if neither of us saw it, then it must've been tiny. So, the wound's tiny too."

"I need to find a phone booth," Jann said.

"Why? Just help me up." Simon thought it was sweet that Jann was being so attentive, but it was wholly unnecessary. "You thumped him in the jaw very nicely!" he said, trying to change the subject.

But Jann wasn't up for it, he could tell.

"I said don't move. I'll be back as soon as possible. Do you understand?" he said, standing up and holding his palms outward as he spoke, as if to freeze his partner's position on the ground.

"There's a telephone right there," Simon said, calmly pointing to the back of a nearby building. He started to suspect that Jann was becoming overwhelmed by the situation, which was a little surprising. He always seemed so unflappable, so confident.

Simon was right about the phone: A compact telephone was tucked into a niche right beside the doorway.

Jann ran over to it. "There's a light!" he said, having discovered a small switch.

A cold blue radiance filled the back entryway of the building and spilled out into the alley. Simon could now see Jann as clear as day. A sign above the back door was also visible. The building was a pharmacy. The back telephone probably functioned like an intercom for the off-hours deliveries, he figured.

Jann picked up the receiver. "It works!"

Under the harsh light, Simon could see that his partner's hands were a bright ruby colour, covered with blood. Jann was shaking so violently that his fingers were struggling to dial 9-1-1.

The volume on the phone was extremely high. From

ten feet away, Simon could hear the operator's voice without straining.

"911. What's your emergency?" a woman said flatly. Her voice echoed down the alley as if she were speaking through a megaphone.

"Help! You've got to send help! My partner's been stabbed! In the stomach! Th-there's blood everywhere," Jann wailed.

"I'm okay," Simon said. "Jeez, don't exaggerate. I'm sure they have more serious …"

But Jann didn't seem to hear.

"Sir, you'll need to calm down." The operator's voice was monotone. "What's your location?"

"We're in an alley! That's … well … it's parallel to Church Street. South of College … Y-you, you've got to come quickly. Jesus, there's a lot of blood!" Jann yelled into the receiver.

"How do you know she's been stabbed?"

"He. He's been stabbed! For Christ's sake! It was right in front of my fucking eyes! I can't see the wound but there's blood all over!"

"Sir, you're going to have to calm down. A unit will be sent right away, but we need an address."

"I said just south of College, literally, just south of College on Church."

"College doesn't intersect with Church, sir."

"What?! – No Carleton then, Carleton Street," he corrected himself.

"You forgot that College turns into Carleton east of Yonge," Simon interjected.

Again, Jann didn't seem to hear him.

"I need an exact address, sir."

"Three fifty Church," Simon read from the signage on the back of the pharmacy.

"Three fifty Church," Jann repeated, having heard. "But we're in the alley. To the east. We're not on the road. Please come quickly!"

"They're on their way, sir."

"Okay. Okay then … What should I do?"

"Are you wearing socks?"

"What?! Yes, of course. Why?"

"Take them off, put them in a ball, and place it directly over the wound, then apply pressure to stop the blood flow."

With this, Jann dropped the receiver and sprinted back to Simon's side. "Help's on the way," he reported breathlessly.

"Jann: I heard the entire conversation," Simon said, seriously worried about his partner's state of mind at this point. "Look, the rate of bleeding seems to have slowed down."

"Don't move," Jann said as he scurried behind Simon to support his head. "You look awkward," he said as he eased his partner's head up onto his lap and began stroking his brow.

"Aren't you supposed to do the sock thing?" Simon gently suggested.

"Yes, yes," Jann agreed. He removed his shoes, yanked off his socks, and balled them up. Then, he carefully peeled away the soaked clothing from around Simon's stomach and placed the socks on top of what appeared to be a very small puncture mark in the centre of his partner's stomach. He then rewrapped Simon's midriff and applied pressure.

"Not so hard!" Simon said. "You'll crush my ribs."

"You shouldn't be expending any energy by talking."

"Are you telling me to shut up?" Simon teased. "What a prick."

"Yes, I'll do the talking for now."

"Okay: Distract me. Put your shoes back on and tell me how nice the floorboards are going to look. They'll be dry by now for sure."

"If you be quiet, I will."

"Deal," Simon said, smiling.

"The floorboards … The goddamned floorboards …" Jann's voice trailed off as he took a moment to put his shoes back on, "they'll look great. They'll be the best fucking floorboards ever," he rambled. "When we move the furniture back in from the kitchen … and the plants and everything … it'll look totally finished."

"You'll move in by September first, right?" Simon confirmed. He closed his eyes. He felt very relaxed.

"Yes, and stop talking … Jesus, why are your eyes closed?!"

"I'm just resting. Calm down, Jann. I'll be fine. Keep talking."

"About moving in?" Jann asked, evidently having lost the plot.

"You don't have too much stuff … I think everything will work nicely together," Simon said, his eyes still closed. He was getting sleepy now.

The unmistakable sound of the fire truck, sirens blazing, grew closer and closer. It was coming from the south.

Simon opened his eyes again. He could see the lights from the vehicle streaming into the alley from a laneway that was connected to the street. The truck stopped.

"Don't they know we're in the alley not the street?!" Jann yelled.

Then Simon heard the great truck switching gears and saw more light – this time, as bright as daylight – fall horizontally into the alley. He realized the truck was attempting, perhaps struggling, to drive into the narrow space.

"Down here!" Jann screamed, waving frantically at the truck.

It was doubtful the firefighters could hear anyone's voice over the loud engine, Simon thought. They know where we are. There's no need to yell at them. This could take a while, he reasoned, feeling content to wait. "I think it's stuck," he said. "This might take a bit."

Suddenly, over a loud speaker, a man's voice said: "To the north." But the truck still didn't move any farther into the alley.

Jann peered down at Simon and touched his forehead with a look of concern. "It'll be amazing, the house we'll set up. Living together will be perfect, just like you imagine," he half yelled over the din of the fire truck.

He was overcompensating, Simon thought, opening his eyes. "Oh, now you'll elaborate?" he said, teasing.

"You'll have your new job with those craft people. We'll save money. Go on vacation. To Spain. Every winter. What d'you think about that?"

"Spain," Simon said, latching on to the idea. He closed his eyes again.

Two firemen ran down the alley, which was now brightly illuminated.

"Step aside. Sir, we need you to step away," the taller of the two said to Jann.

Both firemen swiftly descended onto Simon. They used some sort of sharp implement to cut his shirt and blazer away from his body almost instantly. They plucked the blood-soaked socks off the wound, tossing them to one side, so as to get a good look at the injury.

Jann stepped back to let them do their work. "How could that tiny wound cause such loss of blood?" he asked, staring at Simon's stomach. "Jesus, you're whiter than white," he said.

From his position, flat on the ground, Simon did not particularly want to see what the men were doing, although he sensed they were covering the wound with a more sanitary patch than Jann's socks. He glanced over at the discarded clothing. It was dripping to such an extent that the entirety of the white blazer was now a particular shade of dirty red.

"Holy shit," he whispered. Maybe Jann was right to be worried. But at least help was here. He had faith in the emergency personnel.

All of a sudden, an ambulance came barrelling down the alley from the northern end, sirens blazing. It stopped just five feet away from Simon's head. Two paramedics jumped out and raced over.

One of the firemen stepped back and wiped his brow with the back of his bloodied hand. "Let's speed this up, fellas," he said. "This guy's lost a lotta blood." And with that, the paramedics quickly loaded Simon onto a gurney and into the back of the ambulance.

Jann hopped in without asking. He sat in the very back corner of the small space, out of the way. He was carrying the pile of bloody clothes, Simon noticed.

The ambulance drove very quickly and within minutes it had arrived.

"St. Mike's," Jann told Simon as the paramedics extracted his partner from the ambulance and raced the gurney through the halls of the hospital at a dizzying speed.

Then they stopped somewhere after the entrance to the Emergency Department. From his position on the gurney, it was hard for Simon to tell exactly where they were in the hospital.

He overheard some doctors, he presumed, talking to Jann. His eyes were closed, and he realized that they must think he was unconscious, as they spoke freely in his presence. He didn't mind. He was perfectly comfortable eavesdropping.

"Your friend likely has an inferior vena cava injury," a doctor stated.

"What's that?"

"A vein was severed in his stomach. The vena cava is an important one because it carries deoxygenated blood from the lower half of the body to the right atrium of the heart. It's a bad location for an injury."

"That's why there's so much blood?"

"We'll give him a transfusion."

"What's the outcome here? I mean, he'll be okay, right?" Simon heard Jann's voice crack.

"The location of the injury's a factor. If it's below the renal vein, it has a better prognosis."

"Well, was it above or below?!" Jann sounded exasperated.

"We don't know. He needs surgery immediately."

The conversation ended abruptly.

Jann returned to Simon's side.

Simon opened his eyes and smiled weakly. "I'll be fine. All this fuss."

"You're awake?"

"Yes. I heard about the operation."

"We'll get you right as rain in no time," Jann said, but Simon could sense that he wasn't entirely convinced.

"Call Claire, okay? The number's in my wallet." He knew that Claire could help Jann to calm down, even though the two had never met. She had a sisterly, nurturing quality that Simon knew would smooth the waters for Jann during the operation. Then after, he could have a proper catch-up with her. He wanted to share the good news about the job as well. Much had changed since he had seen her last.

"Okay," Jann agreed. He gingerly took Simon's blood-soaked wallet from his back pocket, extracted a piece of paper with Claire's number on it, and headed slowly down the hallway to make the phone call. He appeared, to Simon, reluctant to step away from the gurney, if only for a moment or two.

"Don't look so glum," Simon said. "I'll be fine. You'll see."

30

Claire's phone rang, waking her up from a deep sleep.

"Hello?" she said, looking at her alarm clock. It was after 1:00 am. Who would call at such an ungodly hour?

"Claire? It's Jann." He was breathing heavily on the line. There was a hard edge of panic in his voice. "Simon's Jann."

"What's wrong?" She sat up in bed. "Is Simon okay?"

"It was so quick ... such a small ..." he said, clearly struggling to explain.

"What happened?"

"Simon."

"Yes. Is he hurt?"

"Stabbed. He was stabbed. By Brian. In an alley. We were out ..."

Claire could sense that he seemed only capable of vocalizing in small bubbles, outbursts of two to three words.

"In a fucking alley. For Christ's sake ..."

"Where are you?"

"St. Mike's Emergency."

"Don't move. I'm coming. I'll be there as quickly as I can. Okay?"

"Claire, he was throwing up blood. Bright red! He just started, all of a sudden, in the hallway, right here, and now they're operating —"

"Do you hear me, Jann? I'll be there very soon. Do you understand?"

"Yes." Then the line went dead.

Within twenty minutes, Claire was bolting past the front desk of the Emergency Department, running down a series of puke-coloured corridors in the middle of the night when the hospital was as quiet as the grave. The tinkling sound of a few, distant telephones ringing, unanswered, and the flickering overheads, the quivering light, made for a strange and deeply unsettling journey. It was surreal — as if she were floating, barely making progress as her pyjama bottoms tickled her ankles, her sweater fell off her shoulders, and her slippers made light smacking sounds against the linoleum floor.

And there Jann was, crumpled in a chair halfway down the last empty hallway. She recognized him from Simon's description. Despite his height, he appeared small and almost childlike, staring down at the floor, as if needing someone to scoop him up.

When he saw Claire, he seemed to recognize her right away, which was impossible. Nevertheless, he rose from the chair and opened his arms wide like the wingspan of a huge owl.

She could see that his eyes, which locked on hers from a considerable distance, were red around the edges and filled with a kind of agony she'd never witnessed before. This man was in great pain. It was horribly raw. You could see it in every contorted muscle in his face.

When she hugged him, their bodies locked together almost violently – her arms wrapped around his neck; his, very tightly around her torso.

They didn't move, except for a slight rocking, back and forth, which grew over time to be steadier and more consistent. They remained like this for some time. There was no need for words.

She knew.

31

Paul never felt comfortable in funeral homes. Who would, other than an undertaker? At thirty-five years of age, he had attended his fair share of funerals – his grandparents on both sides and his Aunt Lillian, who had left him the funds that he used for the rent in the so-called commune – but this time was different. This was Simon's memorial service.

Paul lingered on the front step of the Bloor West funeral home, feeling uneasy about going inside. After a few moments, he forced himself.

These places always had a distinctive scent. Was it mothballs? Or maybe it was some kind of embalming fluid. The thought turned his stomach. Christ, let's just get through this, he thought as he approached the visitation room.

A few people were already seated. At the front of the room, surrounded by a number of modest bouquets, an urn sat on a pedestal. The idea of cremation had always seemed ghoulish to Paul.

He spotted Claire in the first row of pews, dressed in a dark blue dress with a stiff-looking collar. His heart skipped a beat upon seeing her – an intense physical reaction from the core of his being, from his gut, that took him by surprise. She was huddled over a blond man – Jann, Paul assumed – with her arm over his shoulder. Others encircled the two, and it looked as though they were engrossed in an intimate conversation, so he kept his distance.

Then, five rows back, he spotted Beata. Two young adults, presumably her children, flanked her. He recognized her from behind – that bowl haircut by now so familiar to him. He realized how much he missed her, even after such a short time. But what was she doing here? Hadn't she flown to London? He approached her, touching her shoulder.

Her eyes were red from crying, but she looked pleased to see him. She hugged him, then introduced Aisha and Etienne. The kids shook Paul's hand, evidently realizing who he was. So she had spoken of the group therapy sessions, he realized.

Beata's children were considerably older than Paul had expected. Having heard about them for many months, he now realized that he'd imagined them as teenagers, when of course they were fully grown. After all, they had relocated to Chicago all by themselves. But what were they doing here?

Etienne and Aisha shifted over on the pew, making room for him to chat with Beata.

"Hello Paul," Aisha said warmly. "Come sit with us."

He nodded to both siblings and sat down beside their mother. "Good to see you, although not under these circumstances. It's incomprehensible, Simon's death," he said to Beata. "How is it that you're here? What happened to London?"

Etienne was leaning into the conversation, a little more so than his sister. It was clear he wanted to get Paul's take on recent events.

"My children convinced me otherwise," she said, smiling and gently patting Etienne's back. "I really had not gotten over the death of Jafari. Not properly."

"But you seemed so sure about the move." Paul was genuinely surprised.

"I've just started seeing a psychiatrist and I've come to realize something: I can convince myself of a lot of things. I can see things when they're not really there. I'm a determined person, you could say." She paused. "Can you will a person back to life? Because I was trying to do precisely that … And, of course, it's an impossibility."

"I know you loved him very much," Paul said.

Etienne nodded vigorously.

"Even after all this time, I still can't believe I'm in this position: a widow. It's unimaginable that Jafari's gone. This funeral, Simon's death, is bringing it back to me … Such a tragedy."

"Grief's a long and merciless process," Paul said.

"There are phases of it, I've learned. The kids set me up at the Clarke Institute. There's a young doctor, as I said, who has a plan for me."

Paul wondered what that meant but he didn't press. He hoped the psychiatrist wouldn't load her up with drugs that would just numb her feelings. He shot a glance at Aisha and

Etienne to see if they wanted to add anything. They did not appear to want to interject.

"You know," Beata said, "returning from the airport with Aisha, when she stopped me from going to London, there wasn't a stick of furniture left in the apartment. I was very efficient in getting rid of everything."

"Hadn't you broken the lease?"

"Etienne spoke to the landlord," she explained, then added, "He and Aisha drove all night from Chicago to stop me from taking that plane."

"And we are back with her now," Aisha said emphatically.

"Yes. In the empty apartment," Beata said. "We're buying a few pieces of furniture … It's a start."

"I'm very glad to hear." Paul was reassured.

"It's funny, when you strip everything down, take out all of the stuff, and truly start fresh like that, then the ghosts, they fade away little by little."

He tried to imagine her apartment, a blank slate. Perhaps that was part of the process for Beata coming to terms with things, this time in a healthier frame of mind.

Paul took Beata's hand and gave it a squeeze. Thank God, he thought, something good had transpired. He never believed that running away to the UK was a rational option for her.

Just then, a white-haired minister hobbled up to the front of the room, St. James Bible in hand, and the funeral service began. Claire turned around to scan the crowd and nodded at Paul with a look of appreciation.

Where were Simon's parents? Paul wondered. Everyone in the room was young. He knew that Simon's mother and father had rejected their son's "lifestyle," as they would've said, but surely they would not fail to attend his funeral? Paul had to admit that this might be the case.

After the sermon, which seemed a profound mismatch to Simon – was he religious, even in the slightest? Paul asked himself – a few people took the opportunity to speak. These were long-time friends of Jann's, it became evident. They were there to support him.

Claire turned around and gestured to Paul, indicating that he should add a few words, which startled him. What could he possibly say? Even after Jann's friends had taken their turns and as Paul walked up the aisle to the podium, he still wasn't sure what he would disclose or express.

"I'm Paul. I knew Simon, for a time, this past summer," he began, his mind still blank. He saw Claire, out of the corner of his eye, nodding encouragingly, and so he forced himself to continue. "I knew him for one season, you could say. A season where a lot of things …" His voice trailed off. How could he possibly sum up everything they had experienced over the past few months?

"Simon definitely went through a great deal in his life. Many hurdles. Without much support or love around him. Living without letting his true self shine through. For reasons that we all know, we can all understand." A buzz of acknowledgement rippled through the crowd. He wondered how many people were from the gay community.

Then he gazed directly at Jann – there was, by now, no mistaking who he was – and this just about destroyed him. The man seemed worn down to the bone. Paul felt as if he were staring into a pit of despair.

"I'm sorry, Jann. This is so fucked up – Sorry." He glanced at the minister, who was raising a disapproving eyebrow. "I just … can't believe this has happened." He stopped to collect his thoughts.

"We were in a group … this summer … the four of us …" He stumbled over his words, but he felt that the audience needed to understand. "It was supposed to be this great thing … but I'm not sure what we accomplished, to be honest …" He felt close to tears.

Claire watched him, wide-eyed, as if she feared he was going off on a perilous and illogical tangent. And she was right. He could feel himself drifting out to sea. Was he implying that group therapy could have saved Simon? That didn't make sense, not even to him.

"The thing, the person, who transformed Simon's life was you, Jann. You helped him realize that there could be a way of living without denying who you are. You helped him to imagine that another world is possible. I saw a change in him that was profound. Didn't we, Claire? Beata? We all saw it. It was a sea change over the course of these past few months. He came alive. He found himself. He was happy for perhaps the first time in his life. Please find comfort in that, Jann."

Paul left the podium feeling utterly drained. He needed to get some air. He walked straight down the aisle, out the front door, and into the parking lot. He sat at the edge of the lot, leaned up against a cement pylon, lit a cigarette, and cursed himself for his lack of eloquence. What was he even trying to say back there?

Claire followed him out to the parking lot. Without a word, she took a cigarette from him, plunked herself down on the adjacent pylon, and began scratching her collarbone near the neckline of the dress.

The two of them sat and smoked, glancing into the backyard next door where an elderly man was sweeping his patio in a slow, mesmerizing way.

"It's nice that we're together again. The group, I mean," she finally said. "To mourn one of our own."

"I was right about what I said back there about group therapy."

"No, it was a worthwhile experiment."

"Life's more complex than I imagined, Claire. It seems silly, almost childish, to say. What did I think we could accomplish together? Heal ourselves? It was a ridiculous supposition."

"An optimistic one, maybe."

"No, it's the same as my living experiment. The communal house. I had faith in an idea that simplified things too much."

"Sharing a living space, sharing responsibilities? Sounds like a good idea."

"Marxism isn't what it's cracked up to be."

"The commune's still failing to impress?"

"It's because people are more complicated than Marx led me to believe. No, I don't mean complicated. More like, messy. More of a train wreck. We're prone to mistakes – and I'm talking about myself here."

"We're evolving."

"Yes, but everyone's travelling along different paths at varied rates in opposing directions. That means, in some ways, we're utterly unknowable to each other … and ourselves."

"Paul, that's pretty dark. I wouldn't say that at all."

"All I'm saying is that Marx banked on kindness. He assumed goodness, too readily. Not that I'm suggesting cruelty wins the day. What I mean is we're inconsistent, entirely malleable, prone to fuck ups. Christ, we could do anything under any number of circumstances."

"Horrific things. Look what happened to Simon."

"Exactly. What're we supposed to learn from his death? That life's totally screwed up?"

"You can't draw that conclusion. Life may be unpredictable, but it's not futile," she said, crushing her cigarette butt into the asphalt with her shoe.

"Aren't you going back to school?" she asked, changing the subject.

"Yes. It was a late application, but I could enter in January. Larry's been very helpful."

"Good. How're things at the Roncesvalles commune?"

He hesitated before answering. "I … I moved back to the old house on Garden Avenue."

Claire looked shocked. He realized he should have introduced the subject more delicately and chastised himself for his lack of sensitivity.

"I ran out of money," he said, a little embarrassed. "My wife was surprisingly understanding. She needs help with the boys because the sitter's unreliable. And I missed the kids a lot. It was a tough summer."

He wasn't telling the whole truth. In reality, Cynthia was nursing a wicked heartache from the split up with her boyfriend, some guy named Sam. She was vulnerable in a way that he had never seen her before – curled up on the sofa, watching television, or reading a *Chatelaine* magazine without getting dressed for the day. That was the state of things when Paul had gone over to the house to make his woeful declaration that he was out of money. He wondered if Cynthia had fallen apart to the same degree when he had left, compared to when Sam checked out, but realized that this was not likely. What did it matter anyway? He was certainly not seeking to get back together with his wife.

The stark reality was that he had settled. He and Cynthia agreed that he would stay in the family home until he finished his PhD. They had an understanding, you could call it. Not what a person would necessarily dream about, but it was a safe and predictable place to land after a difficult summer. He often reminded himself that life was filled with such compromises, that this was probably best for the kids, and that this was the most logical decision – and shouldn't a person aspire to be logical and responsible, after all?

"Had you told me this would be how the chips would fall, a few months back, I wouldn't have believed it," Paul said.

As he spoke, and caught the tone of his delivery, he wondered if he were presenting this plan to move back to his marital home as some kind of a happy compromise, a good thing, something that tied up all the loose ends of his life in a neat little bow, when in reality, it was the opposite. He was profoundly disappointed, crestfallen to the core – a fact that came into sharp focus the moment he locked eyes on Claire today. He realized how deeply he loved her, how much he had totally fallen for her, and yet there was nothing to be done.

"What about you? How are you?" He suddenly grasped how much he didn't know about Claire – where was she born, did she have any siblings, what was her favourite childhood memory? – and felt a cavernous anxiety, a fresh ache, rising in his chest, knowing that this was the last time he would be able to ask her what really mattered.

"Me? I'm good. Work's good. The manuscripts are rolling in for the next publication season. And you know me: My work's my life. That's just how I'm wired."

Did she realize that he had been hung up on her for most of the summer? Paul suddenly recognized that Claire was much more together in her head than he could ever hope to be. She was a survivor while he was a train wreck. The ridiculousness of his trying to help her, via the group therapy experiment, seemed, in this light, quite striking.

"I'd better get back," she said after a while. "I want to catch up with Beata. Maybe go out for coffee. Want to join us?"

"No, I've got to go," he said. He felt too exhausted from the funeral, and moreover, he sensed this may be the last time he would see either Claire or Beata, that this chapter of his life, chaotic and deeply unsettling, was coming to a close.

As they hugged goodbye, he said, stupidly, "See you around," when they both knew that was not going to be the case.

He remained in the parking lot for a few more minutes, glancing up at the sky. It looked like rain. The weather was turning. Fall was in the air, and the leaves were just starting to change. Someone had a fireplace going, and the comforting scent of burning wood wafted through the neighbourhood.

He walked home, ruminating over Claire: the image of that ever-present pencil dangling from her mop of unkempt hair, the particular way she squinted when the sun shone in her eyes, and how she often squeezed his arm for emphasis.

He found himself reconsidering his old theory that love could be measurably diminished one droplet at a time. He realized how soul-crushing that could be and was forced to confront how unhappy he had been before the summer, before group therapy, before Claire. He knew now, for certain, that love could also be constituted, enhanced, one droplet at a time.

Paul felt, for perhaps the first time in his life, the harrowing dichotomies of existence – the diminishing and replenishing of love; the pendulum swinging from kindness to cruelty; and the greedy edges of sadness that coexist with the urge for happiness and the desire to, somehow, make things better.

Ah, to make things better. That old chestnut, he sighed. He wondered, with all of this heartbreak from the loss of Claire to the death of Simon, if it would truly be possible for him to make things better; to begin again as a person, a revised human being; to go back to the garden and start anew? Or would he need to, somehow, accept watered-down aspirations, unsteady convictions, the sting of omnipresent disappointment? He wasn't sure. Nothing felt resoundingly right to him anymore.

With these questions swirling around in his head, Paul had trekked home from the funeral as if sleepwalking and, oddly, ended up in front of the Roncesvalles commune, not his house with Cynthia and the boys. His legs had automatically transported him to the wrong location. He had to admit, it felt more like home than anywhere else.

He walked the now-familiar cobbled path toward the house, surveying the sorry state of the lawn. Halfway up, he peeked into the living room window, the interior softly illuminated against the encroaching darkness, and spotted Larry on the sofa reading a magazine – *Science,* no doubt. A feeling of nostalgia swept over Paul.

His friend glanced up from the pages, an instant smile flashing across his face as he began gestating, wildly, for Paul to come in and take the load off.

Acknowledgements

Back to the Garden is an original work of fiction. Although I embarked upon years of research for this novel and drew heavily from historical events for context, I also took considerable artistic/creative license. The story, all names, characters, and incidents portrayed in this novel are fictitious. No identification with actual persons (living or deceased), places, buildings, and products is intended or should be inferred.

I have a great many people to thank. First and foremost, I owe an immeasurable debt of gratitude to my esteemed Publisher, Matt Joudrey, who saw the promise of this manuscript from the start.

Four authors, whom I greatly admire, served as beta readers: Rebecca Silver Slater, Ramabai Espinet, Dave Cameron, and Michael Mirolla. Their time and sage advice helped to shape the manuscript.

Top-notch editor Allyson Latta worked with me on a preliminary version of the manuscript. At a later phase, my good friend and fellow editor Rebecca Conolly offered invaluable insights. I greatly appreciated her professional acuity.

I also worked closely with At Bay's incredibly skilled, above-and-beyond editor Sophie Yendole. Her well-developed editorial eye, deep reading of the manuscript, understanding of the story, and remarkably generous spirit helped to shape and develop the work, immeasurably enhancing the characters and their unique journeys. Sophie really got me to dig deeper, and I am eternally grateful. Many thanks also to At Bay's copyeditor Priyanka Ketkar.

And finally, I thank my family: My late husband, Tom Mueller, whose steadfast encouragement bolstered my writing for nearly four decades. I am grateful to our dear child, Saskia, who has been incredibly supportive of her old mum, and who has been and will always be an anchor to my life. I also owe a tremendous debt of gratitude to my sister Kelly Duffin, who read drafts of the manuscript, offering encouragement, and who has been, especially over the last few years, an unwavering support. Thank you to my father, Dick Duffin, who has championed my work and often shared it with his sisters – a family of avid readers with deep roots in, and respect for, education. I am forever beholden to my late mother, Eileen Wykes, who instilled in me an enduring passion for literature and the arts.

Photo: Michael Rafelson

MEGAN WYKES wrote freelance for many years, including a stint at ARTNews Magazine, and worked as an editor for 15 years at Oxford University Press, Harcourt Brace and Canadian Scholars' Press. Her first poetry volume, *Colour Theory*, was published in 2016 (Guernica Editions). Her writing has appeared in arts and literary magazines, including The Antigonish Review, The Dalhousie Review, The Frequent & Vigorous Quarterly, Geist, Hamilton Arts & Letters Magazine, The Maynard Magazine, Misunderstanding Magazine, The Nashwaak Review, paperplates, Qwerty and The Toronto Quarterly. *Back to the Garden* is her first novel.

Thanks for purchasing this book and for supporting authors and artists. As a token of gratitude, please scan the QR code for exclusive content from this title.